Don't Falter

To Sleve
My friend and
with much admiration

Chris

Don't Falter

Christopher Chase Walker

This edition published in 2024
by Eyewear Publishing Ltd,
An imprint of Maida Vale Publishing,
London, United Kingdom

Cover design by Juan Padron
Typeset by Subash Raghu
Author photograph by Emerald Mosley

ISBN 978-1-915406-66-8

The author and publisher gratefully acknowledge permissions granted to reproduce the copyright material in this book.

www.blackspringpressgroup.com
www.ccw-author.co.uk

Also by the same author

Now You Know

The Visitor

To Emerald, with love

PROLOGUE

William was nothing if not the son of his mother and father. By profession, he was a historian, an unsurprising career choice seeing that both of his parents did much the same in their working lives and continued to do so now, in one form or another, in retirement. These days his mother dedicated her time (and a considerable portion of her pension) to a study of fabulism in North Yorkshire folk art and music, while his father was a volunteer librarian of the records at the Nostell Priory. They were both fit mentally and physically, enjoyed fell-walking and wine, and forever pinching each other's reading glasses.

Historian, in William's own case, translated to an associate teaching fellowship at the University of Leeds. Articles of his on Queen Victoria's god-daughter Sara Forbes Bonetta, Victorian inventors Kirkpatrick Macmillan and Robert Thomson (the pedal bicycle and rubber tyre, respectively) and racist tropes in British comedy had been published in newspapers and online magazines.

William was in Brighton for the summer; it was a summer city, he decided on first arriving in its sunlit streets. It began small, in the 10th or 11th century. A fishing village on the south coast of England not unlike small fishing villages once found for hundreds of miles east along the Sussex and Kent coasts, and west into Hampshire and beyond. Where other villages failed and vanished, Brighton survived and grew. Eventually blossoming as a playground for Georgian aristocrats wanting to escape the rites and restrictions of court life, then a weekend-by-the-seaside retreat for London's theatre crowd and day-trippers desiring sun, swimming and sex of every sort. It was his birthplace.

Now approaching his thirty-third birthday, William was drawn back to the city seeking a sort of homecoming. Thirty-three years, history told him, was the age that saw the early deaths of King Richard II of England, King Charles IV of France, Catherine of Sienna, Jesus of Nazareth and Sam Cook, whose *A Change is Gonna Come* always sent William's mother into a daze as she sang along to its lyrics. He wanted to know something of his origin, hidden as it was, before it was too late, should his own time come too soon.

He was also here for work – work of his own initiative and, moreover, of personal interest. A grant from a private foundation was paying his costs. The grant was not extensive, covering accommodation and basic supplies only. The rented bedsit in the Seven Dials neighbourhood came furnished; once William understood the local streets and twittens, he discovered it less than a mile walk from the sea. He lived frugally, preparing his meals at home, with only the occasional drink or coffee out. It was nothing new; William was accustomed to getting by on a modest income. Arriving at the end of May, he would stay until August, at which point he was due back north to resume his duties at the university, where that coming term he would lecture undergraduates on 20th century linguistic identity in Britain and her territories. It was a paid gig, and he was grateful for it. Like junior lecturers anywhere, if he wanted more, wanted anything perennial or substantive, it was publish or perish.

He would, the words italicised in his head, *write a book*.

British music hall and variety shows had long fascinated William. Their sing-a-longs and We Generation warmth. Their working class origins in saloon bars, folksy bawdiness and influence on highbrow visual art and theatre. William came to Brighton, grant in hand, to research Max Miller, who was born, raised and died in the city and whose career arced from the Spanish Flu to the Beatles (on whose *Sgt Pepper's Lonely Hearts Club Band* album cover he was immortalised by the artist Peter Blake). A stand-up comedian, singer and guitar-player nicknamed the Cheeky Chappie for his double entendre and innuendo, Miller was banned by the BBC (think the Sex

Pistols in the 1970s, Frankie Goes to Hollywood the following decade) and adored by audiences, including King George V, King George VI, Queen Mary and the Queen Mother at Royal Variety performances. William would walk the streets Max Miller walked, visit Miller's childhood home, the school he attended and what local venues remained from the era where he made his name. While not the sole focus of the book he intended to write about the rise, decline and hipster revival of music hall and variety reviews, Max Miller was one of the stars.

Early one evening in his second week, William is drawn to a café by a sandwich board offering cold drinks and the day's specials. It is a Friday; he decides to live a little and eat out.

Café Voltaire has tall and wide front windows in the Art Nouveau style. It was named after the French writer, philosopher and Enlightenment figurehead about whom William's mother once taught an evening course. He takes a photo of the café to send to her and seats himself at a table on the pavement with a view of the nearby square, the sea and the pinkening sky. A breeze lifts the corner of the menu weighed down by utensils. They are mismatched, the knife, the fork and spoon. So too the café's chairs, some painted white, others yellow or blue. When William enquires of the waitress if she knows anything of the café's history, briefly explaining his reason for asking, she tells him it was until about a year ago a women's clothing store, and in any case she herself has only worked here for two months. To his dismay, William also learns they are out of croque monsieurs. He orders devilled whitebait instead and a drink called an Iced Zozo.

As he waits, he notices a woman watching him. She is seated alone at the next table but one. The glass before her is garlanded with the creamy dregs of a latte. The only other customers are at a table out of earshot. There is an air of unexpected and undesired intimacy. The way the woman watches him prickles. More: he thinks he recognises something in her look. It bears similarity to glances and once-overs he came to know when he was young and began venturing out on his own, without either or both of his parents, and has never entirely come to terms with. He tells himself to ignore it, that if she has a problem, it is not his to worry about; but finds he has nodded and smiled in a small way, as though to give her the assurance she must be seeking.

The smile is not returned and the look continues. A querying stare, ribboned with alarm and, unless he is mistaken, disgust of some form or another. William is at the point of saying something when to his surprise the woman addresses him. Her tone is matter of fact.

'Before that,' she says gesturing at the café's front windows, 'before it was a clothing shop, it was Café Bertrix for as long as I can remember.'

'Café Bertrix.' William turns the words over in his head and on his tongue. 'So always French, when it wasn't selling clothes?'

'Belgian, actually. Walloon. When it was the café it was before, the couple who ran it were from Wallonia. It's the French-speaking portion of Belgium. In the south,' she adds pointing downward, making William think he wasn't entirely incorrect in judging her earlier look. 'So yes, French – of sorts. I used to come here when I was little.'

Her eyes fall away and she looks east along the high street. William is facing west. Between them is something experience (or hope, he concedes) is beginning to take form. The woman wants, even needs to speak.

William's drink arrives in a tall glass. It tastes of melon and mint and is immediately cooling. He knows what the woman has to say almost assuredly won't help him with his book. To date, his research since arriving in Brighton has been near fruitless. He feels stymied. He feels stuck. The woman is pushing fifty; blonde hair streaked with grey and cut in what he hears himself inside labelling an unlovable bob, perhaps by her own hand. He tells himself that if she had been a child here, then perhaps she still has relatives who can assist him in his work. If they are alive, will they speak to me? Even if they have passed away, there might still be photos, mementos, stories handed down to this very woman herself. He will take what opportunities come as and when they show.

'Stopped coming to the café when it became a clothing shop?' he offers. He mustn't press too hard.

'No,' the woman responds after a pause, half lost in her thoughts and resurfaced memories. 'Long before that. They were a lovely couple, such a lovely couple, the Baniers who ran the place. After they went it was never the same. Not even now that it's a café again. Especially not now.' She makes a small noise in her throat and looks at William in much the same way as before they began speaking. A breath of fear but also now somewhat resigned. 'You must be down on a visit? Doing research, digging around the past.'

William is momentarily taken aback, before remembering mentioning his work to the wait-ress and seeing the woman must have overheard. Between mouthfuls he elaborates a little on his pur-pose. Places like the café may have once been a small establishment on the entertainment circuit.

When the woman pays for her coffee and begins to leave, they exchange names.

'Anna,' she tells him.

Shaking her hand, William says his own. Anna nods and lifts one side of her mouth, as though expecting him to have said something different.

Then almost in one breath she invites him to meet here again tomorrow, says she has some knowledge of local history that will be of interest – and rather to both their embarrassment adds that she is not hitting on him.

'I'm old enough,' she says, 'to have been your babysitter.'

When William returns the following morning, Anna is nowhere in sight. The café is busy. He counts himself lucky to secure a table beneath the awning drawn against the sun and the rising canticles of heat. It is nearer fifteen than ten minutes later than the appointed time before Anna shows. She is apologetic. William waves it away with a remark about his habit of people-watching, a comment that elicits from Anna an open-nostrilled stare. There is an undernote of drink beneath her perfume. Her eyes look puffy and over-alert from lack of sleep.

For the next three and some hours, seated across from each other, William listens to tales of the neighbourhood as it used to be, of Anna's family and friends and a particular girlhood springtime and summer. They are intermittently interrupted by a delivery van announcing, *Caution! Edgar's vehi-*

cle reversing, for every inch or two its driver gains backing into a kerbside parking space. Occasionally he attempts to steer things toward the five or six questions he prepared to guide him in this morning's interview but finds his forays falling flat against whatever point Anna is building toward – and, if he is honest, finds himself increasingly keen to hear. He makes notes; she does not seem to mind.

Yesterday he managed but a handful of sentences on Max Miller. Each of the two days before that it was none. With Anna it's page after page. The detail she provides is extraordinary, like a collage comprised of hundreds of images, hundreds of faces, that together create a portrait of a single subject.

Anna, he pieces together over coffee and scones (and the annoyed glances of the waitress for taking their time ordering second cups and eventually lunch), is a data analyst living in Crawley – a commuter town roughly halfway between the capital and the coast. She has a one-bed flat within walking distance of the train station, commutes to Croydon three days a week and the rest of the time works from her sitting room table. Her apartment has a small balcony on which there are withered succulents she forgets to water. She is childless, has no pets and makes no mention of a partner. Before this summer she hadn't been to Brighton for more than half her life.

'Although it was always near, always just *there*, I found myself driving further along the coast instead. Telscombe Cliffs, Beachy Head... But this year,' Anna pauses. Her eyes meet William's and she looks quickly away. She shrugs. 'I came to see someone from back then. They're in town too. For the summer.'

The manner in which she over-enthuses about her job tells William that Anna, beneath the puff, doesn't find it any more rewarding than he does marking essays or helping his parents with their monthly budgeting. What she says about her work saddens him, much more so for the buoyancy in her voice as she describes it.

'The data I manage are marvels of information. They are tapestries of material, oracles of insight into the habits and desires of individual people. As they are today, as they were when they were children or first fell in love. I can see where and when people have holidayed, what they get up to on weekends, where and with whom they've sought sexual fulfilment. Births and adoptions. Grants and awards. Properties. Infidelities. Lies. It's all there, tracked and available on my screen.

'There is security in data. In my spreadsheets there is order and control. Each cell or group of cells can be linked to another cell or group of cells. The cells and links are endless. On my monitor,' Anna gestures a distance roughly shoulder-wide, 'there are

1,044 individual cells. Should I scroll down or to the side, another 1,044. And should I like, I can open up a fresh body of cells using the tabs at the bottom of the screen. From there I'm free to add new data or, through formulas, linking or copying in data from elsewhere. Same as DNA or customs, things like eye shape and culture, are passed from parent to child and from that child to their own children.

'The data I chart will survive me after I'm gone. But through my role in constructing and analysing it, part of me carries on, even though I take measure to remain anonymous. Tell me, though, who, after time, *really* remembers their forebears? It might be that, as a person, I'm forgotten after my time has passed, where memories of a grandparent might survive another generation or two. But we all end up in the same place. Forgotten – apart from data. In data we live on. I find great comfort in that – comfort and, if I may, compassion. For if not for data and those, who, like me, curate it, those like me who analyse it, great grandparents, great aunts and uncles, sisters and brothers, all would eventually be lost and forgotten.

'There is safety in data. Longevity, even eternity. Amongst those of us in the trade there is a nickname for it. We call it SPG. Saint Peter's Gate.'

William and Anna agree to meet again the following morning. Anna has more to tell him, she says, more that he will want to hear. What it means for his work he knows is next to nothing. But she is right. He does want to hear it. Anna is describing a time around when William was born, a neighbourhood where his parents might have lived, people his parents might have known. Lost friends.

In the meantime, on Anna's insistence, William visits a homeware shop not far from where he is staying and speaks to the owner, who is only too happy to talk on the condition of anonymity. Anna knows of him through her data analyst work, her own research into who people are and where and how they live. The shopkeeper, like Anna, has plenty to say about the past, although none of it has the slightest bearing on Max Miller or any of William's professional research. But like Anna's own story, he finds himself hooked. What isn't covered, between and sometimes whilst ringing up customers, the shopkeeper expounds on at the pub across the street.

Although he can scarcely afford it, William buys all five rounds of drinks. He tells himself the expense is an investment in a story he cannot live without. With each round it is a lie easier to believe and, somewhat conversely, a lie that increasingly bears truth. When the shopkeeper guesses a few of William's professional achievements, he chalks it up to him having seen any of the articles where his photo has appeared alongside the narrative. Few and far between the pieces may have been, but *someone* must have read them. That he asks William if he was in fact adopted is dumbfounding, and the subject quickly dropped.

They are two or three drinks in when the shop-keeper opens up about his one-time work as an iComm, an intercommunity communicator, an informant, and his handler Morkel, who vanished abroad or, like William himself, now lives under a new identity, only for Morkel one of his own choosing.

'Twilight,' Anna told William before they parted, 'comes twice a day, morning and evening. Each has three stages: civil, nautical and astronomical. In the evening, when the sun has set, the horizon remains visible and the brightest stars blink alight. This is civil twilight, civil dusk. It lasts up to three-quarters of an hour before its darkness deepens and becomes nautical. In nautical twilight the horizon fades, lines and features coalesce. It's always the civil and nau-tical stages I think about when I think of twilight. And it's only the evening that counts. In the morn-ing, it's just dawn.

'It was spring and then it was summer. The days were long, the sun shone bright. But the light had gone. The darkness was astronomical.'

ONE
(Thirty-three years earlier)

'And his pen?' Miss Rodmell's voice came clipped, procedural.

Anna closed her eyes and concentrated. 'Contoured plastic body, two colours blue – a dark and a bright – with a ribbed finger grip and clickable nib retractor.'

'Ink?'

'Blue gel. Point five-millimetre nib.' In her head Anna pictured Mr Peters working at the crossword in front of Café Bertrix three days earlier, the slender terraces and towers of his letters. He was seated cater-cornered to her at a separate table. Magritte was at a third and facing them both. Mr Peters wrote in block capitals. At forty-eight he had about his face (most noticeably his eyes and small-slotted mouth) a patina of faded heyday. He wore a mid-length grey mackintosh and a red cashmere scarf knotted at the front. His hair was a smooth dark blond helmet. From the angle of the scarf knot, the position of his coffee cup and the weight of the mobile phone in the chest pocket of his mac, Anna marked Mr Peters for right-handed but feigning to be left with the crossword. The ink formed miniature balls at the start and end of his letters. She was relieved when Miss Rodmell didn't quiz her more about his handwriting.

If asked, Anna could describe Café Bertrix in detail. Years earlier she often accompanied her mother there to buy croissants. Beginning in the early morning the café was alive with chatter and the whir of the coffee grinder. Steam hissed and the air was rich with the isabelline scent of the books lining the café shelves and with the dark bouquet of the coffee and the sweet and nimble bouquet of pastries. It was just as busy with customers outside as in. Every now and again Mr Peters rested his elbows on the table and gazed up the street, or glanced across the road to the square, its trees in early leaf, its long hank of lawn. A sunshot Easter bank holiday weekend, the streets and seafront were humming. Thunderclouds were gathering above the Downs.

The fourth time Mr Peters looked up from his crossword, Anna worried that she had been spotted. Nerves hopped through her. She pressed a hand to her leg to stop it bouncing. She and Magritte, along with six other pairs of teams, had spent the past week keeping watch on 17 Vernon Place, a four-storey Regency terrace house that had decades earlier been filleted into flats. Each of its residents (three couples in their 30s or 40s, a film critic and allotment gardener, a single mother with a five-year-old who still wet the bed, and a transgender widower and wine merchant) had been observed, reported on and cleared.

Only Mr Peters remained. His flat had a separate entrance from the rest of the building, a dozen steps below street level. When he emerged up the stairs that day at 12:26 it was only the third time any of the observation teams had seen him outside of the photos and video clip they had received in their brief. It was the first that Anna and Magritte had seen him in person. They were milling amongst the forty or so families gathered for an Easter egg hunt in the green opposite Vernon Place. The air smelled of cut grass and soil. Birds tittered in the trees.

Mr Peters closed the gate at the top of the steps and turned south. His left hand hidden in his pocket, he carried an umbrella in his right. The umbrella, Anna noted, was full-length with a pointed ferrule. Magritte set off ahead of him, while Anna, careful to maintain a distance of fifteen or twenty metres on the other side of the street, followed as he descended first Denmark Terrace, then Montpellier Road. At Temple Gardens, he shifted the umbrella to under his left arm while waiting for a car to pass.

'Make?' Miss Rodmell had asked Anna earlier in the debrief before quizzing her on Mr Peters' pen. The manufacture of car wasn't critical, Anna knew. How she stood up under examination was.

'Four-seat black Marten C-class. British plates. First three characters GR7.' And before Miss Rodmell could ask, Anna added: 'Only the driver visible. Male, 45-55. Round face, black sunglasses, dark beard, brown or black flat cap.'

'Nothing more?'

Anna thought the rear taillight looked like it had been splattered with paint or seagull droppings, but the car had been too far away and moving too quickly to say for certain. She asked herself if she should mention it now, adding a note of factuality to cement things, and shook her head no.

Miss Rodmell nodded for her to continue.

At Western Road, Anna lingered across the street as Mr Peters selected oranges from the greengrocer's crates on the pavement. Magritte followed him inside. Mr Peters paid in exact change, saying only 'ta' to the woman at the till. Outside the shop he turned west, toward Hove. Magritte trailed from a distance. Anna kept across the street and ahead. It was the closest any of the observation teams had come to their quarry, the longest any had yet to trail him.

Every detail counts, Anna reminded herself. *All of it's gold*. Mr Peters carried the oranges in a canvass bag strung from his left shoulder. His umbrella was again in his right hand. Before reaching Norfolk Square, he paused to inspect the gerbera in front of the florist's before moving on. At the top of the square, he stopped at a kiosk and leant his umbrella against it. With a discreet but discernible flourish, he threw back the tail of his mac and removed his wallet from his right hip pocket. Again paying with exact change (or at least not accepting any in return), he purchased a newspaper and a tin of mints. The paper he rolled in two and stowed in the left pocket of his mac, the mints in the right; and he continued along the same direction as before.

Only now he had slowed up. There was half a pace off his gait. Anna added a further four or five metres between them. Magritte dropped back by a similar distance. That was procedure. Now some distance ahead, Anna stopped as though something had caught her eye in an estate agent's window. That, too, was procedure: Mr Peters mustn't be give too long a lead.

Making some show of it, Anna pretended to examine the property ads in the window display. She rang Magritte. There was no answer. Mr Peters slowing up might indicate knowledge of being followed, or that he suspected it and wanted to determine whether or not someone was on his tail. *The Observed's hesitancy exposes two things*, Anna could hear Miss Rodmell reminding the watch teams at the beginning of the assignment, the lamplight from her lectern angled across the lower third of her face, *paranoia and guilt*.

How would he act if provoked? If pushed, what would he do? Anna didn't know. She looked up the street for Magritte. There were four or five dozen people in the immediate distance heading in both directions, but no Mr Peters and no Magritte. A bus sneezed past. Then another. Anna peered into the estate agency window and tried Magritte again, with one finger pressed to the glass and the phone pressed to her ear, as though she herself was under observation and forced to present a cover. She excitedly described a flat – two bedrooms, feature fireplace and front balcony – down the phone and, on tiptoes, craned her neck, as though whomever she was speaking to was somewhere near and should hurry, before the property was taken off market.

Magritte's phone rang on and on. A fear seized Anna. Something was wrong.

Nothing in Mr Peters' file indicated violence. He presented a lulling indifference suggesting he had only recently shrugged and that the next shrug could be deployed momentarily if only he could be bothered. He was her father's height, clean shaven and his file, Anna rehearsed now to calm her nerves, showed a bookish man (Auden, Chekov, McCullers, Whitehead, Zweig). Three affairs with women roughly his own age over the past seven years. Supported Halifax FC. Preferred the high street to shopping online. Ambrosia count moderate. Gym membership (swim and sauna only) that he never used. Haircut every five weeks at the same Sillwood

Street salon for the past six years. Thirty-five thousand a year income working as an S–, topped up by a small inheritance from his parents who had died fifteen years earlier, a car accident in Crete. No siblings. No mortgage or credit card debt. No religious affiliations. Nothing on IcePie. No porn. No CCTV captures of him loitering outside schoolyards in his mac. What remained about his face and limbs of his once youthful slimness, now seemed souvenirs that topped and tailed a thickening chest and sides. His eyes, grey-blue and set a formidable distance apart, infrequently met those of others and struggled at times to not betray a masked watchfulness and six-days-of-Sunday sadness. Mr Peters could slip radar – no recorded movements, nothing online, no telephone data, no sightings. He could disappear. And no one likes that. When you disappear.

Yet they did. People vanished.

Gone was Marie, Café Bertrix's one-time bowl-bellied proprietress who, with her ringlets and costume jewels, might herself have been displayed beneath any of the glass cake domes at the front counter. Marie's alluring Walloon (*Bondjoû, mi p'tit robet!,* the bewitching *Toutes les couleurs chantent pour vous aujourd'hui*) had seemed to Anna to burnish her (and her above all others) with a sophistication she wouldn't have otherwise known as a child on the south coast of England.

Gone was the long-limbed waiter Monsieur Banier ('Banes' to Anna in her earliest vocalisations, Eugene to her parents and other adults), Marie's husband of more than thirty years. His long and wizardly fingers had mesmerised Anna as he cleared cups of coffee and plates of cake from the tables, or when, holding either end of a bulging croissant bag, he would, with an insubstantial flick of his wrists, spin it sealed.

Gone were many of the café's books that had lined the shelves forming coves around the indoor tables. And gone was the café's *joi de vivre* that, once absent, was as haunting a lacuna as the vanished Baniers. Anna's parents were upset at Marie and Eugene's disappearance. They only spoke about it in hushed tones and had stopped frequenting Café Bertrix. Until following Mr Peters, Anna, although living less than ten minutes away, hadn't been back either.

There was, Anna believed, a veiled world existing beside our own. At times a passage opened between the two. You could, if you knew what to look for, with a determined sidestep or cunning manoeuvre, cross over to the hidden world. There, one's limitations, personal or emblematic, blossomed with new possibility. Other times a hidden world could bubble-up, impose itself and you found yourself caught in it. Only through an act of will could you press your way out, press home again, into the familiar, the navigable. Something was wrong. Something in Mr Peters' background had been missed. Anna didn't know what or the whole of it yet. She knew only the basics, only what appeared in the brief Miss Rodmell had dispensed to the observation teams prior to deployment. When Mr Peters slipped radar, when he disappeared, other people did too. But not this way, but not this way, Anna repeated to herself.

Hurrying back the way she had come, phone to her ear, her temples throbbing and the sea scent of The Channel salting the hot pavement – would it be so unheard of for someone to vanish here in the sunshine and breeze? Here amongst the bank holiday sales and hangover lunches?

A delivery van accelerated from the bus lane opposite. Anna glimpsed from behind it the soft limbs of Mr Peters' red scarf folding casually through a family of three, then skirting and finally narrowing past a tangle of students hefting boxes of drinks and the bantamweight of their joy. Then Magritte further back. And then Magritte was on the other end of the phone, short of breath and explaining she'd needed to follow Mr Peters when he ducked into the courtyard behind the laundrette.

'Describe,' Miss Rodmell said not looking up from her lectern. For this afternoon's debrief she had onscreen before her Anna's written report and Magritte's camerawork.

'At 12:48 Mr Peters turned left into – ' Magritte began.

'Thank you, Miss Malling. We'll hear from you presently. Miss Fetlock.'

'Farnham Courtyard sits behind the southern side of the high street, with entrances either end, top and bottom.' Anna glanced at Magritte. They were at the front of the classroom, standing before Miss Rodmell. Having made detailed notes, Anna had gone over them incessantly in preparation for today's debrief. The courtyard was around the corner from home. Anna had known it all her life as a floral and green-scented cut-through to the high street. All of its buildings were three or four-storeys, custard-coloured with white trim and wide windows, and was red brick underfoot.

'Mr Peters entered from the north, off Western Road. In the centre of the courtyard are eight sheds in two rows of four, joined at the back. The sheds are flat-roofed and approximately one-point-seven metres in height with doors painted different colours.' Anna couldn't resist the urge to show off and, looking straight ahead past Miss Rodmell, continued: 'On the eastern side they are red, green, blue- and white-striped and pink; and on the other sky blue, purple with yellow stars, Union Jack and white. Atop the sheds are flowerbeds atop the shed with plants point-five metres high including wallflower, narciss – '

Miss Rodmell scowled. Anna hurried ahead:

'The Observed travelled past the sheds and stopped in front of 18b, in the bottom right of the courtyard. He waited outside the front door. After half a minute he turned and left the way he came.'

'Nothing more?'

Anna again looked at Magritte, who glanced at her blazer lapel and back at Anna.

'He did acquire a flower, Miss. Put it in the buttonhole of his mac. A small orange carnation.'

'From?'

'We don't – ' Anna winced, remembering the intolerant stare issued her when, two or three months earlier, near the beginning of winter term, she had failed to supply Miss Rodmell with a piece of information. *Detail: the Holy Grail, Saves lives: never fail*: it was drummed into them. 'We think it must have been growing in one of the planters atop the sheds. It was the only moment when he passed out of sight. There was no flower when he left home.'

Miss Rodmell cocked her head. 'Not from the florist's in Western Road?'

'No, Miss.'

'Not from the news kiosk?'

'The exchange was clear, Miss. His newspaper was straight from the rack beside the hatch and the mints went directly into his pocket.'

'A window box? A passer-by overtaking him? A confidant heading the opposite direction?'

Blood coloured Anna's cheeks. Her eyes grew hot and her mouth contracted to the side. Miss Rodmell was called The Shrew out of earshot. She was everything Anna didn't want to become: loveless, unpopular and alone. Anna was frightened of her and consequently compelled to impress her, as though by doing so she would somehow ward off a fate whose finger had begun hovering above her own shoulder. Other than the few seconds Mr Peters passed behind the sheds, he had been under watch. Magritte, even on tiptoes, would have been unable to see over the plants that spiked and curled from the shed roofs. 'No, Miss.'

Upon regaining the pavement, Mr Peters, the orange carnation now in his lapel, had resumed his course down Western Road. Anna kept in front of him and across the street. Magritte trailed from behind. As he passed in front of a bookshop, Mr Peters did a backstep and peered at the window display. Behind the pastel paper chains festooning the window, three dozen or more books were arranged on shelves so their titles stared outward at passers-by. Removing the mints from his pocket, Mr Peters placed several in his mouth. Then he walked away at his earlier un-slackened pace, crossed the street at Brunswick Square, entered Café Bertrix, queued until he reached the counter, where he ordered a pain au chocolat, a bottle of sparkling water and a flat white.

'Magritte followed The Observed into the café after first waiting for someone to queue behind him. Tailing procedure 14a, Miss. I left my satchel at an empty table in front, counted ninety seconds and entered. The woman between Magritte and The Observed had shoulder-length brown hair in a ponytail, pink tracksuit top, black leggings, silver Scorch IV trainers. Age twenty-eight to thirty-four. She appeared to have been out for a run. There was sweat below her hairline and her cheeks were flushed. There was no observed contact between herself and Mr Peters.'

'You left your satchel unattended in front of the café?'

'The café was busy, Miss. It was unclear if The Observed would sit inside or out. Securing an out-side table covered one outcome – the likelier. He hadn't removed his scarf upon entering the prem-ises, indicating his intention to sit outside. Had he chosen somewhere to sit indoors, Magritte would have positioned herself nearby. Trailing procedure 9b.' Anna breathed quickly in and out and again until she felt it slow. 'The outdoor table secured was beside a window, Miss. Depending on where The Observed sat inside, had he done so, he would have remained in sight through the window.'

'But out of listening range. This was a pre-arranged formation?'

'No, Miss.'

'Did you communicate your intended external position to your partner?'

'It was unnecessary. Mr Peters took a table in front of the café. Magritte followed him outdoors approximately one minute later.'

'And in this "approximate minute," Miss Fetlock, between Mr Peters seating himself in front the café and Miss Malling securing the one remaining table, who was observing him then?'

'Miss?' Behind her back, Anna dug a thumbnail into her wrist. The indent was deep and left a mark still visible even the following day. *Get it right*, she told herself. *Get. It. Right.*

'You state that Mr Peters was the first to take a seat. He was then followed by Miss Malling approximately one minute later, and you yourself presumably another two or three minutes after that. It is that initial minute I ask you to clarify. Between *The Observed* exiting the café, hooking his umbrella on the back of a chair, whether as a signal itself to any confidant or used in some manner of signal before hooking it over the chair, setting his order on the table, his newspaper, seating himself, and Miss Malling eventually arriving in position. Who was observing Mr Peters then? More precisely, why did you not occupy yourself outside the café until you were certain where The Observed was sitting, or if, in fact, he'd come for a takeaway?'

Magritte cleared her throat. Anna held her breath. Neither spoke.

'You might also explain why, in your report, you have failed to mention the vase.' Again Miss Rodmell scrolled down the screen before her. She pursed her lips and widened her eyes.

Anna could feel Magritte not looking at her. Ostensibly photographing herself at the café, her almond tart and caffe latte, and messaging these images to friends or posting them on IcePie, Magritte had instead been photographing and filming Mr Peters. Anna was the observer, the memorist and notetaker; Magritte was 'the lens'.

'The vase, Miss?'

'Yes. Every table in front of the café has on it a miniature white vase. Narrow, cylindrical, approximately seven centimetres tall. You will observe,' Miss Rodmell tapped at her screen and one of Magritte's photos taken at the café was projected on the wall behind the lectern. 'You will observe the vase on the table in the upper left corner, where customers have moved it to one side. Another here.' Miss Rodmell swiped through the photos. 'And here. And here. Here we arrive at the one at your own table, and of course here again on Mr Peter's, *The Observed*. You see it?'

'Yes, Miss,' Anna and Magritte answered simultaneously.

'The flowers in the vases are all the same, you will note, including your own, Miss Fetlock, and those of the other tables, save for *the observed* Mr Peters'. A single young iris in each vase – and in Mr Peters' we see it has been joined at some stage by a small orange carnation. For the record, did either of you observe Mr Peters remove the carnation from his person or see him insert it into the vase at his table?'

'No, Miss.'

'You say it appeared on his lapel at some point between his entering and exiting the courtyard?'

'Yes, Miss.'

'And now it has materialised in the vase in the approximate minute you allowed him out of sight. Quite the enigma, this carnation. First it's not there, then it is. Then it vanishes and appears elsewhere.' For the second time that day the power winked off and on. The projector connected to Miss Rodmell's computer shut off with a tidy whoop and its image taken at the café disappeared from the wall. Anna asked herself when Mr Peters could have removed the flower. She was certain she had seen him with it only after he had exited Farnham Courtyard. But he might have whisked it off at almost any point between there and the café table, without Anna or Magritte noticing. But what mattered was, why had he worn it at all, if it was only for such a short time? And why did he remove it?

All the while they were at Café Bertrix, Mr Peters seemed to look everywhere but at Anna. And he didn't look at Magritte either, which was extraordinary: everybody looked at Magritte, as Anna had seen for herself time and again. She had black hair, like bitumen, a burglar's mask of freckles and green eyes. Beginning when she was thirteen and was out with her mother, men's gazes would glance past her mum and percolate on Magritte.

But not Mr Peters. He had watcher's eyes, Anna decided. She felt a sort of pride arriving at the term, seeing how it could also be applied to her own self. Eyes that flicked and filched. Eyes that darted and sipped. Hummingbird eyes.

The one time he could have squared a look at them, Anna saw, was when Mr Peters had pulled a hand down his face, beginning with the high inlets of his hairline, as though exasperated by his inability to solve a crossword clue. For a moment his gaze was hidden by his fingers, and the next his features were dragged downward, revealing the white orbits of his eyes, his nose, his lips, when suddenly he snapped up his pen from the table, clicked it open and began inserting letters into the crossword. Anna could make out only part of it – PLA – the first three characters of a down answer. Mr Peters' bottle of water obscured the rest. But by the number of times his wrist flicked, Anna figured it an eight or nine letter word.

It was then that a group of five – all in their 20s or 30s and smelling of detergent, sleep and (mysterious to Anna) morning sex – passed between Anna's and Mr Peter's tables. They gathered on the other side of the canvass barrier separating the café's outdoor seats from the pavement and began their goodbyes. Momentarily forgetting her assignment, pulled adrift by a hormonal neap of imagining what it must be like to be with someone else, Anna tried to determine who amongst the group were a couple. She pictured herself here at the café with a boy. One of the women had curly dark blonde hair like Anna; and Anna looked hard at the man the woman was with (the man Anna decided the woman was with: the way their bodies referred to each other, the number of times he looked at her, how and how long she looked at him) and indulged herself in a fantasy that this was a vision of herself sometime in the not too distant (and therefore magnificently distant) future, out with friends for coffee before heading home, for which Anna borrowed the description and photos of the flat she had seen earlier in the estate agency window.

When she next looked at Mr Peters, he was upright and shaking his leg as though it tingled with sleep. The newspaper was rerolled and returned to his mac pocket, the bag of oranges hanging from his shoulder. He collected his umbrella from where it was hooked on the chair and left. Anna noted the umbrella was printed in a dark shepherd's check and had a curved wooden handle.

'Time?' The time of Mr Peters' departure would have been onscreen before Miss Rodmell, in Anna's report. Part of the debrief was demonstrating how well you knew the facts, therefore substantiating your own veracity and that of the report itself.

'13:28, I believe, Miss.'

'Go on.'

'For a moment I thought he had forgotten his pen. It was on the table. But as he departed, he put it in his pocket.'

'Which?'

'Left trouser, Miss. He used his left hand to collect the pen. It was...' Anna paused. Again she reminded herself to get it right, and breathed deep before continuing. 'The Observed presented himself as left-handed. This was the final allusion to it, Miss. In case I had doubts.'

'You are saying it was a performance to generate misinformation, that he wanted you to see the pen go in his left pocket so it's there, to hand, whenever he happened to need it again. You believe he knew you and Miss Malling were observing him.'

'I believe he suspected he was under observation. Whether he understood it to be by Magritte and me' – Anna stopped herself from saying *or any of the other teams* – 'I can't say. He was on guard. Without question, he was on guard.'

'Proceed.'

'Mr Peters crossed the street to the plaza above Brunswick Square. After a few paces, he...' Anna turned her eyes toward the ceiling. Miss Rodmell tilted her head to one side and waited. When Anna found her voice again, it had lost some of its flatness, its reportage, and was now rounded by wondering notes. 'He stopped, Miss.' She knew better than to add how it had seemed, by slowing to a standstill, Mr Peters was saying: *Go ahead, take a look – take a good look.* Beyond him the heavy skies were almost overhead and the sunlight had gone milky through a broth of cloud. 'For six or seven seconds he stood perfectly still, looking at the square.'

'*At* the square?'

'In its direction.'

'Or at someone or something in it, beside it or beyond it. Your formation?'

'V-shaped, Miss. The Observed was at the vertex. Magritte had exited the café first, returned to the zebra crossing and was outside the butcher's at the top of Brunswick Place. I counted thirty after Magritte left and crossed in front of the café. The Observed was never out of sight.'

'Neither were you,' Miss Rodmell said, if Anna could read her look.

'A cyclist rode past two or three metres from The Observed. Female. Thirties. Pink hair. Lavender coat. Silver bicycle with front basket.'

'Direction?'

'Northward, Miss. Upslope. There were also two boys on skateboards, three or four metres in front of The Observed and heading toward the seafront. Mr Peters resumed walking after they passed and entered Brunswick Square through the northwest gate. If I might, Miss, the square is approximately sixty metres wide and three times as long, set on a gradual downward slope. From the outside in, it's enclosed by a black iron fence, hedge and gravel path. The path is accessible from without by gates – two at the top, two on each side and one at the bottom. Seven in total. After starting along the path, Mr Peters struck out across the central lawn, in the direction of a clump of shrubs.'

'It was more in the direction of a gap between the shrubs and the copse beyond it,' Magritte said, unable to keep quiet any longer. 'It was my position,' she added, offering Anna an apologetic look for correcting her. 'I was two dozen or more paces to the left of my partner, Miss. The line of sight was...' Raising her arm, Magritte gestured an angle.

'You can demonstrate this on camera?'

'I had it ready.'

'But no shot, I see. Miss Fetlock. Your position?'

'Approximately twenty metres directly back from the square. The road forks in two around it. I took the right and my partner the left.'

'Why did you not enter the square yourself?'

'Suitable cover was inadequate.'

'The bushes? The copse?'

'Could only be achieved after some distance across the open lawn. By maintaining a reasonable gap, The Observed remained in sight on the downslope of the square.'

'In sight without interruption?'

'Momentarily, when he passed behind the shrubs. Five seconds, Miss.'

'No more?'

'There were cars.'

'Stationary or moving?'

'Stationary, apart from one.'

'Total count?'

'Four or five dozen, Miss.' Anna's eyes again fixed upward as she pictured the scene. The only gaps were where motorbikes or scooters were parked, or there were double yellow lines. It had been the same for Magritte, on the other side of the square.

'The moving one?'

'Left from a parked position alongside the fence, approximately two-thirds down.'

'Make and driver?'

'Nothing, Miss. There was no time.' Knowing what was coming next, Anna swallowed hard. She wondered how soon the thumbnail pressing into her wrist would draw blood. 'The value of The Observed,' a tide of relief washed through her when the whole of the quote came back, 'will by my per-formance be served.'

'And Mr Peters?'

'He was there, Miss. Then he wasn't. After the car passed, I looked both ways before crossing for the square.'

'Now there was suitable cover?'

'A campervan, Miss. Parked just above the side gate. In front of it was a second van. Mr Peters passed out of sight behind them. Inside the square were groups of picnickers. Two couples on their own and several clusters of seven or eight and a party of about twenty. Many were on their feet, packing up and shaking out blankets on account of the weather. I might have appeared to be joining any of them.'

'Mr Peters?'

'He should have been just ahead of me, Miss. His speed and direction of travel. I scanned the picknickers for him, his key identifiers the grey mac and red scarf.'

When Anna didn't see Mr Peters, she made as though heading for the largest group. Beyond them, across the lawn, she saw Magritte entering the square through the opposite gate. She had her phone to her ear; Anna felt hers buzzing. Magritte said she would check the copse. Then she laughed loudly and clapped her hand to her forehead. She turned a three-quarter circle in little Geisha steps and, like an admiral or explorer in an old painting, pointed exaggeratedly at the copse. It was her cover, Anna knew. Magritte was pretending to be lost, finding her bearings, or that she was late meeting friends who had moved on from the square ahead of the coming rain.

Anna kept her phone to her ear after Magritte had hung up. She scanned the lower half of the lawn for Mr Peters' red scarf and continued to talk into the phone. This too, like Magritte's feigned perdition, was a cover, in case, having lost sight of him, Mr Peters was now watching her. 'No, no, *no*,' Anna said into the phone. 'We trained for this, we trained for this.' Out of the corner of her eye she saw Magritte heading for the trees. 'If you're looking up there,' she said, 'I'll check down...'

Beyond the picknickers a small dog dashed after a ball, bounding into a cluster of shrubs at the bottom of the lawn. The shrubs were tall and dense and formed a deep circle. Many were in bud or blossoming. The dog dove into them with a crash and a single delighted bark. Heads turned and gulls squawked in the sky. After a moment the dog, ball in mouth, burst into sight once again and galloped back the way it had come.

As Anna neared the shrubs, she saw they weren't as solid as they first appeared. There was a hollowness to their mass. Around the side she found an opening. Anna thought this must have been the way the dog emerged moments earlier, rather than warning herself it was the way Mr Peters had entered ahead of her.

She squeezed inside. Branches chattered in a gust of wind and caught at her hair. The sky darkened. Above the brown scent of the soil, a chlorine-like smell pinched the air. Anna scanned the earth for footprints. None but the dog's looked fresh. The passageway was tight, forcing her to twist and duck. After a few steps she stopped and listened. There was no noise inside the thicket. Pulling back the branches separating her from the central hollow and stepping into it, Anna said to herself *He's not here* and *You've made a terrible mistake*, when in the side of her eye she saw something move.

And there was Mr Peters, the arms of his red scarf blown horizontal in front of him by the wind. In one clean movement he shut the same gate through which he had passed minutes earlier when entering the square and opened his umbrella just as the rain began. The drops were fat – belly-floppers, Anna's father called them – and made a sound like cabinet doors shutting when they hit the gravel path, the roofs and windscreens of the cars. Words from Mr Peters' crossword stuck in Anna's head. CONTRA-PUNTAL. UNMARKED. SHALLOT...

'And the clip?'

'The clip?'

Miss Rodmell waited. After a beat, she picked up her own pen from the lectern and waved it at Anna.

'Mr Peters' pen clip. Dark blue.'

'Wrong.'

the iComm

I see many things in the shop. Many things, many people and what those people are like. Who they are. The first time I realised I could read someone – let's not dress it up as anything fanciful: it's just eyes open – it was a February afternoon, when a customer came in followed shortly after by another man.

Straight away I read something in the first fellow. He was heartbroken because he had ceased to love his wife and it took him hard. There were dark shallows under his eyes. When he passed by where I was pricing a shipment of eggcups that had arrived that morning, I noticed a peculiar scent about him. Pitched somewhere between Emmental and electric fire, it indicated secretion from a souring gland.

The scent was familiar. I knew it in my brother, twenty years earlier, when we were still in secondary school. Samuel would fall in love and, within weeks, tumble right out the other end. It tortured him that he couldn't maintain that initial freewheeling sense of passion and caused him to doubt his abilities as a lover. For weeks, Samuel would be physically sick, unable to eat or keep his food down. His eyes bruised with sorrow and he emanated that curious bouquet of dairy and combustion. Sometimes there was also a hint of juniper giving me hope that he was on the mend. But it never lasted and I grew to suspect it was really just gin.

The man who had entered the shop first was thirty-six or seven, about the same age as my brother would have been, with a dark stook of hair standing sentry over his forehead. Samuel and I hadn't seen each other for over eight years. He had gone to live in New Zealand and met a girl. Together they joined a community that lived 'off the grid.' Their home was a warren of rooms constructed of old car tyres, local stone and reclaimed wood. They had electricity – their roof was blanketed in solar panels – but no internet. Every now and again, usually at Christmas, my birthday and one or two random times over the year, I would receive a letter from Samuel, and I'd send him one in return. It would have been easier to communicate online, through some app or another, but it wasn't his way and, because it wasn't, it couldn't be mine either.

Sometimes when one of Samuel's letters arrived notably later than it was dated, I would examine it to see if it bore any sign of having been previously opened. If the gum on the envelope gave way too easily or looked as if it had been resealed too securely, if the letter itself maintained its original crease. Samuel always wrote longhand, in pen. To the untrained eye it was difficult to decipher; I once joked to him that it looked like the bewildered scrawl of a thumbless masturbator, to which Samuel made no reply. When sometimes there was a smudged word or a bit of matter in the margins, I would ask myself if it was from my brother's own hand, a bit of his breakfast, say, or the carelessness of whomever had intercepted the letter before sending it on to me. Was there more, were there other letters that were confiscated before they arrived? Did all of my own letters make it to him? Only infrequently did Samuel reply directly to anything I had written.

Now, as I watched the man browse wearily through the shop, I began to wonder if he really was my brother. He was scornful of people he considered less intelligent than himself, had overcome a childhood fear of moths but still flinched at unicyclists, often fretted he had left his front door unlocked or the iron hot, was aroused by women's underarms, and still mourned losing his mother more than a decade after her death – all things just as my brother had been or the direction he was travelling before settling abroad. But when the man trickled up to the counter with a retro wall clock and a gift card, I knew it couldn't possibly be Samuel. The card he had selected had a shaggy, blonde-maned pony on its cover. Samuel was allergic to horses. They gave him hives and made him sneeze.

To make double certain it wasn't my brother on a surprise visit and playing a joke, I glanced at his face.

But where there would have been laughter in Samuel's eyes at the searching look in my own, there was only the wrecked mosaic of absented love. The man paid in cash; I gave him change and he left. It was the only time I saw him. Samuel's letters continued to arrive every few months. He made no mention of the incident. Consequently, neither did I.

By the time the man I thought might have been Samuel had disappeared out the door, the second fellow, who had entered moments after the first, approached the counter. He looked at me in a way I couldn't determine if it was suspicion, disappointment at something not in stock, or a veiled sexual offer.

I was wrong, but only after a fashion. Because before the offer came – it wasn't sexual but governed me ever since same as any erotic craving might – first came a quiz, of sorts.

'Striking scent, that,' he said with a deep sniff over his shoulder before turning back to face me. And because I was so pleased with myself for reading everything I had in the first man, I was surprised when he went on to say, 'Bergamot, tobacco with back notes of chili or...is it lime?

I faltered momentarily, before recalling there had been a few young women in the shop earlier who had tested the bottled scents we carried. Some of it must have sprayed onto the nearby shelves or cushions. I could smell it now that the first man had gone, and with him the scent that reminded me of my brother. 'Celeriac, I believe. There's also a blue cedar and fig with smoked pep-percorn. Perfect in autumn and winter.'

'No, I should think the former,' the man replied. And when I didn't immediately say anything in return, he added, 'What that chap was wearing.' Without taking his eyes from me, he nodded back-ward at the shop door.

'Was he wearing one...?' I mused, not wanting to sound impolite by correcting him and mentioning how the other customer had smelled to me.

The second man asked where the men's toiletries were and I pointed to the shelves where the scents were displayed with our hip flasks and metal ther-moses. Had I not before been watching the first man so closely, I could have sworn the second one already knew which way to go. After a couple of steps, he suddenly stopped and clicked his fingers.

'Funny. I should think I recognised him. He wasn't by any chance...' and with that he tipped back his head and arched himself to such a degree that I could tell he had been a gymnast in his youth. He wasn't particularly tall, was stocky-thighed and had filled out in the middle: he resembled a pommel horse. His skin was tan for the season and he wore a copper-coloured jacket, black trainers, black jeans, and his half-lens glasses, for reading up close, were pushed atop his head. His hair was short, unparted and grey. Half to himself he repeated, 'He wasn't...' then popping upright like the bobbing bird desk toys we sold, 'He wasn't Mac McKenzie, the Shrikes bassist?'

I replied that I was sorry but wasn't sure what Mac McKenzie looked like and added that I had never seen the other customer before. The second man nodded and went to inspect the scents.

All the while he busied himself deciding between the bergamot-tobacco and the cedar-fig, I thought about Samuel and how much I wished it had been him. I remembered to myself how he had convinced me to swallow an earthworm when I was six and he was already nine, how our mother once had to collect him from the police station for nicking a street sign to use as a sledge, the staring stoicism he displayed at her funeral breaking like a storm after she was cremated, and many other things as well. So, when the second man returned to the counter with a bottle of the bergamot-tobacco, and I was moving my lips to my brother's name, he said,

'You were doing the same earlier with the other fellow, while he was looking around.' He laughed at my embarrassment and then assured me everyone talked to themselves. 'I bet I was at it just now, about Mac McKenzie. It couldn't have been him. I've just remembered he died. Motorbike accident six years ago. Just this, please.'

I was grateful for him purchasing something. Many people didn't. They would come to the shop, note what we had in stock and say something loud enough for me to hear, things like *Let me think about this*, then go home and buy it online for two or three pounds less than what it cost with us. To my surprise the man also selected a corkscrew from the odds and ends discount box at the counter. Because that particular corkscrew had been in the shop for over a year, I suddenly felt that a new chapter of my life was beginning, and all for the better. I was so pleased, that I found myself saying something about the customer whom he thought was Mac McKenzie. Before I knew it, I'd raced through everything I'd read in the first man, whom I had never seen before and wouldn't see again and whom I had, with a questing heart, mistaken for my brother.

And that's how Morkel recruited me.

THREE

Anna

Girls at Lynton Senior School belonged to one of four houses – Canterbury, Kemp, The Greys or Mallory. No manner of campaigning or pleading, whether by students or parents, could influence the house to which we were assigned. The decision was the Head's. Houses competed with each other for trophies in sport, poetry, community service and academics to demonstrate how much the school meant to us and how much girls meant to each other within their house. Almost no one switched. Those who did and who hadn't established themselves in the eyes of their peers as gifted poets or athletes, or whose abilities were deemed to in some clear and valiant manner help their new house clinch the Lady Lull Trophy, awarded annually to the house that won the most interschool competitions, were treated with suspicion and had to prove themselves through initiation.

Initiations tended to be harmless commands or dares. Wearing your uniform inside out. Going without a bra and deodorant for a week. Memorising and reciting on demand the full names and birthdates of the girls in your new house. Sometimes they extended to acts such as snogging someone else's boyfriend, flirting with workmen tending to the belowground pipes in the street outside the school walls, or downing a shot of spirits before every class for a day.

It was only then, following initiation, that girls who had been re-assigned to a different house were no longer considered an agent for their old one, a mole who would report back on, or sabotage, their new house's activities. I had been at Lynton since I was seven; when reaching Seniors I was assigned to Canterbury, where I stayed until I was transferred to Mallory two days into my Year 9 autumn term. Exactly a year minus a day before becoming a Lynton Rudie.

Rudies were what students at Lynton called Year 10s studying the fundamentals, or rudiments, of tradecraft. I was one of twenty in the three o'clock class; two other Rudie classes met in the morning. Tradecraft was compulsory, along with English, Maths, Science and all the rest. Most everyone but for Maize Addams, Prisha Kumari, the Sorenson Twins and one or two others was already fifteen by that April when we were assigned to monitor the residents of 17 Vernon Place, where Mr Peters lived.

There were around seven hundred girls at Lynton; more than a third were in senior school and not quite half of us were on bursaries or scholarships. It surprised me that my parents could afford the fees, even with the bursary we received (money that was as contingent on my maintaining grades as it was on my parents' income). But even when money was tight, when things needed doing to the house or Dad's work ebbed, I wasn't given over to agonising about it. Any time it swam up to bob on the surface of my consciousness, it was handily quashed by a sense of that's-just-the-way-it-is entitlement – something later outstripped by the amazement that my parents paid fees to, and encouraged me to excel at, a school instructing children in practices undermining individual privacy under the high banners of community and stitch-in-time national defence. Enrolling me in Lynton, they must have thought I would be hidden in plain sight, while trusting their own abilities as parents that this hiding would be more inoculation than inculcation.

Besides, there was hardly a choice. Every school taught tradecraft or something like it. Anyone with an older sibling already knew the basics, its knowledge handed down as though it were a favourite book or local myth. I was an only child and took right to it.

That first day of Tradecraft commenced not with Miss Rodmell taking attendance nor giving us an overview of that term's curriculum, but with an oral report from a dozen sixth-form girls. At the sound of the bell, they proceeded single file into the classroom and stood facing us. My heart raced at the theatre of it. A patch of sunlight angled across the floor and lit the legs of the girls nearest the windows. After a moment, Kitty Whitesmith, who wore her hair in a fringe that she changed from candy blue to grape or apple-red as the spirit took her, stood forward.

'Subject A exited 12 Connaught Place at 07:46, wearing a mid-tone grey blazer with a gold-stitched nightingale crest on the left chest pocket. Skirt, above the knee, green, pleated. Shirt, white with Peter Pan collar. Green- and grey-striped tie inserted between third and fourth shirt buttons. White knee stockings and brown size five Newick lace-up shoes. Black Timberland rucksack worn over right shoulder. Hair brown, approximately twenty centimetres in length, plaited. Eyes green. Approximately forty-eight kilograms. Height one-point-six metres. Complexion fair, with indication of sunburn on nose and earlobes. Make-up, none. Jewellery, none apparent. The subject proceeded along eastern side of Sackville Road, making no observed contact with passers-by. At Blatchington Road, Subject A crossed on crossing signal and proceeded to 15 Clarendon Villas, where she was met by Subject B after three knocks using door knocker. Subject A used left hand to knock. Time 07:58.'

Subject A was Charlotte James. From where she was seated three desks away, I could see Charlotte's face turn burgundy and her breathing hard through her nostrils. It was gratification, gratification shading into arousal. Here was one of the older girls – who, as everyone knew, could speak four or five languages; who, with her hair tucked beneath a cap, had played Percival in the school production of *Guinevere*; who was one of the 'Kemp House Forwards' who had racked up forty-six hockey goals between them the previous autumn – here was one of the older girls who had paid minute attention to Charlotte, who had followed Charlotte that morning and was now standing before a full classroom and, without mentioning Charlotte by name, describing her so completely that everyone had turned to look at her, silently wishing it had been them who had been the subject of Kitty's report. Kitty didn't once look at Charlotte while describing her and her route to school, but instead kept her eyes fixed on the back of the classroom. Now finished, she stood back in line, and Louisa Tompkins stepped forward.

'Subject B exited 15 Clarendon Villas after engaging in what appeared to be a verbal farewell to a person or persons inside. Note, Subject B was dressed in same grey blazer, green skirt and striped tie as Subject A, with the exception that her shirt was Oxford cloth with button down collar. Subject B also wore white knee stockings, with evidence of dark-corded anklet on left ankle. Shoes, black leather T-bar sandals with plaster-coloured soles. Black Herschel rucksack with brown leather strap and brass buckle worn over both shoulders. Black-framed Billy Bomberg glasses. Height approximately one-point-seven metres. Hair black and straightened, shoulder-length with centre parting. Eyes dark brown. Complexion medium brown. Subjects A and B spoke animatedly as they proceeded to Eaton Road, turned right onto Palmeira Avenue and left onto Lansdowne Road, left onto Furze Hill to Victoria Road, where they were met by a group of eight wearing Lynton uniforms. Subjects' topic of conversation is unknown.'

One by one each girl – all now in Lynton Upper Sixth and Tradecraft 3.1 – stood forward from the line at the front of the classroom. With eyes cast into the middle distance or fixed overhead, hands clasped behind their backs or straight along their sides, and in voices all but flattened of emotion, they described a Rudie leaving home that morning and making their way to school. Because there were nearly twice as many Rudies as sixth-formers who'd been assigned to tail and report back on us, to be amongst those who had been followed felt like a privilege.

As the sixth-formers moved from Subject C to D and on, I wondered if there was some deeper order to it, some divine calculation behind who had been chosen for observation. We had studied Calvinism in

Religious Studies; to be amongst those selected for following that morning had an air of predestination.

'Subject J,' I remember Maggie Flowers beginning and actually straightening my back in anticipation. Maggie Flowers, at seventeen, had spent the summer (and would continue spending school holidays and weekends) atop a scaffolding tower, restoring the Pre-Raphaelite murals uncovered at Chippley House a year or two earlier, and ten years later became the youngest woman ever to be appointed a dame. She was considered a brain at Lynton, kindly, and was an absolute demon at darts. After a pause during which she removed her glasses and, folding their arms, clasped them in her fist, she allowed herself a swift sideways smirk and continued,

'Subject J exited 62 Waterloo Street at 07:22 and was met by a man aged 68-75, short white hair, trimmed white goatee, skin tanned with pink blotches. Clothing, blue windcheater, denim shirt, corduroy trousers, oxblood leather lace-up boots, wristwatch apparent below left jacket cuff with outward-facing dial. The man had three dogs on leads, two Border Terriers and a Jack Russell. Subject J and the dog-walker gave the appearance of previous acquaintance and proceeded north along Waterloo Street...'

I wondered where Maggie had positioned herself and how long she'd been watching for me that morning. From its top at Western Road (along which Magritte and I would trail Mr Peters the following spring) Waterloo Street spilled slowly downhill toward the seafront. Along both sides of the street were parked cars – always parked cars – and about every fifty meters a cement planter out of which grew a spindly tree. Every few planters were paired with a wheelie bin for rubbish or recycling. I pictured Maggie crouched behind the bin opposite our house waiting for me to appear, then briskly stoop-stepping behind cars as she trailed me up the street. I pictured her like a hunter in a tree, keeping watch from a window in any of the houses across the way, before slipping out after I had passed, too busy chatting with Terry Peppers to give any notice, and following me on foot.

From my bedroom window and from the sitting room a storey below, on the first floor, I would often see Terry walking his dogs Molly, Golly and Ollie to and from the seafront. Terry was a widower; his husband had died when I was very young, when adults, outside my parents, Aunt Susie and one or two others, still hadn't formed in my mind as individual people, but were part of a vast network of grown-ups who had always been the age they were and whose functions were a mystery, beyond parenting and presents and providers of food and rules. That morning I hadn't seen Terry until I was out the front door. We walked together as far as his flat, at No 52, and would have passed other neighbours on their way to work and who didn't feature in Maggie's report.

'...Height, tall, one point eight metres,' Maggie continued. 'Hair, long, dark blonde, curly, approximately forty-four to forty-six centimetres, worn in ponytail. Eyes, blue. Complexion, light, with freckling around hairline and nose. Estimated weight, fifty-four kilograms...'

Maggie might well have said, 'Exceptionally tall', or 'Tallest of the class'. If she had been watching the whole house, my parents included, she could have said 'Taller than her mother' or 'Tall as the bridge of her father's nose.'

'You get your height from your Grandfather Anton, darling,' Mum told me when I was twelve and already borrowing her skirts, shirts and shoes. Mum and I had the same thickness of ankle and the same thick, curly hair, only hers was brown and cut into a bob longer in the front than at the back. 'He and his brothers were giants, all five of them. If they had stood one on top of the other, in a column, they'd be taller than our house, over three storeys. You get it from him, your grandfather. It skipped your dad. A mere five-eleven, when he doesn't slouch. Anton was one of the pair at six-four, with Arthur. Martin and George were six-six. Johnny six-seven. Your grandfather might not have been the tallest Fetlock, but he had a colossal calmness about him. The sort of person you'd want on hand if there was a baby needing delivery or things kicked-off on the train. He didn't swing it around. But it was there, this calm certainty in his eyes and limbs.' Then Mum handed me a jumper that had been hers and I turned to look at myself in the mirror. I had never met my grandfather. But our house, with my room at the top looking west through the chimney pots to the sunset and the sea, made me think of him, as Mum had described him to me: tall, narrow and calm.

Height I knew about. Height I understood. But I could never grasp acreage, not in relative terms. How it measures against blocks or stretches of the seafront between groynes. Lynton's grounds were perhaps the size of two, two-and-a-half football pitches, split unevenly on either side of Furzewell Avenue. On the southerly side was the junior school and gymnasium-cum-theatre in a modern three-storey building made of green glass extending from behind a prim, white-stuccoed cottage. I remember drawing it, in crayon or marker when I first began at Lynton, as an engorged caterpillar that, despite its diminutive head, had managed to consume so much food that its body had swollen out behind it like a sort of Cubist dirigible.

The image stuck; by the time I was a Rudie, I was never able to look at the building without wondering if it had been the architect's intent to design a structure embodying an earlier stage of the creamy and golden chrysalis of the senior school across the street.

This, the senior school, was girded on its street-facing flanks by high, knobbly stone walls. Openings in the wall were marked by pairs of enormous and preposterously phallic pillars painted a buttery magnolia. Some of the more audacious girls (Georgia Wilmott was one, and Amy Bracewell famously) would pen their boyfriend's name or initials onto the pillars' glans after they'd *done it*, or claimed to have. There were three buildings on the seniors' side of the grounds. The largest and oldest was The Laurels, a four-storey Georgian house whose rectangular shape, mansard roof and row upon row of windows had a homey simplicity to it that it, too, could have been designed by a child. It was unornamented by anything other than clematis. Reading *Pride and Prejudice,* it struck me as the sort of house that had once hosted balls and presided over garden parties amidst the wheeling kaleidoscope of summer, before being transformed into a school.

At home, Mum sometimes still wept out of the blue – and I think Dad cried too, alone. I could push it out of mind at Lynton. Everything seemed possible there. I was happy. Maggie Flowers following and reporting back on me that morning amplified my sense of belonging. I was inspired.

You'll show them, I said to myself, the hairs on my arms standing to attention. *You'll show them you're the best.*

History would see to that. History was coming. History came later.

The Kerckhoff Assumption states that, so long as the key remains hidden, a coded message is secure even when everyone knows it's a coded message. Shannon's Maxim goes one further, assuming all secret codes, like bank safes (or like willpower, trust and love) can or even will be cracked or broken. To that was added the Wyndham Proviso (also known as the Stapleton Condition or, because she had presented it to class with a dramatic hand movement, the Rodmell Finger): *if they are looking for it.*

Those three points, that triumvirate of theorem, reformulation and stipulation, together with the Four Ps (Prevent – Protect – Prepare – Pursue), were the basis of Rudie lessons and activities inside and out of class. As something of a buttress propping up the whole septet was Miss Rodmell's assertion:

'Misnomer, tradecraft means spying.' After she said it, her eyes appeared to follow something floating around the room above our heads. Despite there not having been a power cut of any significance for two or three days, Miss Rodmell had forgone any audio-visual aids after the sixth-formers had trooped out. She stood at the front of the classroom and spoke in a manner suggesting her hands were clasped to her hips. But then in a voice lathered with benevolence, her fingers interlaced and forming a bowl, she continued. 'Tradecraft is about helping and supporting. It's about information, recognising potentialities, recognising signs and,' she held our gaze, 'being aware.'

For fourteen- and fifteen-year-olds it was also about having fun – glorious, un-parented, secretive and, because we were fourteen and fifteen, display-able fun. I thrilled in it. Each Rudie was assigned a partner; Magritte and I were paired from the start.

Week one we learnt to make invisible ink with fruit juice and wrote each other notes. Then it was the rail fence cipher, the Caesar shift, the solitaire (and later, the Affine, the Vigenère) to concoct secret messages and palm them to each other along the school corridors, the gym changing room, the zebra crossing that linked the school grounds. We designated dead drops on the undersides of benches and behind loose lavatory tiles, on noticeboards and lunch hall tray racks. We pressed pushpins into doorjambs and trees, chalked the school wall with discreet strokes to signal a message was waiting at a dead drop, Xing them off when it had been collected. And because all of the other Rudies were in oppos-ing teams of two trying to intercept our messages just as we tried to intercept their own, we laid trails to false or 'double' dead drops. There, we secreted messages of elliptical nonsense or easily decrypted accusations of having a spotty face, pharaonic-styled curses of developing a saggy bum.

Much as I loved them, much as I knew they loved me, and much as I wanted their approval, Mum and Dad detested Tradecraft. They didn't say it so much, but I sensed how they avoided talking about it, how it never drew remarks like English or Astronomy or Lynton in general. I'd be lying if that wasn't part of the attraction, the magnetic grab of defying parental beliefs and teaching – and all of it sanctioned whole-sale by school and state.

When we weren't 'in the field,' Rudie Trade-craft was in a third floor classroom of The Laurels. A line of windows looked south through the trees and across the street at the junior school. Slanting squares of sunlight shone on the floor. There were six rows of long desks separated by an aisle up the middle. Girls sat two to a desk and Miss Rodmell at a table at the front facing the class. In the corner nearest the windows was a lectern, faintly clerical looking and wormholed. In late autumn and winter, when the skies were overcast and dusk began beating down after lunch, and there was a power cut, the classroom would plunge into a vesperal light. Miss Rodmell would remove a battery-operated lantern from the lectern's cabinet and continue the lesson, and girls would continue taking notes by the lights affixed to our desks. Each desk was fitted with a pair of telescopic stems that, when extended, were about half an arm's length and had small solar-powered lights on their tips. The stems were bendy and made of bamboo; everyone called them 'twigs'. They were the invention of Lauren Turner, an 'Old Tonner' as alumnae were known. While a Year 11 at Lynton ten or so years earlier, sometime not long after the power cuts had begun in earnest, she had sketched the twig design (so the story went) in the liminal dark of sixth period Geometry. Over the next half-term, she manufactured enough for her entire year. You extended the twig from where it was fixed to the desk, switched on the lamp at its tip and angled it until you could see.

But that first day of class the room was bright as a penny. And the Wyndham Proviso (or Rodmell Finger) went some distance in explaining why traditional tradecraft was being taught in schools. A secret code can and will be broken *if they are looking for it*.

But if no one is *looking* for it...

Beginning before I was born, beginning some time when Mum and Dad were young and everything began shifting from manual or analogue (or personal) to tech and digital, everyone began looking away from everything that wasn't electronic. If it was in plain sight, it was out of sight. That left a gap. That gap, it was asserted, made us vulnerable. Vulnerability meant risk. And risk meant danger.

Tradecraft classes were a response to that. Pick a school and it was there, in some form or another. You learnt to monitor without tech. You learnt to keep watch wherever you were and wherever you went. On your way to the shops, in parks, on the seafront, at home and in the homes of relatives, the homes of friends. Sometimes I think tradecraft must have made it easier or more compelling to be so devoted to technology. Tech is an impersonal gathering of information, an impersonal harvesting of data – so much data that it is impossible, even with tech, to analyse all of it. Tradecraft was the opposite. You didn't know who was keeping watch, or how many who's were watching. It could be anyone. Was it him, you would ask, the friend of a friend who's come along for coffee? Is it her, the parking attendant? The painter whistling atop the scaffold? That student in the rental flat across the street? You didn't know where to look. So you looked away. You looked back at tech to forget, and were entertained.

There were also the power cuts. They were another reason for teaching traditional tradecraft.

Power supply, like memory and, I'd soon find out for myself, like lovers, had become unreliable. The sun shone, the wind knifed and eddied, but power – electricity – had ebbed as a reliable faculty. The cuts – two or three most months, lasting anywhere from a few seconds to a couple days – began when I was too young to pay them any notice. But by the time I was no longer being bathed by my parents before bed, they began to grow in frequency and duration, until the cuts seemed to have developed a sentience of sorts, one that understood randomisation, the authority of repetition, inopportunity. When it was half-term and airports were jammed. When England's men's team were lining up for penalties. As traffic lights ran through the colours, trains sped toward level crossings... The cuts were blamed on power surges. Or power station short circuits. Or substation faults. Or broken lines. Or busted grids. The heat. The cold. Rain. Ice. The 'wrong kind of sun'. Or the power was needed elsewhere, diverted for global-contract commerce, for security threats that, for reasons of security, went undefined. Or some network of bedsitters brimming with caffeine and cryptocurrency had crashed it for shits and giggles. To show those in power and those in power of power companies a power of their own.

Traditional tradecraft didn't rely on electrics or tech. Traditional tradecraft relied on personal skill and guile. It taught us to keep our eyes open and to keep the information coming.

Besides, it was in our fiction and in our history. It was in our blood.

From its top at Western Road, looking down toward The Channel, Waterloo Street was a cream-coloured cascade, ornamented with verdant and floral patches. All of the buildings were three or four storeys. Many houses, like our own, had bowed front windows. In darker months, light shone through slits between curtains and there was the smell of woodsmoke and scented kindling. In summer, windows were thrown open to draw a breeze and those whose homes had balconies sat outside on foldaway chairs. Music played from inside sitting rooms, behind out-swelling curtains, and there was the sound of ice in glasses and corks ploiked from bottles and sometimes then, after sailing some distance, a *toink* or *tonk* when bouncing off a car bonnet. There was always the smell of the sea.

Home itself was a haphazard collage of furniture and artwork by family friends or was Mum-made, as we called it. Floorboards sounded orchestral notes. Every room was painted a different colour. It reminded me of the patchwork quilt Mum had made for me one Christmas. Fashioned from misshapen off-cuts and squares of samples, it was stitched together to produce a comforting and comfortable whole.

The sitting room shelves drooped with the weight of books and Malkmus, our cat, when he slept on them.

When there was still a month to go before the Crosses would arrive separately, half an hour apart one July day amongst the comings and goings of a party that lapped like a kind of tide between our house and the seafront, I returned home from school one afternoon to a weighted stillness. It was as though someone somewhere in the depth of the house had hissed hush just as the front door clacked closed behind me.

That sounds fanciful. But we were already on alert. A few days earlier, Dad, home alone, found his laptop lit up and running without having switched it on. Six dozen or more audio files had been accessed, all of them password protected. Nothing was missing. No one had entered our house. But someone was looking, and they didn't care if we knew.

I wanted to do right by that someone. I wanted to demonstrate we were okay, and left to be. Excelling at tradecraft would show them. By then nearing the end of a full academic year of it, I was attuned to listen and look out for the unordinary, for things out of place. National security – our lives, our safety – depended on vigilance.

When exactly I began feeling it depended on me must have accumulated gradually, like sea spume or a malignancy.

The silence that greeted me that afternoon hung heavy. Even when home was empty of people, there was always Malkmus. Much like I knew the usual sounds of homecoming and our house, Malkmus recognised the jingle of my keys, and would come popping downstairs to meet me, burbling a string of croaky *mwerps* when I came through the front door. Sometime not long before my third birthday I had found him, as a kitten. He was two- or three-weeks-old, Mum guessed and, with his four sisters and brothers, mewling in the hollow of a tree stump in St Anne's Well Gardens, where my parents along with some friends and their own children had gathered for a playdate. We were told to leave the litter untouched. But when one of the parents whispered they had spotted the mother cat dead in the road, each family who wanted a kitten took one. Years later I began questioning if the dead cat was really the mother, or a different cat whose death we used to justify the taking of another's kittens. In moments of cold anxiety, I pictured the mother cat in the tall grass watching helplessly as we selected which of her young to make our own.

Home was divided into two sections. On the ground floor and walled off from the front hall and stairwell were Mum and Dad's studios, accessible through a door kept double locked. Between Mum's studio at the front of the house, and Dad's in the back, was a second locked door. The locks were to protect Dad's audio and recording equipment. Atop his desk were a cockpit of preamps and compressors and devices with rainbows of lights and buttons; a pair of widescreen monitors; a laptop and microphones angling mantis-like in their stands. Coiled cables and headphones hung from hooks. The rear window was blacked out by soundproof curtains and the walls themselves cushioned with sound dampening foam.

Dad was a voice artist with an Octoberish tenor familiar to thousands, maybe millions. Sometimes when I would accompany him to the supermarket, or he would take me to the library or swim class, whomever was behind the till would glance inquisitively at him when he spoke, attempting to fix his features with where they had heard his voice before. At home, Dad would recite lines he was learning or lines he had learnt and liked. With a knife in one hand and a grapefruit squirting him from the other, I was one of the first to hear his Bertie Wooster. Lying on the sofa with his knees pointing toward the ceiling and a typescript curled in his hands, Mum and I were Mechanicals to Dad's Nick Bottom, and also ran him through *The Lady with the Little Dog* and *Spring Torrents*. He was a brilliant mimic, instantly catching the voices of cabinet ministers or twisting his voice into Glaswegian patter and Glamorganshire farmer. Most of his work was for radio, but there were also voiceovers for television, films and video games.

Mum and Dad each had keys to the studios and a set of spares was hidden under the stairwell runner. The first and second floors above were what we called 'our quarters'. At the very top was my bedroom and another for guests. The loo between the two rooms Dad had dubbed the Towering Shitter on account of its walls narrowing inward above the toilet to a skylight some ten feet above. Below, on the first floor, was Mum and Dad's room, a damp-smelling bathroom dwarfed by a rust-dappled tub, a sitting room with a fireplace, crumbling cornices and access to a narrow balcony that ran below the front windows. Cat hairs and dust were everywhere.

At the back was a box room through which you had to pass to reach a small porch, and the kitchen, inhabited at one end by a battered wooden table where we ate all of our meals, and on the other by an enormous cooker that, with its dashboard of levers and knobs, its grille and spread, looked like it had been refashioned from an old motor car. Shelves ran from countertop to ceiling and were packed with dried goods and spices. Pans hung from a rack above the sink. Above all, the room was dominated by a wide arched window that gazed over the neighbouring gardens.

When I came home from school that afternoon I paused for a moment before clicking my tongue for Malkmus. Puzzled at the silence, I called for him and again clicked my tongue, louder this time, as I climbed the stairs to our quarters. It wasn't until I reached the first landing that I heard the cat flap in the porch door go, and soon found Malkmus marching around the kitchen, his tail kinked in an indignant S-shape. There was a fat streak of water on the floor from where the pint glass that served as his water dish had toppled over. It was one of his peculiarities that he wouldn't drink from a bowl. Malkmus's food, ordinarily dry kibble on a saucer, was a pale, water-swollen mush on the floor. Why the mess, why the tumult that had caused it was unclear. I hardly gave it a thought.

As I began clearing it up, I heard Mum and Dad in the front hall and the bright vernal voice of Aunt Susie. Susie wasn't truly an aunt, not by blood or marriage, but a childhood friend of Dad's. In their youth, I was told much to my disgust and bewilderment, they had once 'snogged each other's faces off' at a party. A surprising piece of news, for I had only known Aunt Susie to like women. Things, I might have learnt sooner, weren't always, nor should they be, black and white.

It was Mum who discovered me in the kitchen that afternoon. The image of her rounding the corner, wearing a look of half-harried relief and saying something over her shoulder about the time, then starting back with a gasp, still blinks into focus uninvited in me – and with it, a smouldering afterburn from the internecine undoing that soon clove me from my childhood, my parents and home.

What had she seen that had made her gasp so? Was it, as I must have told myself then, simply an unexpected someone crouched in the corner with kitchen roll twisted around one hand and clutching something moist and bowely-looking, or was there something more? Mum's eyes when she saw me flashed with a mistrust that at once bordered on accusation and pleaded for acquittal. But acquittal from what?

Later, not that day, but sometime that summer, I understood there was dread there too. As though Mum had seen, in that same instant she saw me, the horror of something unfastened by her own hand, now whirling into form. Her look reminded me of a painting she herself had shown to me years earlier, not long after starting as an assistant curator at the Courtauld Brighton. I must have been about twelve; it was Mum's first job after a long illness during which she had ceased producing any artwork of her own. She had brought home proofs of an exhibition catalogue to tidy up the text written about each piece. The painting, Johann Heinrich Füssli's

Lady Macbeth Walking in her Sleep, was part of an exhibition based on the works of Shakespeare. In it, Lady Macbeth, somnambulant but awake inside to the horror of her and her husband's crimes, staggers wild-eyed and ashen from her chambers. Mum said the painting, and the scene itself, was about regret.

The look on Lady Macbeth's face stayed with me and was an image I used to scare myself with on nights when I felt like a good fright. I would picture the face materialising in unlit rooms, wandering the stairwell, or catching a glimpse of it gawping at me in my bedroom window. Now, on my mother's own face, a look akin to Lady Macbeth's crowding dread.

When I saw it, I looked away. 'What?' I said, hot with shame; how much for Mum and how much for myself I couldn't measure. I opened my hand so she could better see it was only cat food nestled in the paper cloth. '*I* didn't do it.'

Mum instantly composed herself. 'Of course not, darling. No, of course you didn't. Here, let me give you a hand.'

This annoyed me; the job was practically done. As I began saying I could finish it myself, Aunt Susie came in and set down her toolbox with a clang. Now I knew why Malkmus had tipped over his water. It was protest against construction noise from the studios below. He liked routine, nap-able daytime peace and quiet. Susie was here for work. She stood for a moment beneath the arch separating the kitchen from the hallway. Then crossing the floor to where I was crouched, she kissed the top of my head. Aunt Susie was small, an undersized fruit bowl bubbling to bursting with orbs and spheres. Her hair affected in me a buoyancy that, as a small child, would send me racing and, with a squealing leap, bouncing into her embrace. It was an explosion of corkscrew curls whose tunnelling hazel hollows quivered as though abuzz from sly celestial vibrations. If I had grown taller than Mum when I was twelve, Aunt Susie and I were eye to eye a year before that. Beginning around that same time, whenever I saw her the word *unpolluted* always swam to mind.

'After school snack?' she said peeling back the outer layer of kitchen roll in my hand. Aunt Susie was wearing knee-length jeans stippled with cracked paint and oil, a standard look for her. Susie did everything from electrics, to plumbing and carpentry: a handy-hand, as she phrased it. Below her jeans her legs were smeared with wood filler. She perspired a citrusy musk. 'Stay right where you are.' Susie crossed the room and, using the foot lever, popped open the rubbish bin lid. 'Five quid if you make it from there.' She had moved quickly to the far corner of the kitchen. Once there, she seemed to search for Mum's eye and nod.

'On the bounce?'

Aunt Susie shook her head no. 'Swish.'

As I weighed my shot, Dad, all this time like an understudy casting a final look at his lines, emerged as though speaking to a character offstage, on the stairwell landing.

'Yeah, yeah. Fine. Agreed. All else fails, we can sell her for parts. Trust me. Only fifteen, you know, so her liver is still a fine specimen of – Oh! *Hello*, darling.' Dad, with a muppety look for me, held up a quieting finger at his offstage co-conspirator. Then rolling his eyes and whistling dryly, he plunged his hands in his pockets and sauntered with openly feigned casualness into the kitchen. He wore his usual summer get up of shorts, flip-flops and striped t-shirt, beneath which a small but long bowl belly had taken form. Dad was thirty-eight, nearly a year younger than Mum, and his eyes twinkled like a poet's. It was one thing about him that never changed. Because it was summer, his beard was barely more than stubble. Chalky dust was caught in the hairs of his forearms and feet. 'Didn't know you were home, lovely.' He pushed his glasses to the bridge of his nose. Today he wore the pair with round metal frames that made him resemble an emigrant composer.

'Sarah,' he nodded at Mum. 'Susan.' Dad cleared his throat. 'Fine weather we're having. Fine, fine sunlight and... I was just saying to – ' He glanced over his shoulder. 'Oh, it doesn't matter. Who wants a cuppa?'

He started across the room for the kettle. Susie held up a hand. Dad stopped. Susie nodded for me to take the shot. I hit the rim and the wad stuck there, half in and half out, leaking its contents on the floor. Mum switched on the radio. The room filled with sound.

I could smell her shampoo, rosemary and mint, opened up by the steam in the bathroom one floor below. From my bed, I pictured Mum's face in the thin jets of the shower, eyes closed, as though meeting a kiss. A thick strand of hair clinging to her jaw and the water running down her throat. In that pose, she appeared younger than she was, a woman somewhere between her own thirty-nine years and my fifteen. I had woken a few minutes earlier to the sound of the outer studio door closing shut and listened for the locks knocking into place. Although two floors above, and too far to actually make it out, in my head I also heard the scrape of the keys turning the locks. The top one that said *whipperol* and the lower that made a noise like gastric juices on the move.

Thinking it was late, even for Mum and Dad who sometimes worked at night, I checked the time and saw it had gone half-one. If I couldn't get back to sleep, I would need to take a sleeping pill – or a quarter of one, considering the hour. I was prone to waking in the night. Typically, it was exams and worrying if I was a good enough friend to so-and-so, or if so-and-so was ignoring me because I hadn't gold-starred something they had posted on IcePie. There was all of that but I knew, too, that it had begun years earlier, when Mum was ill and she would vanish in plain sight. Now there was a voice telling me to keep a lookout, something inside insisting I keep guard.

Tonight, it had been the two of them in their studios. I followed their sounds as they came up the stairs to our quarters. Dad was half-singing, half-humming a song as he went from the stairwell to the sitting room, where there was the brisk, woody clatter of the curtains run closed along the rails. Moments later, empty mugs in hand, he went clanking to the kitchen. Meanwhile Mum had gone straight from the stairwell to the loo. The bathtub tap came on, whining as it strained for hot water. Then, almost in delayed response to Dad in the front room, the clicking of the shower curtain pulled to length across its rail and the hot hiss of the shower. I thought it strange Mum should wash her hair at this hour.

Incidental as they may have been, there was something about the sounds that sat with me, somewhere in my room, with neither name nor identity, as I lay awake picturing Mum's upturned face leant into the shower and how it had appeared when she had found me in the kitchen that afternoon, hurriedly masked with motherly normality – then Dad and Aunt Susie, a beat behind their cues and uncertain of their lines, explaining in detail how they had been busy mending the ON AIR light above Dad's studio door when I had arrived home.

Something didn't sit right. It was like thinking you'd glimpsed a bird flying in reverse or perched upside down – but when you looked again, all was as it should be. Outwardly Mum and Dad appeared the same as ever, only now seemed in want of some sort of assurance or validation. Tonight's sounds had the air of a performance, a second act to underscore the afternoon's nothing-much-to-see message, its just-getting-on-with-things message and here-we-are-at-home-on-just-another-weekday message.

Mum's face had been a parody of that. But not a parody of faces you see in art. In art, it was common to see people – particularly women, Mum once told me – looking mournful or pained. Her own face was almost without sharpness; only her eyebrows, thin and dark, had any real angularity. That and a pink scar like a tick-mark below her bottom lip from a childhood bicycle accident. Mum had a wide fore-head and narrow chin. It was a shape, a face shape, she had shown to me in pieces from Rubens to Velasquez and El Greco. After time, I started noticing it for myself, in paintings and on people. The shape came to define femininity in my mind, as much as more obvious things like hips and breasts. While at work or listening to someone speak, Mum's lips contracted into a dash so tight you wouldn't think a teaspoon would fit. In repose or when she thought she was alone she would tuck her bottom lip beneath the top. Best of all was joy, when her mouth grew – or exploded – into an immense, open-toothed smile, like the entrance to the funhouse ride on the pier. It was a contagious smile; I looked for an outline of it in my own. Our eyes were the same pale blue, with the left at a slight sag to the right.

Although Mum didn't believe in god, religious art (and its centuries of pained women) held a special attraction for her. We often travelled up to London, to its museums and galleries to view their permanent collections and exhibitions. On the promise of a Calippo or Cornetto, there were day-long excursions to manor houses and stone churches adjoining out of the way two-road townlets with names like Steeping Alciston and Fenny Fittleworth. We would set out on foot from empty rural train stations, along empty roads, before breaking off down stony dirt paths through head-high lavender and rapeseed, eventually reaching our destination and their time-darkened murals depicting St Sebastian or St Lewinna or the Three Marys.

'It's a fetishisation,' Mum said to me with crisp certainty. We were on a train home from visiting Middle Filching Manor to see its restored Smetham drawings. I was too young to know what fetish meant but was aware of the way the man seated across from us in the train carriage glanced at us both at hearing the word, the inquisitive flare of his nostrils. Mum enlarged the photo on her mobile screen she'd taken of one drawing. 'Look at their faces. The Virgin Mary, Mary Magdalene and Mary of Clopas are portrayed looking mournful, weeping. That's their beauty, their pain. Or their suppression of it.'

FOUR

The Dome café was sunlit and busy. The air was bright, as though washed vigorously only that morning. Voices, like a murmuration of starlings, swelled and dove with the hiss and bang of the coffee machines behind the bar. At a table near the centre, Alastair's arm was crooked halfway behind Anna, along the back of her chair.

'Hooper's conspicuous. Tell Bennet to grab a cuppa and switch with him. Do it now.' Alastair's eyes, high green and given to flashes and darkenings, sought Anna's own when he spoke, although the words were for the two boys at the table behind his outstretched arm.

Anna nodded, as though responding to Alastair. Nodding was good: it was something. She hadn't said anything for how long now? she asked herself. Not since she spilt her coffee. It was still there on the table, in a cold brown sea of tissues and down Alastair's leg. One of the boys at the next table tapped Alastair's instructions into his mobile phone and sent them on. Anna, despite the certainty she could now smell the sweat under her arms, raised her hand for the dozenth time and raked her hair back. She was in Lynton uniform (she thought of the skirts at home, the t-shirts and vests, the ankle boots that made her feel sophisticated, at least six-teen), mutely paling or blushing and convinced that, should she be sent on a manoeuvre herself, or just collect her rucksack and go, she would trip or invol-untarily sprint. There were a few – more than a few, she noticed suddenly – Malkmus hairs on the cuffs of her blazer, but she daren't pick them off now, lest she draw attention to her untidiness. Perhaps he hadn't noticed? Alastair. Alastair Broyle.

How many Tops were in on the operation Anna wasn't certain. She and Magritte, who was sta-tioned near the northeast exit with Danny, another of Alastair's team, weren't officially involved. Only the boys, no Rudies. Rudies were at Lynton and nowhere else. At other schools, Tradecraft stu-dents had no name. But at Hanover Park Boys they were Tradecraft Ops – Tops. Apart from Alastair and Danny and the boys at the table over Alastair's arm, Anna counted four more plainclothes Tops amongst the dozens of exhibition goers flowing in and out of the adjoining halls. The narrow, vine-gary-looking boy named Hooper stationed on the mezzanine above the bar, and another at each of the ground floor exits. She wondered also about the boy working at a sketchpad three tables over, but he looked too old for Year 10, looked older than even Alastair, who had a year on the other Tops and two on Anna.

Alastair pointed past her at one of the sculptures, oversized and suspended by wire from the ceiling high above. The ceiling was long and barrel-shaped; a line of skylights, like the eye of a goat, ran the length of the room and the sculptures floated almost aquatically in the sunlight. 'We'll make out like we're talking about those things, the art stuff, beginning with the starfish.' Squinting, Alastair traced a slow finger in and out along the figure's limbs. 'Keep looking at it while I carry on for a minute. Nothing showy. Just look as though I'm talking about the starfish. Then you take over. Point first at the jellyfish, then the blue whale, then the seahorse, at the other end, so you guide me around the room to look over my left shoulder. Say something about each. *Don't* rush. Ten, fifteen seconds per sculpture. Got it? Here, look this way. No, at me.' Alastair's eyes were noticeably asymmetrical, the right set at a downward angle from the left. 'Do you know anything about sea life?'

Anna, who knew about sea life as much as the next person, shook her head no. She stared upward past the dolphin posed in the act of leaping, at the skylights beyond. Sunlight shone hard through the windows, summer was in high bloom. It was June; school broke up three weeks to the day; and Alastair Broyle, Anna told herself, now knew her name. She felt him looking at her. Seconds passed. Her head swam. She shook it again. Then, from somewhere, she found a voice that was as much her own as her mother's.

'But I can tell you about the pieces,' she began. 'They're by Emily Kindberg. She did the *Sacred Cow* for the fourth plinth in Trafalgar Square, also the *Golden Bough* at the Courtauld Brighton. Each of these,' Anna continued, finding confidence in the sound of her own voice and circling her finger overhead, 'are in twelve colours, primary through tertiary. No black or white. And each piece is made of one thousand nine hundred and sixty-nine individual pieces of paper. She doesn't explain why.'

Alastair's lips parted, like he had been shown up for a dilettante and mislaid his defence. Of the two of them, until today, only Anna knew anything about the other. Alastair had been a yeasty whisper of a boy until the previous summer when, reportedly, his initials had twice been daubed on Lynton's phallic pillars but mysteriously painted over a day later both times. He had a quick, sultanic face and a prowling voice that Anna heard in her body.

'Why what?' Alastair bunched his lips.

'Why always that figure, that amount of paper for each piece.'

'I thought perhaps why sea creatures to begin with? It makes me think. There are one, two, three...' keeping his arm along the back of Anna's chair,

Alastair tipped back his head, then his shoulders, and silently (and with deliberate languidness) counted the remaining sculptures with his free hand '...eleven of them. Maybe there's something in that? Eleven times one thousand nine six nine. Or divided by. Anyway, *only* that figure? No. I don't buy it. Who's counted it up? Other than what she says, this artist, what's the evidence? What's keeping Bennet?'

'Half a minute,' came the reply from the next table. 'Stuck in a queue.'

'Tell him to forget the bloody tea and get in position. Hooper's about as subtle as a meerkat. We need another of you. Any more Rudies around? Keep going about it. The art.' Alastair jerked his chin up at the dolphin and leant closer to Anna. His hand held firm where it was on the back of her chair.

Anna's head fizzed and fluttered. Would there be photos of the two of them on IcePie? For a few dozen Ambrosia points, she could buy an image from the Dome's CCTV. Or Magritte, had she taken any pictures? If Alastair saw her taking photos of them, would he tell them to leave? And if he wanted to look over his left shoulder so much, why hadn't he done it when counting the sculptures just now? With youthfully feigned unawareness Alastair held himself in an almanac of poses seemingly borrowed from classical sculptures and oil paintings, poses that displayed his swimmer's slender brawn, his alertness or him brooding. His hair, an odyssey of curls, had performance aspirations of its own. In its auburn whorls were peninsulas and horns, gyres and waves. Was it the whale, the jellyfish and then the seahorse, or the first two the other way around?

It had been Magritte who suggested she and Anna go to Brighton Dome after school that afternoon. Ordinarily, they might have gone to one of the other's houses, the shops or to the seafront for a swim, but Magritte had to collect tickets at the box office (Father's Day was that coming weekend) and on Tuesdays the café did two-for-one iced coffees. They had just ordered their drinks at the bar when a boy wearing a cricket jumper and shorts angled himself against the counter beside Magritte. The boy had bright eyes with long lashes and wore his hair in a tidy quiff.

'I can get these.'

'Can. But. Won't.' Magritte hovered her mobile phone above the payment screen. She looked the boy up and down like he was bad milk. 'Shouldn't you be out throwing balls at someone?'

'I'll throw my balls at whom I like. *Not* you two.' The boy raised his eyebrows, as though to say: *understand*? Then assuming an affronted look: 'You really don't *remember* me?'

'...From?'

'From! From the mists of the past.' The boy's fingers danced up and down as he waved his hands away to the sides. 'Ten, eleven years ago, *Magritte Malling*. Ten, eleven years ago, you lived in the ground floor flat at 28 Shanklin Terrace. Upstairs, through his own front door, in his little box room with, fittingly for this reunion, an aquatic-themed mobile above his cot, was the magnificent young princeling, empaupered in his little blue realm. Ring any bells? We used to nap together. You had a silver dress with puffy sleeves, a hobby horse named Daphne Gallop, ate crayons and – '

'Donny...Porter?'

'Danny.'

'You had a dog, a chocolate Lab.' Magritte's voice was matter of fact.

'Irish Setter.' The boy arched an eyebrow.

'And a kitten who would...'

'Paw and suckle at the dog's – her name was Sasha – teat.'

'There was a canvass swing in the front window.'

'A hammock, actually. But I think you *might* already know that. You're testing me. As you should, as you should. If you'll permit me, your parents had – ' the boy quickly described in enough detail the flat Magritte had lived in for her first four years that Anna saw her shoulders take a more natural, less armoured shape.

'So you're what, out buying old playmates after-noon coffee?'

'Mud pies, too. *If* you still like them. But really, it's something else. Top stuff, you see. Come. We can't talk here.'

Moments later and they had woven through the café to where a boy with his back to them drank tea from a cup and saucer. On the table in front of him was an uneaten scone and a paperback book open at his elbow. Anna set her drink down and surreptitiously wiped her palms dry.

There was something disingenuous about the way the boy remained immobile, as if he hadn't sensed their arrival or heard Danny say his name. His spine erect, his jaw set, his eyes were cast with alert intensity at the giant squid dangling above the tables in the far corner. After a beat he stood and turned. Alastair held his shoulders back, so that his arms fell slightly behind his body kept pushed forward at the pelvis. With his right arm straight and turned outward and his thumb all but touch-ing a crooked middle finger, he raised his left from the elbow and, in an almost dismissive gesture, his eyes took in Anna, then Magritte, before landing on Danny.

'Two minutes. Take the table at one o'clock.'

'One! It's already gone four.' Magritte laughed, pointing at the oversize clock on the mezzanine.

'I believe he means one o'clock there.' Danny nodded toward the tables at the far side of the bar.

Alastair's face hardened. 'No. I don't. I mean my one o'clock.'

Danny's eyes darted away. 'Roger. Come on Ems. Does anyone still call you that? You can be my... *déguisement amour*. But promise you won't try and kiss me. Far too much of *that*, thank you very much, when we used to go to bed together.' Somehow it was understood that only Magritte would go with Danny, and Anna would stay behind with Alastair. Pairing off as couples was Trailing Procedure 16d, known amongst Rudies as 'plausible grope-ability' or 'kissing cover'.

Alastair drew out a chair for Anna and sat beside her. 'Anything?' His eyes flashed. Thinking Alastair was asking if she wanted a drink (thinking he was indeed speaking to her), Anna tried lifting her iced coffee, but felt it hold fast with condensation to the table top – and with a jerk give way, sloshing across the table and over the side.

'No sign,' came a boy at the table behind them. 'Tissue?'

'No.' Alastair continued looking at Anna, who was already yanking napkins from the holder on their table and pressing them into the spilt coffee. 'Got it covered. Here,' his tone softened. 'Let me help. We should laugh at this.' He did. But all Anna could do was say sorry again and again in a bronze whisper.

No, Anna decided. No, she wouldn't buy a CCTV image of them for IcePie. If he was at all interested in her, Alastair could spend his own Ambrosia points. And no, she wouldn't worry about what order she pointed to the overhead sculptures, saying a few words about each. Having found her voice she had a half a mind to say what was on it. Alastair got under her skin, his way of examining her with his gaze while speaking to the boys on the next table. And when he did talk to her, she didn't much like being given instructions when she didn't know what was happening. Still, *something* was happening and she couldn't shake the desire to play along. Alastair. Alastair Broyle. She felt silvery inside. The seahorse came last – the seahorse and its question mark of a body. Pointing at the blue whale, Anna began,

'Why did you send Danny for us?'

A smirk lifted Alastair's ear. 'Do you mean, why didn't Danny and I act like a couple ourselves, or why didn't I approach you myself? The blue whale.'

'Largest creature on earth. Yes, why not the two of you here, at command central or whatever you call it?'

'Keep your voice down. Or you go. It's the same procedure with Rudies. You tell me.'

'Because you would have been all over each other and wouldn't keep watch?'

Alastair shook his head and looked away. 'You can't be too much of a Rudie. The seahorse.'

'Because it makes two couples. You cover more ground. Here and...' she inclined her head in the direction of Danny and Magritte.

'His idea, actually. One of his better ones. Making use of available cover.'

'What, like a parked car or a shrub?' Anna feigned offense.

Alastair waggled his head. His eyes danced. 'More like a lamppost.'

Anna crossed her arms and wound her neck back. 'A *lamppost*?'

'You know what a letterbox is, don't you? This café is a letterbox. Messages left and messages collected. Our subject of interest is here to post a message to his contact. The seahorse.'

'The seahorse,' Anna started – and stopped, while she thought what to say next. As a small child she had a storybook about seahorses. From it she knew they changed colour when courting, displaying their emotion in bursts of pinks and purples, in shades of green, and would swim side by side, their tails coiled round the other's like people hold hands. She could still recall the scent of the book's inner spine and it comforted her now.

'Subject arriving in three, two, one, now. Two o'clock.'

'Whose?'

'Yours. Northeast entrance. Moving to one o'clock, the pamphlet display.'

'Got him.' Alastair looked past Anna, then back at her again. 'Summarise and alert all.'

'Subject is lone Asian male, 40s, clean shaven with short greying hair. Three-piece cream-coloured suit, blue shirt, green-striped tie, shopping bags in both hands.'

'How many bags? Danny have eyes?'

'Checking.'

'No. Don't turn around.' Alastair gestured to Anna and again laughed for show. 'Gives the game away. Patience. Danny report yet?'

'Waiting. Subject has set his shopping on display table. Appears to be selecting pamphlets and... Subject has five bags. Repeat, five bags.'

'Pamphlets?'

'He's selected one. Two. Three. No, two. Subject has returned one to display table.'

'Priority Danny gets the one put back. Soon as subject moves away, Danny counts to twelve and retrieves it.'

'Roger. Subject has collected shopping and moving toward bar. Twelve seconds beginning now. Subject approaching three o'clock, four...now six.'

'Bags?'

'Five. Confirm five bags.'

'Note any shop logos visible. Danny collected that pamphlet?'

'Verifying.'

'Confirm Bennet's in position.'

'...Confirm Bennet...Confirm pamphlet retrieved. Subject is now placing order. Bartender is female, blonde ponytail. Age, forty to forty-five. Ears pierced with gold hoops. Uniform is white shirt, black tie and waistcoat.'

'Subject's bags?'

'On floor by his feet. Now count six bags. Repeat, six bags.'

'Enquire Bennet to confirm reception of sixth bag en route to bar.'

'Checking...Negative. Bennet reports subject had no contact with public.'

'Confirm anyone leaving bag at bar prior to subject's arrival.'

'Not known. Eyes were on the subject. Impossible to know bar was his destination. Confirm subject arrived at bar alone.'

'Note to check Hooper's and Bennet's cameras for anyone leaving bag at bar prior to subject's arrival. Note Porter possible failure to supply accurate count. Instruct Porter to return to pamphlet display and retrieve top two of all pamphlets.'

'There must be twenty different – '

'Do it.' Alastair looked through Anna. Then he rolled his eyes. 'Whole bloody place is a letterbox. Could be anything, anywhere or any– '

'Sir. Subject now receiving bar order. Takeaway coffee, large, black. He's waved away a lid.'

'Watch the payment.'

'Eyes on payment...Cash.'

'Bastard's not leaving a trail.'

'Subject collecting bags. Confirm six bags, now carried in one hand.'

'Which?'

'Right. Coffee in left. Subject moving northwest through the tables. Seven o'clock, now eight...'

And there he was, in his three-piece suit straight ahead of Anna, squeezing sideways, almost hiero-glyphically, through the tables of exhibition goers and pensioners, his right arm bent behind him at the elbow and wrist with the shopping, the coffee held head high in his left. Anna had just caught sight of him (his lips forming an O to help him finesse his swivel, to round his twirl) when an elderly woman in a wheelchair pushed off backward from her table and caught the man on the hip.

Now the coffee flew from the man's cup. Now his body curved away from the splash as it clapped across his lapel (also his shirt, tie and waistcoat). Now the man's shopping jerked up and struck the heads of the people at the table in front of him, then swung the other way and crunched against heads of the people at the table behind. Everything stopped. The man stood blinking. The woman in the wheel-chair sat blinking. Anna sputtered and laughed into her hand. Such a dramatic spill – she thought of Hokusai's wave – erased the shame of her own. The sea sculptures overhead swayed in a breeze unfelt if not seen.

the iComm

I am an ordinary person. Look around and you won't find anyone more ordinary than me. I have ordinary needs, ordinary desires. I am a small business owner, running my own shop. I live in a flat. My bills for the shop and flat I pay on time, without question. I enjoy music and films, sunsets, flowers, and a well-trimmed hedge. I am ordinary. I am. Anyone asks how or why I could have been an iComm, an inter-community communicator, I tell them it was two things. There was Milan and there was death.

Milan. One morning in the shop, some months before I met Morkel, I overheard a woman talking on her mobile phone. She was telling a friend how, on a recent trip to Milan, she had been upgraded from 'cattle class', to business. While this particular woman was buckling in, and the jetway was still attached to the plane, one of the stewards approached and instructed her to gather her overhead luggage and follow him to the front of the aircraft.

At first she thought she was being escorted off the flight, and worried that her – *you know*, she said down the phone with an upward glance to see if any-one was listening (I quickly toppled and made busy restacking a column of coasters). But before they reached the door, the steward, gesturing grandly, presented her a wide seat with an adjustable back that reclined flat, slippers and a blanket. The plane needed balancing, he explained handing her a menu. She was being upgraded. 'Madame,' he said. 'If you please...' Glass of prosecco and nuts.

Now I had never been to Milan and had never myself flown business class. But I knew then that, given the chance, I would do both. Milan didn't matter so much; it was the upgrade that interested me. Since meeting Morkel it felt like I, too, had been re-seated. Since meeting Morkel I felt I was doing my bit to keep things balanced. It was for the greater good – the good of us one and all. I asked myself, who wouldn't say yes?

There was Milan, and there was also death.

In the beginning, there is life. And in the same instant, there is death. You can't have one without the other. If life or consciousness is like a mirror permitting us to see ourselves in the world, death is the dark backing that makes a plate of glass a mirror. I almost died. But first there is my mother, who did.

As it happens, it was a plate of glass that killed her. As it also happens, my father was walking at her side when she died, holding her hand. They had gone to the marina to meet friends for lunch. Afterward, full of shellfish and wine, they were approaching their bus stop when death made its play. The sea wind loosened a window on Piedmont Tower, then newly constructed above the west quay, and sent it sailing down, swift and whole, finding my mother right above the shoulders...

My own brush with death came early; only much later did I truly understand it. When I was still not yet two-years-old I had an infection. This infection took the form of a discoloured lump on my neck, an angry nerve that had swollen out 'like a meatball' according to my mother, a nurse both at home and at work. Unable to comprehend the story when told to me at a young age, the infection lost its identity and became instead an actual meatball – beef most likely, although possibly lamb – that had lodged in, and was surgically cut from, my throat. As the years passed, I grew aware how often I would find myself fingering the scar on my neck as I wheeled a trolley past the pasta display at the supermarket, or when encountering anyone whom I took to be a visiting Swede.

Much later, when I was grown and already running the shop, I mentioned the incident to my father in one of our now maundering conversations, how I had almost died at less than two-years-old from choking on a meatball, and asked if he remembered the incident. My father cast his eyes up as though called upon by a passing cloud to calculate the cosine of some complex equation or another, slapped his knee in the same manner his own cidery father had to the shanties he had sang down the pub, and creased over laughing.

'Not a meatball,' he managed after a full minute of slobbery puffling. 'The size of a... Who feeds a baby – ?' and with a snort was away again. At that point Reginald, my father's cat, popped through the kitchen window and stared at him before, having crept closer (and with an outstretched paw), appearing to take his pulse.

Until then the story, to my mind, was that, at fifteen or sixteen months, I, fair-haired and ducal in my highchair, had been issued a meatball for my tea, gobbed it whole and almost died from choking. The meatball, having advanced halfway along my windpipe, had needed to be cut from my neck by a surgeon. After years of fingering the scar (and wishing above all the slice on my mother's neck had been as insignificant as my own), what I still didn't understand was why the object hadn't been forced from me there and then at the family table. Why hadn't I been hoisted blue-faced from my seat and administered the Heimlich? Given my father's love, coupled with his penchant for tidiness, after a sharp abdominal thrust or three the meatball would have launched from my lips and, with a knightly plop, landed in the casserole dish from whence it came.

But no. It had been a simple if aggressive infection, an angry abnormality that came millimetres from asphyxiating me. Only an emergency razoring by my mum eased the swelling against my windpipe (she was a nurse, as I say, at home and at work). I was thirty when I gathered the truth.

So. There we have it. You must seek and speak the clear truth from the beginning. Otherwise people live their entire lives misinformed. That is my logic. An iComm provides the truth. An iComm chaperones the truth. And for it, the small rewards. What I saw and heard I passed along. Morkel and I met once or twice a week. Typically he would come to the shop, purchase whatever – an astronaut pen, a bar of cedar soap – and we would while away twenty or thirty minutes if it was only us. If others were about, he would suggest a date and place to meet. Sometimes it was ping-pong at one of the outdoor tables on the seafront or in St Anne's Well Gardens. After a best of three, we would sit on a bench and talk. Other times it was badminton and a steam at the health centre, where we racked up double Ambrosia points for all the exercise (Morkel knew how to work the system). Only once did we go for boules; I found I had a natural talent for it and swiftly won three-nil. We never played again.

Other times, if I hadn't done anything socially for a while, I would get in touch with him. But it was really Morkel who arranged things. He seemed to know when I was free, so only rarely did I need to decline or suggest an alternative. After a few months of light sport and shop talks, we began meeting at his flat.

I say 'his' flat, but really Morkel was only staying there temporarily, he explained, owing to a spectacular misfortune that prevented him from living at his actual home for the foreseeable.

'The whole place needs redoing – *every*thing,' Morkel told me shaking his head. He went on to explain how, after years of sacrifice and saving, he finally had enough money to convert his cellar into a habitable room. He had always dreamed of a basement kitchen, where he could while away weekends entertaining friends. His hasselback potatoes with a truffled Béarnaise, he let me understand, had them queueing.

'But three weeks into construction the builder shifted a beam that had evidently been bracing everything up. You couldn't see it at first, but the house began to list. Not just mine – oh, no – but the house next door, and next door but one. Terraced, you understand. The alarm was only raised when...' Morkel arched himself backwards like before when trying to recollect Mac McKenzie's name that time in the shop, then popped upright again '...Sally, who lives next door, left to walk her dog. She opened her front door no problem, but now it wouldn't close behind her. The jamb had shifted. Everything was...' Holding his hands upright and parallel to each other, Morkel made a creaking noise and slanted his fingers to one side. 'I had ten minutes to grab what I could before the place was sealed off.'

Morkel told me the street. A few days later I was in the neighbourhood and went to see for myself. Sure enough, there was his house behind a wilderness of scaffolding, like a medieval tower under siege. It was a tall end of terrace townhouse; only the front façade and a portion of the side wall remained. Both were now propped upright by scaffolding angled across the street as far as the pavement opposite. The sky was visible through the second floor window (what with the roof having spilled in). From the side the house was a bravura of crumbled plaster and broken brick, opened up as though burst by a bomb. Morkel had favoured Victorian colours; the rooms were painted deep blue, deep brown, maroon and charcoal. It would be a year and a half, maybe even two, he explained, before the rebuild was complete.

'His' flat, then, was in Buckingham Road, just up from Brighton Station. It consisted of a ground floor sitting room with a curved bay window and parquet floors, a galley kitchen overlooking shared gardens in back, and a bedroom sandwiched in between. There were flats below and above and not a sound from either. Here, a table with matching chairs, a cafetière, a lamp with a paper shade. There, a sofa, a cooker, an unspeakable rug. There weren't any shelves; and it was my impression that if I should open any of the kitchen drawers there would be but a lone saucepan, a fork, a spoon, a single knife, if anything at all.

There was definitely a pair of cups, however; the coffee Morkel served was excellent. And it was over coffee one afternoon that he asked me what I knew about the Hassop Five. Until that day, I had casually conferred to him whatever insight I had on customers, deliverymen, fellow shopkeepers, regulars at the café and pubs I frequented, neighbours and people whose paths I crossed at the supermarket. I wanted to impress him. Information meant Ambrosia points. We'd talk, and the points would appear in my account. Usually it was forty or fifty, on occasion seventy-five or eighty and, at Christmas, a clean two-fifty. They added up. Never before had Morkel asked about anyone in particular.

The Hassop Five were a group of environmental activists arrested months earlier for protesting the Brightside Lane fracking site in Derbyshire. The three women and two men were charged with grievous public nuisance, a new elevated charge brought into legislation for offenses deemed to materially injure or incapacitate a significant portion of the populace. Penalties were severe, designed to punish and deter. The Hassop Five had halted a convoy of trucks by clambering atop the lorries delivering fracking equipment to the worksite – the drills, the chemical tanks, the towers and pumps. They stayed for nine days, until their supplies ran out. Angela Gissing, Simone Roberts and George Coombs received forty-three-month sentences and were stripped of all Ambrosia points, tens of thousands between them.

The remaining two – Mark and Hannah Cross – had quietly vanished whilst awaiting sentencing. Their faces and names were everywhere. Beyond what had appeared in the news and online, I couldn't think what more I knew.

'Probably holed up in some Alpine bothy or Laotian hut.' Morkel handed me a photo of the Crosses taken at the Brightside Lane protest and winced at the sun in his front window.

I thought of Samuel. 'No chance. Not with her pregnant.'

SIX

Anna

There was no warning for the switch. One afternoon, on the second day of my Year 9 autumn term, almost exactly a year before I became a Rudie, Miss Buxted asked me to stay after class. Miss Buxted taught English; amongst Lynton girls, she was a favourite. She gave the impression of playing less strictly by the rules than other teachers. That and her warm as-it-is manner encouraged us. Sometimes she would dress in period costume and conduct class as though she were the author of one of the texts we were studying, or one of the characters. We read *Mansfield Park*, *A Month in the Country*, *Mademoiselle de Scudéri* and poems by Antonia Hemmings and Wendy Cope. Anything sexual in the texts she dealt a wry smile and bright eyes. It was my final class of the day. The room smelt of sunlight and pollen. Through the open window was the sound of gulls crying.

'Now then, Anna. First things first.' Miss Buxted sat down beside me at my table. Calling students by our first names was one of the things that endeared her to us. She had a low mauve voice, pale eyes and wore her hair upswept atop her head in two large curls pinned off centre. About the same age as my parents, she appeared unwed (and therefore ineligible for the

Ambrosia marital bonus points lottery). After asking about my summer and listening as I told her about all the swimming I'd done, how I'd mistaken a nappy for a jellyfish in the shallows near the old West Pier, and how, at home during the August heatwave, we had kept shirts folded in the freezer to slip into for temporary relief (which drew a shiver and a laugh from us both), Miss Buxted said,

'Something was brought to my attention yesterday after class.' She inflated her cheeks and let the air out slowly. Miss Buxted was wearing a collarless jacket over a button-down shirt and a loose, floaty skirt. She fished something from her pocket and kept it covered in her hand. I tried to think what I'd done wrong and stared at the table, hoping to look penitent. 'You must forgive me for being the one to tell you,' Miss Buxted continued. 'Over the summer the school conducted a House Assessment. You know what those are, I think.'

'Yes, Miss.' I nodded.

'Every girl knows, I'm sure. Only the point is you *didn't* know. The Assessment results should have been communicated to you and your parents before now. It was for...for fool's reasons they weren't. Do you understand what I'm telling you? It was an oversight, and house transfers are *not* a punishment.' Miss Buxted rested her hand on my arm. Rules prevented teachers from touching students. Handshakes were permitted, but nothing more. 'I know you've been sailing along at Canterbury, and it's because you're doing so very well that the Headmistress has reassigned you to Mallory. It's a paper switch more than anything and won't affect any of your classes or friendships with the other girls or – oh, Anna darling, don't. No, no. Come here.'

I don't know for how long I cried. But all the while Miss Buxted held me to her. That made it worse; I so wanted to impress her, and there I was, blubbing away. But eventually I sat up and dried my eyes. Miss Buxted's sleeve was marked with dark patches by my snot and tears. She pretended to not notice. That *really* made things worse.

'Better?'

'Yes, Miss.'

Miss Buxted folded her hands on the table; whatever she had removed from her jacket pocket earlier was still hidden beneath them. 'If anyone had asked me at your age if I thought I would become the sort of person who quoted things to others, I would have been appalled. Quoting always seemed so...arrogant, don't you think? Nevertheless: *In time all undertakings are made good, All cruelties remedied, Each bond resealed more firmly than before.* Have you read any Robert Graves? No? I thought perhaps at home, something your father was rehearsing. A war poet. Graves, Owen, Sassoon, Edmund Blunden...They're not on the curriculum these days. Unfashionable now. Or too...we spent an entire term on them when I was a student here.'

I marvelled at her. 'Miss?'

'Oh yes. English Lit was in the room next door. This room was Classics. News to you? Well, well, well. Secrets still exist. Good to see you girls don't know *everything*.' Miss Buxted's eyes delighted like they would later that term when discussing the symbolism of J.L. Carr's Alice Keach finding Tom Birkin alone in a church garden and, handing him something to eat, saying she knows how much he likes a 'firm apple.'

It was then that Miss Buxted revealed what she had been hiding under her hands. A small, finger-worn velvet box, it had a clasp at the front and miniature hinges at the back. Thin cream-coloured piping ran along the seam of its lid.

'Go on, open it.' Inside, the box was lined with fraying silk. A brooch, circular and no larger than a penny, was fixed into the bottom half. A ring of gold traced around the outer edge of the brooch. In its centre was a single oak leaf, rendered in a now coppery ormolu. Miss Buxted pulled it free and instructed me to turn to her.

'Now this,' she poked the pin at the back of the brooch through my blazer placket and fixed it to its clasp. 'This was the Mallory badge I was given when I arrived at Lynton in Year 10. There!'

I touched it with a fingertip. My own school-is-sued Canterbury badge was a plastic button with a safety pin on the back. Like most girls, I wore it on my rucksack. Only head girls and those who held house offices were issued the enamelled sort. This was something altogether different.

As though reading my thoughts, Miss Buxted said, 'In my day everyone had these. Not so for years now. Gone the way of our war poets. But never mind about that. I'm giving it to you, as a welcome to Mallory. It's yours. For keeps.'

I tried to think what to say.

'You prefer an ordinary one instead?'

After a moment I shook my head no. 'It's only... what if I lose it, Miss?'

'You won't. Look at me. You won't. And I know you won't lose this either,' Miss Buxted drew an envelope from her jacket pocket. 'The obligatory let-ter to your parents. Nothing in it you don't already know. Boring bit of bureaucracy quite frankly. Have them sign it and bring it back with you tomorrow. Agreed? Good. There's just one more thing.' Miss Buxted dipped her chin, pulled back her shoulders and caught my eyes. '*Ut melius recta se in malum* – To right the wrong. The Mallory motto, in case you're asked. No, don't put it in your mobile. By heart. Repeat. Melius, that's right. Close, it's *mal*um. Mal, as in badly or ill, in malevolent, malfunction, malice. Once more for luck. Good. Only for the ears of Mallory girls, you hear? There you are now. Off you go.'

That evening when we were finishing dinner I remembered the letter. As Mum signed it she was saying something about twice spying a neighbour staring at the back of our house when Dad suddenly held up his hand for her to stop. He pointed at his mobile phone on the kitchen counter. Its screen was alight. Mum checked her own mobile where it had been left beside the kettle. Its screen, too, was on. Mine was the same. All three microphones were listening. We sat in silence. After a time, the scan stopped. Dad poured himself a drink. Mum shook her head no to one. She left without a word. From down the hall the sound of her popping painkillers out of the pack and the bath coming on. Dad topped himself up and went to lie down.

SEVEN

'Open that, will you? Show you something.'

Anna did as instructed and opened the bottle of ale. Her father removed six glasses from the shelves and bunched them together on the kitchen counter. One glass in the centre was ringed by the other five. It reminded her of a drinking game she had played when staying at a friend's whose parents were away for the night. Each player, all of them Rudies (and most of them Mallory), had a glass of wine or cider. They took turns bouncing a coin at the glasses collected in the middle of the table. Some of the players held their heads back at an angle, letting the coin roll off their noses to bounce on its side at the glasses. Others bounced it flat. Whosever glass the coin landed in had to down their drink. If the coin landed in the centre glass, everyone drank. They had played their way through four bottles of wine and two of cider. Anna didn't know how much she had to drink but had thrown up in three different rooms and into the lightwell outside the cellar window. That had been six months ago, at Christmastime.

This afternoon Anna wondered if her father had only just found out and was punishing her by making her repeat the game. Outside their house and in there was no breeze and the summer heat felt like weight. The bottle of ale had been left sitting out and was warm. Fruit flies swarmed above the kitchen drain and the compost bin beneath the sink. There had been more crawling atop the bottles of vinegar and cooking oil before they had been moved into the refrigerator for safe keeping.

Rummaging around a drawer, Anna's father removed a roll of cling film and a ball of rubber bands. 'Any idea where we keep the skewers these days?'

Anna, still thinking she was in trouble, didn't say *Where we always do*, but fetched the skewers from where they were stored in another drawer. Alice Andrews was having a party Saturday week that Anna didn't want to miss. She worried that even if her father was teaching her a lesson by getting her to drink warm beer until she was sick again, it was only part of her punishment, and she would be forbidden from attending Alice's party.

Nick poured a few centimetres of ale into a glass and added a squirt of washing up liquid. Then tearing off a piece of cling film, he sealed the glass and fastened a rubber band twice around its rim. A taut semi-reflective sheen peered up at them.

'Skewer.' He held out his hand as though he was a surgeon requesting a scalpel. The skewer was wooden and slender; Anna's father used its pointed end to poke holes in the cling film, delicately wiggling it to widen each hole by half. 'You want them to get in,' he said, waving fruit flies from his face. 'But not out. The ale is the lure. They're wild for it. The washing up liquid snares them – see how it forms a film on the top.' He placed the trap beside the drying rack. '*Voila*! Now you do the rest. Put one down here,' he tapped the cupboard beneath the sink with his foot. 'One atop the bin and the rest wherever.' If there's any ale left, it's yours. Only don't neck it. Wouldn't want you vomming all over the gaff.'

Amongst Brighton's residential roads and high streets are twittens. Twittens, from the Low German *twiete*, are narrow alleyways and etymological cousin to the words betwixt and between. Bordered on each side by tall and knobbly stone walls, Boundary Lane was one such twitten, a sly and slender passage shaded by trees on either side, not five minutes from Anna's home. She was cleaning it of litter; picking litter earned her Ambrosia points through the GoodWorks programme. Boundary Lane was also one of half a dozen dead drops prearranged between her and Magritte.

Each pair of Rudies was assigned to pass messages to each other without being caught by an opposing pair of girls watching them. It was homework; only Miss Rodmell knew who was keeping tabs on who. Anna and Magritte practiced 'rinsing' themselves of their unknown watchers before approaching any of their dead drops. From home, to retrieve a message from beneath the bench in St Anne's Well Gardens near to where she'd found Malkmus, Anna would zig-zag through back streets, turning left and right and doubling back until she entered Churchill Square shopping centre through the stationer's, take the stairs down one level and exit through the back of the store into the heart of the shopping centre itself, hike up the escalator, exit through the east entrance, board the first westbound bus, disembark after four or five stops and catch a bus heading the opposite direction as far as the yoga studios at the top of Waterloo Street, travel up Brunswick Road where the McKinney family had been forcibly carted away at Christmas, before making her way past the Buddhist Centre and entering the gardens through the Furze Hill entrance. To retrieve the message from Boundary Lane today, Anna had come straight from home. She carried a litter picker and a bin bag that streamed behind her like a banner. Collecting litter was something she did twice monthly for the past three years. Today it was cover. It was a bluff.

Sloped and straight running, Boundary Lane was not ideal for leaving or, especially, Anna felt, retrieving secret messages. Anyone positioned at its top or bottom could keep watch. An opposing pair of Rudies, if they were clever, would cover both ends.

Upon spotting Anna collect a message, they could close in from the sides. There would be no escape.

But Anna had an advantage, in two senses. The first was time. Boundary Lane was five hundred feet, end to end. Collecting litter from the clumps of grass growing from the tarmac or caught in the baseline nooks of the walls took twenty minutes or longer. Any Rudies would need to show themselves if they wanted to catch her in the act. At the sight of a classmate peeping her head out, Anna could put a face to her watchers, would abandon the dead drop and could rinse herself all the more thoroughly the next time, now knowing who was tailing her.

All of the rubbish was the second advantage. The dead drop wasn't tucked behind a loose stone in one of the walls, nor lodged in the fork of a tree. It was in a crumpled can of ginger beer Magritte had discarded as she passed through Boundary Lane the evening before. Should Anna be cornered by the Rudies watching her, she could, with a shrug, present them with a bin liner half-filled with ordinary-looking rubbish, and show them on her mobile screen her thirty-eight month history of GoodWorks litter picking as further evidence that everything was legit, nothing more than routine.

Starting at the top, Anna began working her way down the twitten toward home. She wore thin vinyl gloves but was nifty enough with the litter-picker to not have to crouch and collect much with her fingers. The gloves were blue and added to the show. It was Saturday morning. Boundary Lane was dappled in sunlight. A couple holding hands smiled as they passed. The twitten was just wide enough for them to walk side by side. Anna watched them grow smaller as they travelled downslope. It would be her someday, she told herself. Her and Alastair, hand in hand. The ginger beer can would be somewhere halfway along, near to where the couple were now: at either end was too risky. A week had passed since making fruit fly traps with her father. Alice Andrew's party was tonight.

Anna resented litter picking. Its anti-glamour, its air of servitude. Most of all, she was ashamed of the way her family persistently strived for Ambrosia points. It came across grabby; other families amassed points casually, as a matter of course. Earning Ambrosia points was expected of everyone. Even the elderly. Even children as young as five were at it by gaining good marks in class and through activities like visiting pensioners or growing flowers to save the bees. The Fetlock's Ambrosia count took a hit when Anna's mother fell ill. She stopped working and stopped spending and would have been pronounced a drain on community resources if she hadn't also stopped seeing the doctors (after having initially allocated twenty-four hundred Ambrosia points to advance up the NHS queue). Anna would ask herself why her mother couldn't just get on with it, recover, find a new job. Other people got ill: people got ill all the time. *They* worked. And her artwork, why couldn't she pick up a paintbrush, a camera, or even *one* of Anna's crayons? Why did she just sit there, day after day? And why couldn't she, Anna, instead of litter picking (which, being what it was and outdoors in all weather, earned her points and a half), why couldn't she secure a cushier Good-Works gig like Sonya Baskin who helped tend the rose gardens at the Pavilion, or Cassie Garver who read stories at a crèche. Was it her mother's doing? Had her mother's lassitude and inactivity prevented her, Anna, from accessing all but the bottom tier GoodWorks activities?

Punishments of this sort were rumoured. Someone slides off piste and their entire family goes on a list. The Mortons. The Marshalls and Woods. The Diamond-Gills. Everyone knew their names, knew what happened to them. Anna had been turned down from serving as a playground warden, a singer in the community choir that toured retirement homes and hospices, even as a stone scrubber in the restoration of St Peter's nave.

Litter picking it was. Other than Boundary Lane, Anna also tended to Waterloo Street (including Ivy Place and Kerrison Courtyard), Brunswick Street,

Chapel Lane, Donkey Mews, Cross Street, Little Western Street, Upper Market Street and Lower Market Mews. On heavy days, she would fill two bin liners with rubbish, log it on the GoodWorks system and collect her precious Ambrosia points.

Afterward, she would examine herself in the mirror for signs of shame, hood her eyes and practice looking blasé, how to style it out if anyone taunted her about litter picking. But the shame must have shown; she felt others must see them – the Fetlocks as a family, as a productive unit – as less. There had been no school hall jibes, no classroom aside or slipped tongue of a neighbour. But in private? When she wasn't there, what did everyone say *then*? When would it surface? What, she worried most of all, would Alastair make of it?

After deliberation with her parents, Anna consented to contributing one-third of the Ambrosia points she earned to the family pot. The rest she retained for her own purposes. As her points amassed, she spent them in her head. New boots and a necklace. Trips with friends. Things that would tell her parents how much she loved them, that helped them live.

Her mother's illness began when Anna was eight or nine and never wholly cleared until she was eleven. Just as there was pain in the Marys and Lewinnas and Sebastians depicted in the icons and oils Anna had once travelled with her mother to view and sketch, it was as much in her mother's eyes as it was in her body and limbs. The first symptoms appeared after two of her parents' friends were raided on the grounds of breaching public safety. They multiplied when a couple up the street were arrested. Sciatica. All-day headaches. Labyrinthitis. Torpidity. After four bouts of cystitis in three months (and blotched skin and nosebleeds) Sarah Fetlock had been forced to resign her position as co-director of the Brighton Art Walk, in which every July artists opened their studios to visitors and artwork was installed on the seafront, in squares and public gardens. The Art Walk brought tourists. Tourists spent money and earned Ambrosia points for spending it. Artists earned money and earned Ambrosia points for creating art that sold and for spending money earned from selling their art. Artists were viewed in some quarters as likely subversives; through opening their homes and studios they demonstrated they had nothing to conceal. They exhibited artwork and exhibited transparency. *Right this way*, declared their sandwich boards at street corners, at entrances to courtyards and twittens. *Nothing to hide here, come and see for yourself*, said their open doors.

It was this dichotomy, and many others like it, that bit at Anna – and not just at night when she drifted on the fringes of sleep and was vulnerable to internalised doubt. On one end, the warmth and love of her parents and Aunt Susie, the only family she had. On the other, the broader, sometimes numinous family of society, its vigilance, persuasive punitiveness, its protectiveness, and everyone else she knew. Altogether it felt like an exercise they had conducted in science class. A bar magnet laid bare on a clean surface. Iron shavings sprinkled round the magnet arrange themselves according to lines of magnetic force. All lines of force are equally strong. They are greatest at either end of the magnet, each pole pulling in the opposite direction. Which pole would gather the greatest iron weight? Which pole would prove the most attractive?

It all depended. That was Anna, aged fifteen.

With Sarah Fetlock ill, the family was reduced to just a single income. Ambrosia points grew fewer and were hoarded. And the only artwork Sarah undertook was the daily decoration of the bedroom window. Each morning she drew a chair to it and sat with her head rested against the glass. Sometime later, approaching midday, she would return the chair to its place beside the chest of drawers and move to another room. The impression left on the window by her forehead and hair resembled an Ordinance Survey map, its whorled elevations and concentric depressions.

Other days Anna's mother would pass hours in the sitting room, in a chair turned to face a wall plastered years earlier by Aunt Susie and left unpainted.

Only once did things leak outside home. It was early in her mother's illness, before she stopped leaving the house. Anna's father was in London, performing in a radio recording of *Nicholas Nickleby*. The long hours meant it was easier for him to stay nights at an Airbnb near the studio for the duration of the recording, rather than train it the fifty-odd miles to and from home twice a day. When Sarah Fetlock woke Anna that weekend morning at half past six, she was already dressed.

'Croissants, darling,' she whispered to Anna. 'Come and wake, pillow monster. Let's treat ourselves to some delicious croissants.' In her sleepiness Anna believed they were, after many months, returning at last to Café Bertrix and would see the Baniers. But when she mumbled Marie's name, her mother said they were going elsewhere.

A walk that might have taken twenty minutes took over an hour. They went by back roads, stalking through Brunswick Town, the still empty streets of the North Laine (Sarah ignoring Anna's insistence that they had already passed through Cheltenham Place and North Road), before hiking up to Seven Dials. There, half-seemingly by chance, was a coffee shop, its windows cool and pristine beneath a blue- and white-striped awning. The breeze swirled in such a way that even thirty or forty metres along Anna could smell the croissants baking, a sweet buttery scent that made her tongue swell in anticipation.

Pushing inside the door, Anna's mother nodded at the boy behind the counter. She weaved through the empty tables, Anna trailing behind and aware, to some degree, that something wasn't right. Perhaps a student at one of the local universities, with lank hair gathered in a bun at the back of his head and a glistening spot on his chin, the boy tricked up a crooked smile. 'Not *officially* open yet. Five minutes. But what can I getcha?'

Much to Anna's surprise and delight, her mother ordered six croissants, rather than the two she had expected. The boy selected these from a basket on the counter and dropped them into a bag. When he checked the time on his watch, Sarah Fetlock said,

'Velveteen collars are all the rage.'

This, too, was a surprise, evidently to the boy as well. He looked at Anna's mother as though she had asked if she might squeeze his spot or cut a lock of his hair.

'Beg your pardon?'

Anna's mother repeated her strange phrase as flat and unmusically as before. Confusion ran circuits around the boy's face. He licked his lips and touched the bun at the back of his head. Sarah Fetlock repeated herself a second time, now enunciating each word with a sibilance Anna recognised from when her mother was teaching her to read. Then, as though she had traded in a rack of Ambrosia points for a hatful of surprises, she stepped part-way around the counter and, nodding slowly, placed her hand on the boy's...

A few hours later, when Anna's father heard the story, he set off at once for the coffee shop. Anna was in her room when he returned, and crept downstairs to hear the news.

'All sorted.'

'He didn't report it? Nothing to the Ministry of...or on IcePie?'

'Hadn't got round to it. Or too worried he'd done something himself that would land him in trouble. Leaving the shop door unlocked before opening or serving you at no charge. Nothing, though. I checked.'

'And?'

'And I explained you were pregnant – '

Sarah shushed her husband and said Anna's name. Nick continued, quieter than before. 'I explained you were pregnant and suffering from a particular morning sickness that makes it difficult for you to find the right words. Temporary dysphasia.'

'...He bought *that*?'

'Fifteen quid for the croissants, a fiver tip and a hundred Ambrosia points probably did more.'

It was a relief, Anna overheard her father telling Aunt Susie when she stopped round later in the week. He had been prepared to fork out five hundred Ambrosia points to buy the boy's silence. Only at the last moment had he changed his mind, figuring too large a sum would heighten suspicion. The one hundred points, he explained to the boy in his deepest, most solemn tone, was his token of thanks for being so understanding and not distressing a pregnant woman and her family. Same as Café Bertrix, the Fetlocks never visited the Seven Dials coffee shop again.

Anna knew her mother couldn't be pregnant. For years she had pleaded with her parents for a younger sister or brother, asked for one at Christmas and on birthdays, and left a written statement, ostensibly from Malkmus, seconding the request and testifying to his yearning for another child to play with.

You're all we ever wanted, they told her at the start of her campaign. Then, *You get all our love. One is enough* and *There isn't any money*.

Finally, when Anna was twelve and had her first period, the true reason. The doctors had found cysts on Sarah Fetlock's ovaries after Anna was born and she heeded their advice to have them out.

Anna's desire for a sibling remained strong. Its roots were deep. The evening before her second birthday, her mother had settled Anna in her cot and leaned forward to kiss her goodnight. 'Tomorrow, little one. Tomorrow, you'll be *two*.' And Anna, thinking she would be divided, unwillingly split in half, howled into tears. A sibling, she imagined for years to come, would solve things.

Some distance ahead a stone dropped from the twitten wall. Anna stiffened, her senses switched to high alert. The stone was smooth and round, about the size of an apple. It rolled downslope and eventually rolled itself out. Curtains of hot air shimmered above the roadways. Anna's shirt clung to her back with sweat. There were ten days until summer holidays began, three weeks until the Crosses would arrive. From time to time losing Mr Peters still bit at Anna. It did again now. There was something indefinable about him. It was nothing that raised the hairs on her neck, more a nagging sense of apprehension at his unreadability, his inoffensiveness and economy of memorability. Each time she tried to fix on him in her head, land on something definite, he wriggled free. She told herself he was only ever an assignment, a daylight exercise, that was all. Anna scanned the walls for Rudies. Then using the litter picker, she dropped the ginger beer can in the bin liner and moved along. Magritte's message was the password for tonight's party. Not Alice Andrews', but the one they would go to from

Alice's. Freddie Heathfield's. Freddie was a Top at
Hanover Park Boys. The party was on the seafront.
Alastair would be there.

EIGHT

the iComm

'For example,' I practiced saying to Morkel, imagining him with me in the shop. 'It's always a certain type of man between the ages of 45-65 who buys the oversize *fin de siècle* or interwar Europe posters. Don't tell me you've not seen them? This way please, the racks are just at the back. Here, look. They're larger than our range of picnic blankets – and the blankets, I assure you, seat four people easy. They sell to young single women six-to-one.

'Now. Feel the heaviness of the paper, 300gsm, matte finish. That's durability. They're not going anywhere. Men who buy these maps are newly aware of death. The maps reassure them they won't be forgotten. Notice how the inkwork, the patches of pastels, paint the shapes and summits of vanished realms – look, here's Cisleithania... Bohemia... Moravia...Danzig – so too may generations continue appreciating these men's conquests, their lives. The maps comfort them there will be a record of who they are. In that way, they sense survival.'

Morkel had shot out of his chair when at his flat the week before I told him Hannah Cross was pregnant. Was I making fun of him, he demanded.

Was I having a laugh? He snatched the photo of the Crosses from my hands.

But I know the look like I know my own brother. Samuel had the same expression as Mark Cross in a photo of himself and Lindsay he had sent me when she was two months gone. They were, Samuel explained in the letter that accompanied the photo, between addresses and were waiting on some work (him) and payment for work done (her). In the meantime, they were staying with various friends and repaying their hosts by cooking up bolognaises and stews that could be eaten for days.

Three or four months later came Samuel's card telling me their new address and the news that Lindsay was due that December. I did the maths and, remembering the photo of the two of them, understood what a man looks like when he's in a squeeze and discovers he's a father-to-be.

When I had finished explaining myself (never referring to Samuel by name or as a blood relation, anonymising him instead as 'a one-time neighbour's friend'), Morkel blew a sharp blast of air through his nose and put the photo away. I think we were both embarrassed by the scene. He offered me another coffee and I accepted. We talked on. I left before the rain and we shook hands at the door.

Despite patching things up, I was still eager to justify myself – my worth – if Morkel was going to stick around. Otherwise he might as well be halfway round the world. Not like the Crosses. Like Samuel. I would have done just about anything to see him again.

The Map Men wouldn't do. Yes, it was true these men sensed death was looming that much nearer, but so what? It was inconclusive about anyone in particular, too wide-ranging. So when Morkel and I next met up, I gave him Ella Keats. Ella was older than me by seven or eight years, in her early forties, with a smile straight out of an advert for antiperspirant or financial planning. She had downy skin, pale eyes and a directness I might have found attractive in someone else. In her I could see roiling resentment of her mother's lovelessness and intellectual disappointment in her father. Piled together, it spelled trouble for her husband. Ella had made up her mind which of his faults drove her wildest and waited for them to show. When they did, or when she grew impatient, she would have a fling, using her husband's insufficiencies as justification. When a fling came to an end, she would seek atonement through redecorating the house and making presents of kitchen gadgets for him, bought from the shop. I never did discover his name. But if I ever found myself in want of observing a maple and mirrored steel bonbonniere when it's at home or witnessing a laser-etched aircraft-grade aluminium rolling pin in action, a sonic beer-foamer or hand-held cheese-smoker, I knew as I know my own name that Ella's husband's kitchen was the place to be. She was a Grade A customer. Worth fifty points off Morkel.

Once, a few months before he moved abroad, Samuel made a curious remark. We were having a drink at the Croupier's Arms and had been talking about the shop (with what remained of my share of the insurance pay-out from our mother's death, I was preparing to go into a lease for it) when he said there would never be a revolution, so long as people have money. The Hassop Five were middle-class, if not the horsey, weekends in the country type. Angela Gissing was a conservationist carpenter specialising in restoring centuries-old beams and barns. Simone Roberts, a children's book illustrator. George Coombs supplemented his income as a composer through operating a microbrewery for stouts and porters. Hannah Cross had been a senior grants officer at the Roundhay Charitable Trust, and her husband Mark a geography teacher (also kite enthusiast and allotment gardener) in Calderdale.

How and where the Crosses were now living, I struggled to imagine. They had been among the three hundred or so protestors at Brightside Lane, Derbyshire who had halted fracking at the site for two weeks. For the first four days the protest was peaceable. Demonstrators gathered in the lone road to the site, chanting beneath homemade banners. The fracking equipment lorries they blocked sat hulking and immobilised amongst the crowd. Food and water were shared. At night there were campfires and song. When on the fifth day a group – leaked reports later pointed to insurgents outside the ranks of protesting families and pensioners – heaved a hailstorm of stones at the incoming police reinforcements, retribution was swift. Armed officers surged from the wood and police on horseback charged from behind. Protestors ran three-sixty. Those who stayed were kettled and arrested. Several bolted themselves with locks to the fracking site gates. Others linked arms and were dragged apart. Whether it was the screams, the threat of stampede and arrest or the ornery thrill of defiance, a handful hoisted themselves atop the lorries and, with rucksacks of supplies, flew their banners from on high.

These were the Hassop Five.

To look at him, Mark Cross was unexceptional. I remember thinking it was just as well he was a father-to-be. I could picture him quietly minding his child – a daughter: I would have staked the shop on it – climbing on a playground apparatus, or him tending to a backyard barbecue while talking box sets with other parents as their children gorged on crisps and lemonade. Thickset and tall, he might have played rugby at school, if there hadn't been a pacifist, almost vegan look about him. He was a volunteer firefighter, a blood donor and probably a much-missed face at the pub, now that he was on the run. I had nothing against the man. Only his hair bothered me. And his beard. They were uni-length top and bottom, with a pointless fringe on each. If you flopped one for the other, he'd look absolutely the same. It was an absence, a rejection of style. He was the very sort of person who wouldn't buy so much as a chimp-shaped refrigerator magnet from the discount box at the shop.

Protestors weren't what they used to be. There were fewer of them. When Samuel and I were boys, marches and strikes were commonplace. Dustmen over pay or recognition and teachers for the same reasons. University faculty over pensions. Friday walkouts by schoolchildren for the environment. I myself took part on a few occasions. Samuel was the more committed of us and was something of a leader at our secondary school. But my heart never beat for it like it did in him. It was with some relief when the Ambrosia system was deployed to rectify things. Those students who walked out in protest were docked ten points (in those days a considerable sum), which were distributed as bonuses to students who upheld the rules and attended class on walkout days. I could forgo the protests on the grounds of pecuniary prudency.

What Ambrosia points couldn't curb, shaming stories on IcePie did. Even if some people overreacted, I still believe the measures were justified. When the greater good is being served, the nation as a whole, from trembling great aunt right down to the newest of newborns, needs to be on board with it. We're stronger together. Everyone I talked to said the same.

I didn't draw the line with home inspections either. They began about a year or so before Samuel went abroad, when I was still the right side of thirty. It's not as though inspection teams used force when coming to discuss things with you. They knocked on the door or rang the bell like a neighbour or a friend or a courier delivering flowers. And if you had to give up your morning, an afternoon or an evening while the inspectors made certain everything was agreeable, then that, my friend, is the price paid.

Besides, chances are you did something to warrant a visit. I never bought that hokum about inspections being random, a sort of anti-lottery to make us think it could happen to anyone at any time, thereby keeping everyone in line. Who would do such a thing? And who, I really want to know, who would stand for it?

There had to be a reason, an algorithm at the very least. It could be you were thought by co-workers to be feigning illness and skiving, by neighbours to be cheating on your partner or taxes, or you had been clocked researching something suspect online (I give you mental health, DIY electrics that risked burning entire streets to the ground). All good and just. All to keep us safe.

What rankled me most about the Hassop Five is they missed the bigger picture. I understand completely *why* they felt the need to protest against fracking (the contaminated drinking water was, admittedly, a problem, if a localised one; so too the earthquakes and the spike in infant-elderly diseases), but the nation needed energy. Homes needed it. Hospitals and transport needed it. Commerce. Once, for an entire fortnight at the shop, we suffered power cuts every two hours. Unlock the door in the morning and switch the kettle on: nothing. Half-ten, it snaps off again. Ringing up a lunch hour sale, bang it goes. Again at teatime. Off once more just in time for the after-work rush. And the weekends when it was make or break – the weekends were a *disaster*.

At the Roundhay Charitable Trust, Hannah Cross had been responsible for assessing funding applications and issuing grants. Initially for the arts (with a strong line in traditional music and dance), she later branched into projects supporting young people – youth entrepreneurs, LGBTQ peer support groups, Girl Guides. Outside of work it was more do-gooderism. Guide dog puppy rearing and looking in on elderly neighbours. But for all that supposed decency, for all that supposed community spirit, Hannah, of the two Crosses, was the real insurgent. Even in photos I could see dissidence rippling away in her – unilateral, bloody-minded, self-concerned dissidence behind the *thinnest* polish of community rah-rah and hooray. It was in her eyes, her braless breasts, the way her lips curled back to reveal her teeth in shout or smile. Her hair was even shorter than her husband's, a pugnacious green-dyed fuzz that hurt my scalp to look at. Side by side with him, she stood barely as tall as Mark's shoulders and would have needed to twist her chin up several degrees to look him in the face. Meanwhile, what did she do but look down at the rest of us? Our ideas, our needs.

Only a child could fix that. Motherhood would suit her. It was her place. She wouldn't go losing her head over it.

Morkel promised a pile of points for the Crosses, an absolute mountain. He encouraged me to do everything I could to find them. He showed me more photos and videos. Of her, of him. Some I recognised from television and the papers. Others had an amateur or hurried feel. Why he should be so hot after them he never said. Nor why he thought they might be holed up in Brighton. Perhaps it was some obscure clue, like an eyelash shed by a cat burglar, a taunting calling card left in a looted safe?

Or just a hunch.

There was nothing connecting them to the Fet-locks.

NINE

Anna

Sometime not long before Alice Andrews' party Malkmus stopped hugging me. Our hugs began when he was small and getting to grips with his attacking skills. He would stand on his hind legs with the pink pads of his forepaws outstretched above his head, preparing to pounce. I would scoop him up when he did it and he would cast his forearms around my neck, filling my chest with his purr. Over time he learned I would cuddle him when he stood erect and would announce he was in the mood for a hug with a bubbly *mwerp*, before standing for me to gather him up. Mum said he would grow out of it one day, when he was a moody teenager. But it was only when I was a Rudie, with summer holiday fast approaching, that he eventually stopped. It was something lost and it hurt.

Alice Andrews lived in a hulking stone building with views of the sea. It was in almost direct line with our own, five streets west, in Lansdowne Place. From its harlequin-tiled front patio and broad front door, to the framed Blundens and Dunbars, the vast fireplaces and Alice's own bedroom overlooking the fernery at the back, their home was stamped with well-heeled refinement. It may have been a flat, compared to the three floors of our own house, but where in ours there were drifts of cat hair and dust, an atmosphere of make do and mend (and a room called the Towering Shitter), Alice's seemed a fundamentally more respectable existence than my own.

We were both Mallory, although not close. I had the impression that I was something of a novelty to Alice, the rough-edged acquaintance awarded the elevated status of friendship by way of doing me a favour, a notion amplified by being invited to her party. It felt like a box ticked. Not that I was any less eager to go.

Although not directly responsible for hiring actors, Alice's father, as BBC Drama Chief Lieutenant, commissioned pieces that provided work to the likes of Dad. He was a Federeresque beauty, with a sculpted face and an intense, dark gaze that seemed to take in the world and command a place in it. I always lost my words in his presence. Alice's mother had an OBE for her work restructuring the Ambrosia system, and published articles in the *Economist* and *Spectator*. She was slender and assured, all cheekbones and eyes, the sort of woman who could hold her own in evening dress and eyeshadow after having been up since dawn doing GoodWorks at a children's hospice or clearing paths on the Downs. I couldn't imagine her so much as sneezing, let alone suffering a palette of illnesses that would incapacitate her for years.

Alice's party was a blur of percolating hormones, outfit and make-up alterations, punctuated by fits of hysterical laughing. There were eight or nine of us, and everyone aquiver. Only when Alice's parents disappeared to the upstairs neighbours for dinner did I feel the tension ebb that I'd say something triggering a buzzer and my ejection. But even then my anxiety didn't vanish entirely. Alice's party, she said savouring the words, was really only an *amuse-bouche* to the party on the beach. Freddie Heathfield's party. A dozen or more Tops. Upper Sixth girls from Lynton and elsewhere. Alastair.

Since meeting him and being conscripted into his operation that afternoon two weeks earlier, I looked for him whenever I passed through the school gates on my way home, thinking he would want me for a second leg of surveillance, another stakeout at the Dome. I checked and rechecked the phallic pillars for his name or initials, telling myself I wouldn't, absolutely would not, paint them there myself. The idea frightened and thrilled me. Alastair's name wasn't scrawled on the pillars, nor did I see him in the flesh loitering outside the gates on some made-up pretext. He'd posted nothing about us on IcePie. No messages. But he had evidently said something to Danny, who passed the cyphered entry code for

Freddie Heathfield's party to Magritte – and Magritte to me in the ginger beer can.

The party was some distance from Alice's, further west along the seafront, on the private beach belonging to a string of Art Deco houses on the fringe of Hove Lagoon. The walk took the best part of an hour and felt like minutes. Although the sun still radiated pink above the horizon, it felt like we were hurrying toward night. Freddie Heathfield's parents were property developers rumoured to have once tried buying the Pavilion to make it a luxury hotel, and to own entire streets in Kemptown. Their neighbours were film actors and popstars. For all of that, Freddie was a thin, quiet boy with a narrow chest and floppy hair who looked like he risked breaking an arm opening a can of tuna. He was seventeen and graduating top of his class. A year later he swam out to sea never to return.

Behind the lagoon was a wide walkway with a parade of beach huts facing the sea. The huts were uniform shape and size, painted pale green with peaked roofs. Only the doors displayed variety, decorated in candy stripes and Quality Street-coloured solids. As we neared the final hut, a boy presented himself and stood in our path. Tommy Denton. He instructed us to form a queue and approach him one by one with the password. It was impossible to think that none of us didn't know it by now. Magritte leaving it for me in the ginger beer can was just home-work, a bit of Rudie fun. When it came my turn to approach Tommy and say the words so that only he could hear, I broke out in giggles. It was only after five or six attempts that I managed to say it cleanly: *Beep, beep hurrah.*

Tommy tried looking stern and officious about the whole thing. But there was a pleading there too. For a year or more until the start of spring term he had been the boyfriend of Sadie Hartinger, a year ahead of me at Lynton and once a Canterbury House Rudie. Sadie wasn't amongst the girls invited to Alice's party. Nor had she been invited to Freddie's. She was no longer at Lynton. The last I had seen her was the week following Easter holiday. Magritte, Lor Laughton, Jakki Ringmer and I were on our way to assembly when we spotted Sadie being escorted to the school gates by the Head and two men whom I didn't recognise as teachers. Outside the gates, two more men waited beside a car, together with Sadie's parents. Her father had a sort of amphibious expression and her mother looked as pale as a cloud.

My first thought was someone must have died, a grandparent or a sibling. Or their house had caught fire and they needed to stay with relatives out of town. But why escorts – why *so many* of them? I could understand Sadie being looked after in the grip of some tragedy or another. But four escorts, the Head and both parents? And when it came to it, why were two men waiting either side of her mother and father? I tried making a mental note of what they looked like but was too taken in by the secret drama of things to look away from Sadie. I felt the answer must lie in her face and watched for it. Just before she passed through the gates, she did a quarter turn back at the school as though hearing someone, even the school itself, call her name. I think she must have known this was the last she would see of Lynton, at least as a student. But before she could turn completely round, one of the men escorting her, perhaps thinking Sadie was going to bolt, placed a hand on her shoulder and moved her forward toward her parents and the waiting car.

It was only then that I saw, in addition to the Head, the two men accompanying Sadie were women. I thought now I *had* seen one of them before, an supervisor or administrator in the school office – but equally she could have been a half-familiar face from town, someone I'd glimpsed while out picking litter or at the shops. And it was only later that I realised I had seen something of what I'd been looking for in Sadie. Whether she had turned to look back at the school or to dash away, I couldn't say for certain. But the half-recognised woman accompanying her had evidently thought the latter and had forced her forward. Whatever was happening, she could tell Sadie wanted to run from it.

Later that day I saw just how much – and how little – was intended to be seen. 'It's Goldilocks,' Magritte said, and at first I didn't understand. 'They go in too hard and everyone panics. Half the school would be in a state. Parents too. So they don't come and tear her out of class, do they? They wait for assembly, when there's a crowd of us gathered elsewhere and her removal is largely unseen.

'But then it's no good if *no one* notices. Go in too soft and there are no witnesses, no one to corroborate things,' Magritte went on in a low whisper. We were alone; she couldn't have said what she was saying otherwise. Even saying things to close friends was freighted with risk. 'Think about it. It's not like they came to her house over Easter hols. And this morning, they didn't turn up at breakfast when everyone was in one place. But arrange things so one parent is picked up at home or on their way to work, the other one the same, maybe at work or waiting for the train. Then it's Lynton for Sadie when there's a controlled handful of witnesses. Three events, three audiences. A few photos or a video on IcePie and everything leaks from three sources, each incident authenticating the other two. Everything counts. The place, the time, the manner. Everything Goldilocks. Everything just right.'

After Sadie and her family had been detained, Tommy Denton was signed off school with flu. Had anyone asked, he would have gone on at end about fever, night sweats and self-isolation. But everybody knew better than to ask. All traces of Tommy's and Sadie's relationship disappeared from IcePie. Tommy and his family would have been summoned for questioning – summoned, visited and trailed. Flu was just a cover.

Many of Tommy's fellow Tops would have preferred to keep clear of him: he was tainted by association with Sadie (whose family's transgressions we wouldn't ever find out, although it was strongly rumoured their cleaner had found something hidden beneath the floorboards). It created a tessellating tension. To openly avoid Tommy risked drawing unwanted attention to themselves. What did *they* have to hide? Hadn't they themselves also known Sadie?

Consider the evidence, each would have been told were they also visited by an inspection team. *Here you are with Tommy and Sadie in a photo taken not six weeks ago – do you care to explain the nature of your relationship to the subjects? You are noted as visiting the Denton residence regularly over a period of fourteen months – what was the purpose of your visit on…You don't recall? Well that* is *unfortunate.* The closer anyone had been to Tommy, the more likely they would be scrutinised had they shunned him. Had he not been invited to Freddie's party, then all the more closely the Heathfields and other partygoers would have been examined. Or so it was understood.

Tommy knew all of this, of course. And he couldn't say anything about it. Only through repeatedly proving himself above reproach (and trusting he was still under watch) could he hope for absolution. That was his motive for standing sentry outside the party, and simultaneously the reason for the pleading look I saw in his eyes when it came my turn to repeat the password. I pretended to not notice. What it would take for Tommy to feel he was fully exculpated might never show.

'Aren't you coming?' I turned and called after him. Everyone had already passed his checkpoint and were crunching across the seafront.

'Soon.' Tommy kicked a stone that flew into the night and skittered in the distance.

A high wall separated the public seafront from the beach at the back of the Art Deco houses. The sky glowed from behind the wall and the sound of voices and music grew as we neared. Tommy had directed us to a wide wooden door, sixty or seventy metres beyond his checkpoint. After knocking and receiving no answer, we tried the door and found it unlocked. It slid sideways and we entered. Inside was like a carnival, a great burst of light and sound and gaiety. Beginning at the nearest house and stretching far beyond were three, four hundred people swirling in pockets and pairs. Fairground games pinged and whirred amongst laughter and shrieks and chatter. A man in a grass skirt and coconut breasts played Hawaiian-sounding dance music from a stage erected on the beach. Word went round that DJ Dexter Digits, himself a resident of the enclave, was playing the headline set. We were among the youngest of the guests and stuck together in a pack. I nearly jumped when a woman hissed at us to shut the gate. She was one of a group wearing plus-fours and silver-beaded dresses that flashed in the light. The air was warm and salty-sweet. I had a 12:30 curfew and already it was nearing half-ten.

For the next quarter of an hour we wandered through the crowd. Light breathed from the sea-ward-facing backs of the houses and strings of coloured baubles dangled above our heads. Each house had a theme: 1920s, 1980s, Mods, Rockers, Punk, School Uniforms. I was self-conscious that my gingham dress must signal I was here only by grace and favour. There was no sign of any Tops. Alastair wasn't anywhere. Which house – and which theme – was Freddie Heathfield's was indiscernible. We split up in pairs, agreeing to look for the boys and message the others when we found them. Magritte and I headed for the house furthest along.

'You turned down my offer of coffee at the Dome,' came a voice from behind us. 'But may I interest *mademoiselles* in a drink?' It was Danny. He had a bottle of sparkling wine and three glasses. As though reading my relief that he wasn't dressed in any particular fashion either, as he poured out the drinks his eyes bounced from one group of fancy dress wearers to the next and he gave a terse assessment of each. 'Dressed like a cone of oily chips. Shoulder-padded cockatoo. *Far* too old for that much flesh. Embarrassing. *Naff.*' We clinked glasses. 'Come as you are, I always say. Be yourself.'

In the hours that followed I was anything but – anything but myself or who I wanted to be.

'No, really,' I said and saw that I ought to say more. 'I love it. It's amazing. It's...'

'Only you seem quiet. Another world away.' Alastair turned his chin to one side and tilted his head at an angle. Then he laughed, as though seeing how absurd he looked.

I took a mouthful of my drink and winced inwardly when I saw my pinkie raised in an affectation of ladylikeness. For the hundredth time I glanced at the crowd below, and further out, at the dark mass of the sea. We were alone at one corner of the balcony Danny had led Magritte and me to after collecting us on the beach. It didn't strike me until later that a similar scene had played out before, at the Dome, with Danny acting as the go-between that paired off Alastair and me. The balcony was mostly Tops and girls my own age or older. That only a few were dressed in 80s outfits in accordance with the house theme made me breathe easier – that and Ingrid (or Mingrid, as she was known behind her back) Carpenter, who had cleavage and a reputation, was tossing her hair at someone other than Alastair. I had two or three glasses of sparkling wine and only switched to lime and soda when Alastair handed one to me.

At first he had been at the opposite end of the balcony, talking with a few fellow Tops. Occasionally our eyes met, and once he seemed to nod in my direction. I noticed, too, a couple of the boys he was with glance my way. I had turned to watch something Magritte or Allison had pointed out on the beach below when I sensed Alastair behind me. He wore a tight red t-shirt with a gold lightning bolt emblazoned on its front. It showed off his chest and arms. We were the same height, something that, if I could have put a word to it, felt like destiny. As we talked – or as Alastair talked and I listened – I was vaguely aware that Magritte, Danny and the others had quietly shifted away or said they were going somewhere and hadn't returned. I thought this was life, this was proof that life was happening – happening to *me* – and sipped at the lime and soda, as though by taking it in small doses it would somehow make the night last longer.

'Tell you what. Finish that and we'll do ourselves a tour. Unless you want to bring it with?'

I shook my head no and swallowed the remainder of my drink. I wanted my hands free.

On the beach we made a long pass through the crowd and skirted the rim of the dancefloor fanning out in front of the stage. *Life*: the thought near shook me when I saw Alastair was guiding me away from everyone, toward the beachfront beyond the houses where the light limned into shadows.

'Here, look at this.' Alastair stopped suddenly and collected something at his feet. He held it up for me to see. It was a spider crab shell. 'Feel it.' He put it in my hand.

It fit in my palm and was pointy on top, fragile as meringue. I started to hand it back to him, but he waved it away. 'It's for you. It's yours.' He stroked it with a fingertip. I would have to tell him I needed to be getting home. But I didn't. Not yet. Adrenaline swam through me. It was everything I could do to not shake.

Sometime later we were at the peace statue at the bottom of Waterloo Street. The sea groaned in the near distance. One of us turned to the other and the other, sensing it, did the same. I felt myself going red. It began on my chest and spread upward across my shoulders and throat. I know it was red because Alastair told me, 'You're turning red.' He touched my cheek and held up his finger as though I might see that my own redness had rubbed off on him.

'So are you,' I said before I knew it.

Night didn't show things: I had seen the quote printed in large, italicised font in Mum's book of Brassaï photos. Night didn't show things, it suggested them. I didn't see what I needed to see. Not the red. Not Alastair. Nothing was clear.

TEN

Sarah Fetlock listened to the front door close. Anna was off to meet Magritte and Nick had set out early that morning to cycle to Arundel and back, a ride of nearly seventy kilometres he did twice monthly to clear his head. She was alone. There was work needing doing in the downstairs studios, painting final touches. The blue. The green and cream. But that could wait: Anna would be gone for hours. Sarah made a cup of tea and was sketching a to-do list at the kitchen table when she heard something in the stairwell. It was a small sound, inquisitive, unlike someone knocking or the post clunking through the letter slot. She left her cup beside the sink and went to the stairs to listen.

Halfway down, on the landing between the first and ground floors, a wasp bumped against the window. The window was small and opened outward on a pair of hinges. Through it you could see into the gardens and the backsides of the houses behind their own. The window was bare. Curtains or blinds would have invited attention. Neighbours might ask *Why do they always keep blinds drawn in* that *part of the house? What are they hiding?* and sooner or later an inspection team would show. Sarah turned to go back to the kitchen when for the second time she thought she heard a noise from below.

'Anna? Anna, darling, is that you? Did you forget something?'

Sarah descended to the lower landing from where she could see the front hall. The rush-like runner on the stairs softened her step. The runner began outside Anna's bedroom on the second floor, flowed down the stairs, across the landings and stopped at the base of the bottom riser. The wood of the stairs showed either side of the runner and was worn of lacquer. The banister, where there was one, shone with a fevered burnish.

The front hall was empty, the doors closed. The wasp emitted a truculent buzz and tapped at the window. Sarah opened it and the wasp flew away. The air outside was clean and bright. In the distance she could glimpse the rounded crests of the Downs, green under a blue sky. Sarah rested her forearms on the sill, closed her eyes and pictured the scene from behind, pictured it on a canvas the size of the window, in muted Hammershoi oils. Then as a three-quarters life-size photographic print. A woman, her head and shoulders framed low in the window casing, summer sky and clouds towering in the distance. Her face turned to one side revealing the curve of her cheekbone, the loose curls of her hair. Her yellow cardigan with green patches covering the elbows, her faux suede skirt. There was tension across her shoulders (it was in the shadows, in the lines); was the figure looking away or looking within? To her right was a plant atop a stool. The plant had eye-shaped flowers and long green leaves shiny beneath a coating of dust. Above the plant was an etching of copper birches and a watercolour of Blake's bespangled oak. On the wall opposite was an oval mirror speckled with silvering and giving off a flat, pewtery light.

Instead of blinds the Fetlocks had suspended a wooden drying frame from the ceiling above the landing. Using a rope kept secured to a cleat in the wall, the drying frame could be lowered on pulleys to the window's height; draped with clothes it obscured the view into the stairwell from outside. No one would question that. If anything, they would see the Fetlocks were doing what they could to ease the strain on the National Grid, thus reducing the risk of power cuts, and would receive an annual two hundred Ambrosia points for using natural methods – sunlight, air – instead of a tumble drier. When the drying frame was lowered and hung with clothes, they had to duck and waddle to get past. Only Malkmus could negotiate the stairs unfettered.

Better a painting than a photo, Sarah decided. It was what had come to mind first and she had learned to follow instinct. To paint it, she paused – to paint it would be to give life to things in a way a photograph couldn't. She would live with it, the long labour of painting. Live with it mentally, emotionally, chemically, would bend her back to it as it took form, as it grew from conception to recognisable body, to something that was named and spoke for itself. What would she call it, this painting of a woman in a window? *On the Lookout* or just *Look Out*? Perhaps a collage instead? Sarah opened her eyes and scanned the buildings to see who was watching.

Two days earlier it had been a deliveryman. And long before that, Anna and the birds. The Fetlocks had been a full house when the deliveryman showed. Anna was reading on the balcony outside the sitting room windows, and Nick and Sarah were in their ground floor studios. The buzzer sounded. Then a knock. Then Anna shouted from upstairs there was a delivery.

Sarah left her staple gun on the studio floor and stood up from where she was kneeling. She had been stretching canvasses and her knuckles were red raw. Crescents of blood marked her cuticles from pulling the canvasses taut and stapling them to frames. Wrapping a cloth around her fingers she closed the door to Nick's studio at the back. The door to her own studio she left ajar. The deliveryman buzzed and knocked again. Anna again shouted 'Delivery.'

'Yes?' Sarah held the front door open. She hadn't been expecting a package, but it might be something for Nick or Anna. The deliveryman wore a uniform and cap and was gazing up at the first floor. Sarah wondered if Anna was looking down at the man, or if it was merely her feet he saw propped up on the balcony rails. School had finished the previous week. It was summer holidays.

'Oh,' the man said and seemed to forget why he was there. 'You had me...' he gestured toward the balcony. 'And then here.' He shook his head and unhitched an electronic device from his belt. 'Long shift.' The deliveryman was about Sarah's age, had narrow brown eyes and smelled of soap. A photo ID in a plastic sleeve was clipped to his chest pocket. Bluebird Couriers. Alan something. He and Sarah looked at each other.

Sarah smiled. 'Do you need me to sign for the...?' Her voice trailed away when she saw there wasn't a package.

The deliveryman consulted his device. It was hand-sized, with a screen and buttons on its face. The device scanned numeric codes on packages and had once taken signatures by stylus. Now they took fingerprints. Sarah glanced at the man's badge again. Alan Watkins.

'Collecting a package from Mrs Montgomery.' Alan Watkins pulled his shoulders back and smiled boyishly. Was he flirting with her? Sarah shifted her body to one side of the doorway. The deliveryman looked past her, into the house. Sarah resisted the urge to turn to see what or who he was looking at. She let her hand fall from the door and used it to tighten the bandage around the other. She shook her head.

'Wrong house, I'm afraid. Not number 26, is it? Backwards, I mean. This is 62. Fetlock.' She thought she had better smile again and did. The man might be a scout checking houses at random, on any of an array of pretexts. He would report anything suspect, triggering a full-blown inspection like before, when Anna was small. That time it had been a team of four: one standing guard at the front step while the other three went room to room. When it was over, Sarah let the kitchen tap run until it was hot. She filled two buckets with soap and water. Using cloths, Nick and Sarah cleaned the banister handrail by spindle, the bare bits of step either side of the stairwell runner. Then it was the doors, the walls, the floors, the window frames, tabletops, toilet and tub. Neither spoke. Each bucket they emptied in front of their house between parked cars.

The Fetlocks had passed that inspection. But inspectors could always return. They didn't need a reason: it could just be a lucky dip. Scouting was something else, a different, more guileful layer. They hadn't been scouted before. Or had unknowingly and passed. Sarah needed to stay calm. She had practiced it.

'Fetlock.' The man consulted his device. He held it head high this time, as though to get a better signal. Sarah considered he might be taking a photo. Of her. Of the front hall and stairs. The landing. She ran through in her head what she had been working on in her studio and reminded herself that Nick was editing an audio file in the back. It was legitimate work for both of them. Nick would be wearing headphones and incapable of hearing what was happening at the front door. But Anna could hear. Anna would be listening.

'No. Here all right. 62 Waterloo Place BN2 – '

'This is Street, Waterloo Street.'

'Oh. Now wait. Wait.' Alan Watkins took a half step to the side and slanted his device so that if he really was taking a photo, it would now capture a section of Sarah's studio through the open door. This time she listened if anyone was behind her. She wondered if Anna was on the stairs. 'Still, the *postcode* matches up and...' He re-angled the device and pressed at its buttons.

Sarah felt her forehead tighten. Perhaps it wasn't photos he was taking. It could be video. She mustn't be abrupt: it could indicate she had something to hide.

'And you *are* resident here?'

'For donkeys.' Sarah silently congratulated herself for sounding genial.

'Any Mrs Montgomery staying with you or...' He gestured up the street. 'A neighbour?'

'No.' Sarah thought she'd spoken too quickly. She made a rueful expression. 'Sorry. No one that I know. And no guests or family with that name either. Three Fetlocks: Nicholas, Anna and Sarah.' It was no secret: it was all on record, all online.

'And everything up to date with...?' The deliveryman stepped back and examined the Household Accordance plate affixed to the face of the house. Once or twice a month the Fetlocks would catch sight of Peer Glimpse doing the same – Peer Glimpse, so named by Nick for journeying house to house in Waterloo Street and pausing to study everyone's plates. These were brass, shield-shaped and stamped with a column of three lions with a strip at the base bearing the date until which the plate was valid. All plates were registered with the Ministry of Public Safety. They marked cooperative households, individuals and families who demonstrated compliance with the vast social and administrative protocols governing daily life. Peer Glimpse made note of any house whose plate had passed its expiry date or had been removed, leaving behind a grimy outline of itself. Unlike Community Inspectors, who could enter people's homes, Peer Glimpse didn't wear a uniform and went no further than the front step. His impetus and sanction – and his name, his own address – was a matter of speculation. Sarah thought perhaps Peer Glimpse had been replaced by an official scout, someone with authority.

'All up to date.' There were another eight months before their plate wanted renewal. 'We make certain of it.'

'And there's definitely no package for me?' The deliveryman again looked past Sarah into the front hall. 'Or a letter from…?' He gestured at the balcony.

'Nothing, I'm afraid. Wild goose.'

'So it seems, so it seems.' Alan Watkins consulted his device again. 'Will need your print all the same.' He glanced at Sarah's bandaged hand and managed another look into the house.

'Scraped it.' Sarah unwound the cloth and held her hand up for the deliveryman to inspect. 'The pains of art.' She told him what she'd been doing and, thinking quickly, turned to grab a flyer for the Art Walk from a stack on the stairs. The stairs were several paces along the front hall; she walked calmly, without rush. If he was taking photos or video, that would show him. The deliveryman examined the flyer and pushed it in his chest pocket. Using her good hand Sarah pressed her forefinger to the device's screen.

'Know you next time,' said the deliveryman.

'Likewise.' Sarah smiled again and offered her hand to shake. She allowed him to see her looking at his name badge. 'Alan. And good luck finding Mrs Montague.'

'Montgomery.'

'Montgomery. My mistake.' Sarah remonstrated herself for trying to trick him. She shook her head. 'Good luck with Mrs Montgomery.'

Later, when Anna asked if the deliveryman had been scouting them, Sarah examined her daughter for any sign of anxiety. When she was six, Anna became frightened of birds. She thought they were watching her – watching her and reporting back on her. Not to the local authority or to a government department or corporation outsourced by a government department as Alan Watkins may have been (there was no way of checking, not without raising suspicion), but to God.

Where Anna had come up with the notion of birds serving as the eyes of God confounded her parents. They weren't a religious household. But the feeling of being watched – no one needed to leave their home to sense it. At the Fetlocks, it was the television that had done it. One weekend morning, when Sarah had taken Anna to Café Bertrix to buy croissants and to say hello to the Baniers, their television had started recording – not something *on* television, the performance in the room: Nick. There was a video camera above the TV screen and microphones nestled amongst its built-in speakers, by now all standard issue. Nick sang along to the song in his head as he drew back the sitting room curtains and opened the balcony windows. A short time later, while everyone was breakfasting in the kitchen, the sound of Nick singing to himself earlier in another room:

...The early morning sun...here she comes...

They found more recordings. Sarah and Nick bickering about a Center Parcs booking. Sarah spraddle-legged on the sofa and Nick's head moving between her thighs. Susie on her mobile phone chasing an order of plaster and lime. Anna talking to her teddy bear, her stuffed dragon and platypus. Nick tiptoeing like a minotaur into the sitting room and gobbling a chocolate coin from the Christmas tree. The back of someone's knit jumper obscuring the shot and Eugene Banier's voice imploring: 'Whatever else, we *owe* it to ourselves.' Seven minutes of Sarah sitting motionless in a chair facing the wall. Malkmus twitching in his sleep. Malkmus pawing a porcelain beaker off a bookshelf...

Sarah made to look as though she was reconsidering the stairwell decorations. It was for show, in case someone was watching her in the window. With a week to go before the Crosses arrived, and after Alan Watkins at the front door only days earlier, she couldn't take any chances. She removed the watercolour and etching from the wall to her right and, carrying them high across the landing, in full view through the window, held them one above the other in front of the mirror on the wall opposite. She tried the mirror where the pictures had been, stood back (again in full view of the window) and shook her head no, rolled her eyes. After returning things how they had been, she descended to the front hall and tested the front door was shut tight. She looked through the eyehole and there was no one. The outer studio door was locked, its keys beneath the runner on the fifth stair as they should be. There had been no further sounds. She listened again now, and still there was nothing.

Nor did anything look amiss in her studio, where everything had its place in no particular place. Things were left where they had been used or at some point shoved out of the way. The staple gun and bucket of gesso beside a stack of sketchbooks. Tubes of paint rammed into shelves on the far wall and brushes pointing upright from chipped mugs. The hole-punch she had used to make a collage of eyes and lips from magazine photos was at the foot of the easel in the front window. The floorboards were speckled with paint. The windows latched shut. The ON AIR light above Nick's studio door was unlit, as she knew it must be. Even still, she tested the knob to make certain the door was locked. Finding it so, she turned to leave when compulsion got the better of her and she unlocked it to look inside.

It had long puzzled Sarah how the two studios, one in front of the other, could be so distinct from each other. They even smelled different. Flicking the light on, she inhaled the showroom scent of electrical equipment mingling with the aroma of cinnamon tea and a whiff of bicycle oil and weed. Where her own studio was large, tangled and airy, Nick's was compact and set to order, as though awaiting inspection. Indeed, there was even a framed certificate that permitted the rear window to be closed out by soundproof curtains.

Today the curtains were open, allowing a milky light to pass through the wired glass. Sarah pulled them closed. Then reaching inside the bookshelves opposite Nick's desk she drew the top lever, stooped, and drew the bottom one. The shelves were deep and filled with typescripts in vertical cardboard files, and the leavers were concealed behind panels in the shelves' casing. Susie's work. The bookcase swung outward, on oiled hinges. Inside, beneath the stairs leading up to their quarters, was the Tokyo Suite, as dubbed by Nick after the cell-like micro-apartments available to young Japanese workers.

This is where they'll live, she thought to herself. When the time comes, this is where they can be found. Her tea had gone cold by now and she would get to work painting the final touches. The blue. The green and cream.

ELEVEN

the iComm

It was a fine day – a fine day at the end of an extraordinary week. Beginning in May, business had picked up. There were still days when we sold next to nothing and the future looked bleak. But with a frequency bordering on regularity we started seeing more paying customers. Some days it was an extra cushion or two that sold, a steam-resistant shaving mirror or a pair of cashmere throws. Others it was handcrafted candles by the boxful, rugs and glass vases, heritage wrapping paper at £4.99 a sheet. That particular week so much stock went that it looked as though we'd been robbed. Sales figures totalled what would have ordinarily taken a fortnight or longer. After closing the shop and meeting Morkel for ping-pong in Jubilee Square (my backhand was unstoppable: I won 3-2), when I arrived home there was a letter for me from Samuel.

Rather than reading it straight away, I pushed the sofa across the floor, opened the window, opened a bottle of ale, helped myself to some nuts and sat down, my feet up on the sill. It was tempting to play some music; I had several albums that had been Samuel's and it would have been fitting to listen to any one of them now, reading his letter. But I wanted to feel the sounds of summer breathing on me through the window. The snatches of laughter and birdsong. The popped cork and bicycle bell. The sun was above the buildings to the west and the scent of cut grass and green things growing filled the air.

As usual, I took note of the envelope to see if it looked as if someone had opened it before me. It unsealed no problem and the pages inside bore no signs of having been previously read. I decided it was probably never the case that someone was reading Samuel's and my letters. Or if they had been reading our letters, they had stopped after concluding we were clean. Wouldn't they leave us alone once we had been stamped kosher, or would they pay even closer attention, thinking we had outfoxed them all this time? If it had ever begun, where did it end? Anyone who applied to emigrate underwent inspection. There were fees to pay, paperwork and processing fees, fees for irregularities uncovered by the inspection and for forecasted lost contributions – taxes – to the national pot. Samuel hadn't bothered with any of it. He had simply left and not returned, and his citizenship had been sequestrated. His name was on a list. And because it was, it stood to reason, as family, mine would be too. Perhaps not the same list, but a list all the same. Was anyone really bothering with letters anymore, wasn't it all digital now?

It occurred to me Morkel might know. But if I asked him, what would come of it?

No, I decided. Asking Morkel wouldn't do. It was an unspoken, if understood, particular of our relationship that I didn't seek information from *him*. The question risked snapping our familiarity and routine. There was always enquiring elsewhere (cross my fingers it wouldn't get back to Morkel). I formed a notion of presenting myself to the Home Office, some clerk or another at the postal service, and pacified myself with their roundabout reply:

'Look, we look, okay? We've looked, and you're okay.'

Samuel's letter read ordinary enough. The job he landed the summer before last running snorkelling outings for tourists had blossomed; they had expanded from one boat to three and he was now a partner in the company. His income had doubled. Along with some builder friends, he and Lindsay had constructed a new north-facing room to their home that, despite the skylight, kept cool year round, just the way I liked for a good night's sleep. Lindsay was growing organic flowers and selling them at a local market. Their daughter, Melony, now going on four, was learning the trade. She had had them in fits when, bundling a poesy of irises, she was stung by a honeybee and after the tears announced that it 'hurt like a motherfucker'.

I was happy for them – happy especially to hear in my head Samuel's laugh, a gurgling whistle, like someone puking down a flute. Samuel had gone into Christchurch and seen a shop that reminded him of my own, with a HELP WANTED sign in the window. He emphasised just how much he knew I would never give up my own shop and admired me for building it up from nothing. I was invited to visit as soon as I could if I could find someone – a notice in the window too? – to cover my absence. I would have considered this an ordinary invitation from one sibling to another encouraging a get-together, if he hadn't signed off with:

Trindley,
Samuel

That pulled me up short: Trindley. Soon as I saw it, the blood raced out of me and I read the letter again. Every other line seemed to provide a clue, and by the end I was certain I saw what Samuel was really saying. They had some money now, enough that they could provide for me while I found my feet; there was my own room waiting for me; and there were jobs to be had. The invitation to visit was really an offer for me to come and live with them. Even the flowers were potent with meaning: irises, a sly warning from my big brother to be careful, that people were watching and I could get stung. All of it was carefully worded to sound perfectly ordinary to the outside observer.

But for 'Trindley', I would have thought exactly the same.

When we were boys, Samuel had been obsessed with a neighbour's dog, a pert, tricolour Basenji with white paws, named Trindle. Try as he did through ball games or sneaking up on Trindle while he dozed, Samuel couldn't get the dog to speak. Basenjis are a barkless breed, a fact Samuel refused to accept and fuelled his obsession times ten. It was a dog: surely it would bark at *something*.

Over time, the word Trindle became shorthand, a secret word between us, meaning keep your mouth shut. Trindle: when I stumbled upon Samuel trimming his pubes in the bathroom mirror and he guessed (correctly) I would tell everyone at school. Trindle: whenever he helped himself to a mouthful of Dad's Tia Maria. Trindle: when he would sneak out at night to see a girl.

Part of me wanted to screw up Samuel's letter, envelope and all, and toss it out the window. But suppose someone found it and, thinking it curious to find a foreign letter with personal information lying on the pavement, delivered it to the authorities in hope of an Ambrosia reward? Never mind the Ambrosia points *I'd* be docked for littering, there would be questions, there would be interviews.

Suppose I chucked it in the bin or burnt it? I could deny having even received the letter. Unless, of course, it was already known and recorded I had. Someone could be watching even now, noting my expression, what I did next. Foolishly I was in full view of the world, there in the open window. I daren't look up or move.

I wasn't prepared for any of it. It's that, I think, that smacked hardest. I wasn't prepared for it. And I did *so much* to be prepared. Copies of all financial documents – personal and for the shop – were ready to hand if inspectors came. Morning and evening, I went through in my head what I'd done that day, the night before, that week, as though testifying before a judge and jury. I rehearsed what I would say to people: stories, jokes, opinions, alibis. Even did things like take special care with the butcher knife. It had been Samuel's, a present from a one-time girlfriend to whom he had expressed a culinary interest. When he left, he gifted the knife to me. Every time I used it – garlic, parsley and other herbs, pizzas – I learnt to wash and dry it straight after I was done and stow it at the back of the bottommost kitchen drawer. If it was left in the sink or in the drying rack, I would think to myself: Could this be the time? The time being the time someone broke in and used it to lop my head off.

And there was the man across the street who routinely walked about his flat in nothing but underwear and sometimes starkers. I could *never* do that. It's one thing if you've had a wash and are hurrying from bathroom to bedroom to get dressed. But this fellow! He was no stranger to preparing steamy cappuccinos and sandwiches in his briefs. Watching television and bleaching the sink, taking phone calls. He went online wearing god-knows-what-tiny thong. Once he cooked *and ate* an entire roast in tangerine Y-fronts with white piping.

What kind of man would do that? A man unprepared, that's who. What if there was a gas leak or fire? What if a deliveryman or an inspection team was at the door? A neighbour in distress? *He* was distressed, sloping around so unprepared. I would never consider it. I am, above all, a normal person. I must stress this point. I am normal. I am ordinary. If there was ever a bang-on-average person, it's me. At home, I am always fully clothed in trousers, shirt and shoes, from breakfast to bedtime. In bed, I am in pyjamas, my wool-lined moccasins pointed away from the bedside exactly where I swing my feet to the floor, my dressing gown hanging from a hook on the back of the door. You can't just tell someone to drop everything and move right the way round the world. You need to prep them first.

Three days later I decided I would go to live with Samuel. I don't know if I would have come to the same conclusion, let alone come to it so swiftly, if it hadn't been for a dream. In it, I was bound in heavy rope that stretched taut left and right of me. To one side, Samuel was pulling with a powerful nonchalance, and Morkel dragging hard at the other end. The ground at my feet was the dirt of the football pitch Samuel and I played on when we were boys. Suddenly, I was yanked in one direction and saw that Samuel and Morkel were on the same end of the rope, the opposite end now stretching into emptiness. I fell on my side; it was a soft landing. I was hauled up, dusted down and embraced. Then a silver tray was produced from somewhere, with scalloped edges and cucumber sandwiches cut in triangles. I woke.

I would go. It meant abandoning the shop and everything I had put into it. The pay-out from my mother's insurance, all the hours behind the till and arranging items into attractive displays, keeping the accounts in order, washing the windows myself inside and out to save money...All those hours alone.

Or to put it another way, all those Samuelless years.

Before I could leave, I would prepare. Hoard as much cash as I could and use only a portion of my Ambrosia points toward flights, leaving behind a quarter to a third, a sacrifice making it appear as though I intended to return. Flying directly to New

Zealand would raise suspicion. Instead, I'd purchase return flights to Dublin or Porto or anywhere else, spare no expense renting a local cottage, send a few postcards gushing about the scenery and weather and, after two or three days, book myself on a one-way ticket to Christchurch or Auckland. Business class, of course, like my customer and her pampered flight to Milan. It would cost a bomb. But thanks to the shop's summer run of sales, I had some money. No fortune, it must be said, but enough to be getting on. Fake a few orders in the weeks before I took off, skip on the lease and a few invoices for the final month and I'd have more yet. And I wanted to make something of a present for Morkel before I left. He was my friend, after all. There was nothing he'd like more than information on the Hassop Five couple who had absconded from justice. I would gift him what I could about the Crosses.

Even, I dreamed, deliver them to him.

TWELVE

Anna

I sometimes ask myself what hurts more, losing someone in the first rush of love, when everything is heady and ripe and there for you to reach out and take, or losing them in love's decrescendo, when things are routine, even flat (and don't half wind you up), but their presence is essential to your sense of comfort and wellbeing? I sometimes ask myself, if a month had to be carved out of the year, which I would forfeit, May or November?

Not counting the day we met at the Dome, Alastair Broyle was five occasions that summer: Freddie Heathfield's party; another party the night school ended; twice more before Alastair went to National Training; and once after he returned and school began.

At first I was hesitant. There had been warnings from Mum and Dad. Mum cautioned me about boys in general. There's no rush, she said. You'll *want* to rush and have him all to yourself. But pull back and let him come to you instead. If he's for real, he'll show you his worth. 'Besides, holding back,' she added after a beat, theatrically bunching her hair, 'makes you even more desirable.'

Dad was more direct. 'Boys are scum,' he told me. 'Fickle, frightened liars down to their bones. Trust me, I know boys. I used to be one.' When Danny posted something along the same lines on IcePie, I was compelled to listen.

I was hesitant, too, because, when I saw Alastair a week after the end of school party, it was for a picnic in Queen's Park. I had avoided the park for ten years, since I was five. The last time was a picnic that was no picnic, a sprawling playdate of children and parents. I and one or two other children armed with sandwiches and crisps had ventured away from everyone to feed the geese in the pond, where a man seated on a bench exposed himself to me. How I understood he was doing something he shouldn't, that he was doing something wounding, is unclear. He lifted his penis out from his flies and pulled at it.

My first reaction was to step closer: I had it in my head that he was tearing up bread for the geese and would share some of it with me. When I saw what was in his hand and what was in his eyes – a sneering, joyless vengeance – I fell over. Those two or three steps toward the man saved me. If I hadn't moved closer, I would have dropped in the pond. Mum and Dad were summoned from the nearby parent and child encampment. I remember shouts, crashes through the trees. The man was caught. A care worker visited me at home three or four times. She said the authorities were making certain the man would never do it again – to me or to anyone. I was grateful. I made the Civil Authority Committee a card to thank them and sent another at Christmas. My sense of gratitude grew as I did. It compounded. I felt indebted.

Now I was back in the park where the man had exposed himself, there to meet a boy, eager to be a part of his beauty. I asked myself, was I stepping in the right direction? And whether I was or wasn't, which way would I fall?

Although Alastair and I hadn't declared ourselves a couple on IcePie, everyone knew about us. The night school ended there was a gathering on the seafront below Kemptown. Six or seven dozen Lynton girls and Hanover Park boys and girls and boys from the mixed schools, BHASVIC and Stringers. A permanent twelve-foot-high horseshoe of pebbles shielded us from the rest of the beach. We lit a fire in the basin and gathered round it. A breeze pulled the smoke over The Channel. Every few minutes someone new arrived. There was laughter and yelps and corks flew at the stars. In the daytime, the basin was a nudist beach. After dark, it was rumoured to be visited by men seeking quick, anonymous sex. There was a tacit agreement everyone would keep their mouths shut about what we got up to, a *pax artypay*, Danny called it. No one entirely believed things wouldn't leak out. But after a few drinks and with the summer stretching before us, any doubts about anyone informing on you ran out with the tide.

Still, the party was unlicensed and many of us underage. We took it in turns keeping lookout from atop the horseshoe. Along with Alice Andrews and Prisha Kumari, Danny, Magritte and I had been seated near the fire for close to an hour before Alastair marched over the crest with half a dozen Tops. He either didn't see me or didn't want to know me. I worried he was cross at my having been immersed in revision since walking me home from Freddie Heathfield's. I was diligent about my studies, my bursary depending on my grades. Alastair was greeted with shouts and a tackle and disappeared toward the water with a pack of Tops. Magritte, Alice and I opened another bottle of cava. Boys took it in turns leaping over the fire, landing with crashes that sent pebbles skittering. We cheered them on, shouting *Higher! Higher*! and marks out of ten. Wooden pallets were tipped onto the flames. The lookouts atop the horseshoe were now visible in the firelight. The boys kept leaping, doing criss-crosses that were nothing if they weren't near misses. Ricky Law, I remember, did a running back flip. Without seeing him coming, Alastair dropped himself down behind me and wrapped me in his arms and legs. 'Hello you.'

'Hello.' I rested my head against his shoulder. The fire was like a spotlight, the two of us on stage, everyone else the audience. Alastair took the cava bottle from me and put it to his mouth. His swallows bumped down my spine. Then his arms were around me again and we held the bottle together. 'Aced my exams,' he told me. 'Five hundred Ambrosia points reward from the 'rents for it too. You and I,' he said drawing his face nearer mine, 'should spend it together. And I mean *spend* it. I've been thinking about you. All the things we can do.'

'Thought about you too,' I managed back. And tilting my face towards his, tasted the wine on his lips. Everyone saw. Magritte, I knew, would have it on camera. I pulled his arms tighter around me. The side of his hand was against my breast. I let it stay. Then someone called his name and he was off again – off with the boys. A short while later, one of the lookouts shouted the police were coming. Three cars and a wagon, their blue lights bouncing off the seawall, streamed down the slip road to the beach. Everyone scattered. For the next two hours there were rumours of substitute parties. Magritte, Danny and I, Georgie James, Claire Penfield and a few others linked arms and sang down the houses as we trooped from Sussex Square to Park Crescent and up to Seven Dials in search of the next venue. Everything was dead and each new lead delivered less promise. Someone produced a bottle and we drank it off in St Anne's Well Gardens. Alastair messaged

X. I told him where we were and XXX back and watched for him to come sauntering from the shadows. My phone died waiting for him to show. Danny vanished with Poppy Hind's brother and Lucie Roth sicked-up on the playground slide. Alastair had kissed me in front of everyone. Everyone had seen it. Magritte posted a photo of it online: it was official.

IcePie with my little eye a Rudie no more.

Alastair removed a clear plastic tub of olives from his rucksack and held it high for us to marvel at. I shifted on my knees closer to him. Already on the blanket in front of us was a small cutting board of cheese, jars of sweet pepper pickle and aubergine pâté, a baguette and a bottle of elderflower fizz. Other than the bunch of grapes I had swiped from the party at home, Alastair had supplied everything for our picnic.

'*Look* at the juices.' Alastair angled the tub this way and that. 'Deep golden deliciousness. They're marinated for twelve weeks by Donatello, our neighbour down in Charmouth. His is the cottage next door.' Alastair opened the olives and offered them to me. I took one.

'Killer isn't it? Now try one of the purple ones. Nobody does them like Donatello. Next time we go, I'm going to get his secret recipe. He'll give it to me, I know. Donatello calls me *nipote* – nephew, in Italian. He loves us. Two years ago, Dad helped rescue his belongings when his roof collapsed in a storm. We had his furniture and some of his artwork – *including*, you'll like this, liking art and all, *including* an original Marc Chagall – stowed at ours for six months while he waited for the thatchers. It's only small and just a sketch but worth a ransom. Now, every time we go down, he comes round with food by way of thanks. Pepperoncini, artichoke hearts, pancetta at Christmas. You ever tried limoncello? *So* amazing. I'll get us some next time. Some people drink it over ice, but Donatello says to store it in the freezer instead. Everything he brings us he makes himself. I went to see him this morning and he loaded me up with all sorts.'

'Wondered what.' I was smothered in sunblock with perfume dabbed here and there and still in a mood. Alastair was an hour and a half late. Tomorrow he was going away again, to National Training. Today's ninety minutes lost felt like theft.

'Yeah, totally wonderful. Defo. Donatello defo wonderful. His name is Donatello, but he was born here. Parents, too, if I'm not mistaken. Sorry, what's that again? You won*dered*?'

'Nothing.' I set about opening the pâté and the pickle. 'Just wondered what…'

'Oh, you mean why we had to meet now instead of earlier like I planned. Give it here.' I handed

Alastair the pickle, knowing I could have unscrewed its lid myself.

'Figured something must have happened. But it was only your neighbour, Donatello. Grape?'

'Not yet. We'll wait for the cheese. Train cancelled, actually. We always catch the nine-ten home. Seats booked. Taxi to the station booked. Bags packed. But hello! *Wrong kind of sunlight*.'

'*This*?' I waved my arm at the park. The grass was scorched brown but for a few shaded strips and the sun drew hard on our shadowed patch beneath a tree. We were part-way along the downslope on the northern end of the park. Up and to the left were tennis courts behind a line of trees. More trees below us formed a figure eight around the grotto and duck pond. It was pushing thirty degrees.

'What? No. Well, same sun, natch, but on the tracks down in Axminster. That's the nearest station. Wrong kind of sunlight warps the tracks if it's too strong and too sharp an angle and you add too much weight all at once. Or the driver can't see. Or the signal box overheats.' Alastair shrugged, causing the muscles in his arms to leap and flex. 'What have you.'

For a few moments we watched a pigeon peck at the earth. I unwrapped the cheeses and broke off chunks of bread, wondering as I did if Alastair would prefer I used the knife. He had left with his family the morning after the end of school party for their cottage in Dorset. It was remote and messaging each other had taken some doing. Then the hour and a half lost today. Already things between us felt like they belonged to a different season. Alastair opened the fizz.

'It was crazy,' I started as though he had asked what I had got up to waiting for him to show. 'By the time I left...' to come and see you, I wanted to say, '...for here, there must have been more than two dozen people around the house. Funny, I mean, not crazy.'

'What's the difference?' Alastair bunched his lips and tilted his head at me.

'Nothing. I mean, okay, maybe they're the same.' I felt the breath go from me, I so wanted to say the right thing. 'But doors opened at eleven, right? Nobody's there for the first hour. Not a peep. My parents and Aunt Susie, but nobody else. Suddenly there's a group of four. Then it's eight or nine. Then three more show up. A couple more here, another couple a few minutes later and suddenly there are guests all over the place. A real party. Usually it's not until later that things really get – '

'Wait, where's this?'

'Home. Remember? It's the Art Walk.'

'Oh, yes. Of course. I almost forgot. Being away and all.'

I could tell Alastair didn't remember anything I'd told him about the art shows, so I helped him out,

'It's all over the city today and tomorrow, sixty or seventy venues.' I pulled the Art Walk map from my back pocket. I had brought it with me to show Alastair I was in the know, and for something we could do if things weren't going right in the park. The map had curved under the weight of my bum. Handing it to him shaped like that felt lurid and unattractive. I quickly flattened it on the blanket. Alastair rested his elbow on his leg and his bottom lip on his fist. He was wearing loose-fitting shorts. The hairs on his thighs had bleached gold in the sun. 'You just follow – '

'How do you know where to go?'

'It's a map. You – '

'I can see it's *a map*. My Tops unit came bronze in the South Downs orienteering competition. Would have won, too, if Stubbins hadn't turned his ankle.' Alastair's voice changed from defensive, to assured and now disparaging. 'So what, you go from house to house looking for art? What's at number twenty-one, here, for instance, and why is it in blue when number twenty-two, wherever it is – way over here – is purple? There must be...'

Alastair turned the map over to the exhibition listings on the back. I held my breath.

'Oh, *I* see. Pink is...pottery. Green...sculpture. Makes no sense, but anyway. Blue for painting and if I'm not mistaken there's one...' Alastair flipped the map over to face him and traced his finger up Southover Street to where we were now. 'Says there's a place just over there.' Without looking up he pointed to the far side of the park. The veins in his forearm were popping in the heat. 'In Albion Hill, round the corner from me.'

'We could go and see, if you like. After this.' I didn't want to be the first to eat and presented him the board of cheese.

'So who goes? Bread.'

I put a chunk on his plate with some grapes. There looked too many, so I broke a few away and put them on a plate for me. Sharing, I told myself, he would see we were sharing. 'Lots. Eight, ten thousand,' I exaggerated, thinking I would seem more interesting, the bigger it was.

Alastair examined the listings again.

'And people actually buy stuff?'

'Plenty. I mean, not always. Not everything sells.' I thought of how Mum put small red SOLD stickers on pieces to convince prospective buyers things were being snapped up.

'And *who* goes?'

'From all over. We keep a guest book for people to sign. Lots are down from London and Surrey and

Kent.' I cast my eyes up at the branches shading us and listed on my fingers. 'We get Amsterdam. Bruges, here and again. Places in Poland and France. Japan once.' I glanced at Alastair to see how he took that one, but he was looking at his feet. 'Australia. Italy. Cornwall. And here, of course. Lots are from here. Most, in fact.' I could have killed myself but rabbited on. 'They're different groups. People here for the weekend, and my parents' friends, through work or wherever, and friends of my Aunt Susie. Our Donatellos, you might say.'

Alastair pushed out his jaw and nodded.

'It's always a big party. People come round, have some drinks and the buffet, wander over to other venues or down to the seafront for a swim if it's like today,' I traced an arc back and forth with my finger. 'Pop back for more drinks, go for another swim, come back for more. Sometimes stuff sells. It can be quite dear. Mum's stuff, I mean. There's even one,' I said, thinking about the cityscape that had one of the false red dots on its tag, 'going for eight and a half thousand. Last year a photographer came and – '

'Wait, came why?'

'To photograph everybody.'

'An inspection you mean?'

'Inspection? No. The party.'

'That's what I mean. Because he wanted to get people at the party.'

'Yes, well, no. *Get* them, all right. But not *to* get them. It wasn't an operation or anything. Not those kinds of photos. Just to photograph the party, as it was happening. People having fun, just as they are, casually. And it was a she. The photographer.'

'Was anyone there?'

'Tonnes.'

'No, but any*one*?'

'Well the photographer – Mimi Pretend, that's her professional name – is semi-famous. Mum says her stuff reminds her of Andreas Popalov. The warmth, at least. And there's a photo of hers, Mimi Pretend's, which started in the Kona Gallery and is now at the Courtauld.' Alastair looked confused, so I added, 'You know it, the one down here, the old Church Street barracks. My mum works there. Assistant Curator when she's not doing her own stuff. Artwork, I mean.'

'Art is good,' Alastair said chewing his food. He leaned back on his side, revealing a sleek pack of muscle above his hip. I glanced at it then quickly away before he could see me. 'And your mum's an artist. My old man's in energy. Mining, you could say. But really it's energy.'

'I wonder if *he* is?' I stopped myself from pointing and nodded over my shoulder instead. Alastair was looking at his arm and hadn't seen me.

'What? Of course he is.'

'Him?' I nodded again toward the man crossing the park.

'Who else? I know my own father.'

'That's your dad?'

'Where?'

'There. Him. That man.' I felt my Rudie voice kick in, as though I was paired with Magritte in the field. 'Two o'clock. Straw boater, striped waistcoat, white tee, green bandana on his neck. There.'

'That's not my dad.'

'No. It's Mr Peters. We could never figure him out.'

'One of your parents' friends, from the party or something?'

'*That* would be something. No, not that I've seen.'

'I thought you thought he was my father.'

'He's from class.' I felt breathless. Mr Peters looked everywhere but at us, yet I was certain he knew we were there.

'Just a teacher, then.'

'No. An assignment. Rudie stuff.' I quickly told Alastair how Magritte and I had tailed Mr Peters to Brunswick Square that Easter.

'And you didn't think to take him up again after he shook you? We totally busted that bloke at the Dome a week later, you know. Okay, look again. Got him? Now away.'

'I know how it's done.' My tolerance was ebbing. Yet I stayed. I obeyed. With the surprise appearance of Mr Peters, I had something that had hooked Alastair.

'Where now?'

I nodded downslope. Mr Peters had stopped about six metres from the trees surrounding the grotto and was looking at something ahead of him. It was like before, at Easter, when he paused at the top of Brunswick Square as though to say: *Go ahead, take a look. Take a* good *look*. I had gone over it in my head again and again, each time searching for something in him and each time coming up with less. Not a blank, not nothing. An abstraction. A wash.

Moments later, Mr Peters was on the move again. He disappeared behind the trees.

'Now where?'

'Subject of sight.' My Rudie voice again. 'Treeline, seventy meters, five o'clock.'

'He could be watching.'

I didn't respond.

'The grotto, you're certain?'

'If I were a boy, one of your *loyal Tops*, would you really keep asking?' It just came out.

Alastair pretended he hadn't heard. He was on his knees and pushing the picnic into his rucksack. 'What's that again?' He zipped his bag shut. We both stood. Alastair pointed at my feet. 'The blanket was my grandmother's.'

'You told me.'

'Grab it, will you? Just...no, don't fold it. Over your shoulder. Quick, before we lose him.'

I started for the grotto when Alastair turned me towards him. We were out of the shade and the sun shone hard. Alastair pulled me close, curving my body into his. I dipped my chin. Alastair turned his to the side. He pushed the hair from my cheek and our mouths met, off centre at first, then swam together. My hands felt for his shoulders, the flow of his back. Adrenaline raced through me, jolting my body. Ten seconds, twenty, the hour and a half I'd waited for him. Alastair's eyes would have been searching the trees behind me, but I didn't look to see. Then we were on the move again, my hand in his and the other clasping his arm.

'Arriving six o'clock.'

I started to ask how he knew what time I needed to be home, when I saw he was citing Mr Peters' position. At six o'clock this evening, Mum was auctioning a one-off print to raise funds for a local children's hospice, and I'd agreed to be there for it. The hospice's managing director was attending, as were some of the wealthier people known to my parents and Aunt Susie. I was expected to meet and greet. Mr Peters' straw hat could be glimpsed moving through the trees – six o'clock, seven – where it paused long enough that I half wondered if he'd rested it atop a shrub. Then it vanished.

The grotto was quiet save for the sounds we made hunting for Mr Peters' dead drop. We were certain it was there somewhere. Alastair kicked at the dirt, saying we should have split up, one of us tailing him while the other stayed and searched. He was gone and we were alone. Alastair standing like the Statue of David in a shaft of sunlight. Alastair examining the orange magnolia head found amongst the rocks and moss. Alastair pulling me to him. I could feel him against me. I didn't know what I was supposed to do next. I knew he wanted me to do something. I did my best.

I saw her. For the first time, I saw her. Sometime in that extra hour and a half at home after Alastair messaged he was running late, I found her in the kitchen. She was stirring milk into a cup of tea or holding a plate of food. Our eyes met, or nearly did. She looked at me and glanced away, or I did. She was there. We said hello and didn't speak beyond that. In years past, only the front hall and Mum's studio had been open to the Art Walk. Now, like a sun expands in radiance and mass before it explodes, things had spread to the first floor. There were pieces up the stairs and on the landings, in the front room and on the walls outside the kitchen, where there was nothing. Hannah Cross was heavily pregnant. Sweat stained her shirt beneath her arms and where it was stretched taut over her stomach and breasts. I guessed she wanted to get away from everyone. It was baking indoors and you couldn't move for someone else's elbow or hip. The cords of the venetian blinds swayed in the open window.

I saw her. She brushed a dead wasp off the table onto her saucer or plate and tipped it into the bin. Another crawled on the window frame. I started to point it out, but it lifted away as though on string.

THIRTEEN

Early Sunday morning at the Brighton Station coffee bar: deliberately distressed armchairs, jardinières of fern and petunia, echoing loudspeaker announcements punctuated by whistle shrills from the concourse. Anna and Alastair sat opposite each other at a table. Sunlight slanted through the station roof. It was the day after their picnic in Queen's Park. Alastair was going away again. Five weeks of National Training – NaTra, in the parlance of Rudies and Tops – in the New Forest. After that, a sixth week in Charmouth with his family, enjoying the fruits of the gift-bearing Donatello.

'Timing of it gets me,' Alastair said after they had been served their coffees and a cinnamon swirl to share. 'Sticks in my craw. I don't like it.' Staring into the mid-distance he tapped a fist on his rucksack. Anna puzzled his meaning. Was he working up steam to end things because he was going away, chucking her now because of the six-week separation that lay ahead? Yesterday in the park, in the grotto, had she done something wrong? Too little, too much? Or was he merely complaining, thanks to engineering works, about the half-hour delay until his train departed? When Alastair spoke again, it was like a silver ring tossed into the flood of her heart. It wasn't the two of them or even the trains, it was Mr Peters.

'Of all the people, of all the days, just when you're there, in the park, he shows. Bloody odd, wouldn't you say? You're *certain* it was him?'

'Of course,' Anna said with a note of indignation. They had gone over all of it yesterday, after the grotto. 'So why?'

'Yes, precisely. *Why*? Three months ago, Easter weekend, you trail him. You observe him going about town. Fresh fruit, newspaper, mints and stopping for a coffee. All above board, completely kosher. That leaves his detour into Farnham Courtyard between buying the paper and the café. *Why* the detour? Why *there*? Is there anything special about the courtyard or, as I suspect, was it to gauge if he was being followed? Lure you – '

'Magritte,' Anna protested, instantly regretting her defensiveness.

'Would you have done any different than your partner? Methinks the same. No, he improvises. Lures you into – if not a blind alley, then somewhere he can determine whether or not you just happen to be out poodling along same as him or same as how he wants to be seen, or if you were indeed tailing him. Which you were.

'Then there's the buttonhole mystery. When was the flower inserted and again *why*? Where did it come from? Not from the florist's, you say. Okay, I'll buy that. I think, between you, Magritte *and the florist*, one of you would have seen him pinch a flower head and pop it on.'

'Also, there weren't any at the florist's. Carnations.'

'So he gets it from somewhere else. The kiosk is unlikely – he made a clear exchange. Newspaper. Mints. Cash. We could make enquiries about the vendor, but my instinct says no. That leaves Farnham Courtyard. Flowers there?'

'Yes. But again carnations, no.'

'And no hand off, no brush pass?'

'Not that we could see.'

'Still, it mightn't take much. Not if they were pros.' Alastair chewed his lip. 'But I'm inclined to think one of you would have noticed. Thus logic tells us either it was present all along and you didn't notice, or he had it hidden about his person.'

'There was nothing. No flower. Red scarf, umbrella, canvas bag – yes. But no flower. It would have stood out a mile against his grey mac.'

'Ergo?'

'His pocket.'

'Precisely.'

'It would have been his right pocket – he was right-handed.'

'Which pocket is immaterial. But okay, his right. That makes sense. Yes, right pocket. Right hand...'

Alastair mimed the movement Mr Peters would have made reaching into the pocket of his mac and drawing his hand upward across his chest. '...Left buttonhole. As he enters the courtyard or exiting? My money's on the latter. You're some distance up the street, your partner doesn't have eyes – let's assume she's circled somewhere out of sight while he exits – and one, two, three four...' Alastair repeated the pocket-to-buttonhole movement. 'He fishes it up and pops it in in full stride. Regains the street and is on his way again. He pauses outside the bookshop to buy himself time to think...'

'Or check the reflection.'

'*And* check the reflection. Good. That's good. Checks the reflection to see who's watching him, buys himself a few seconds to think what next. All of it looks like he's just out for a wander, casually considering a book in the window display. Do I buy it? Will it be a good read? Do I want something else instead? The coffee and crossword are more of the same. Perfectly ordinary. Perfectly natural on a bank holiday Sunday.'

'He hooked his umbrella on the back of the chair. Miss Rodmell – '

'You said.'

'So maybe it was a signal.'

'Maybe. Maybe not. *Not*, not in my opinion. No, the carnation is the key. He keeps the umbrella, it's the carnation he ditches. Question is, who's seen it? Is it while he's wearing it or...?' Again Alastair thumped a fist on his rucksack.

'Or when it's left there, in the little vase, for someone to see later.' Anna silently congratulated herself for completing Alastair's thought.

'Yes. A distinct possibility. For someone to see later or someone already there at the café. Keeps it on, sends one message. Ditches it, means another. All safe? Abort? Which is which?'

Alastair stuffed his fists under his arms and shook his head. 'But no, I don't like it. Rubbish. Suppose he leaves the flower for someone to spot once he's cleared off. The café is busy, his table gets taken soon as he goes. The new people accidentally knock the vase as they're sitting down. They're what, the size of this?' With his cup Alastair tinked the saltshaker on their own table and it fell on its side. 'Or someone shoves two tables together and everything gets bunched up so that a passer-by or whomever can't spot the signal. Too risky. Too much left to chance. No, it *has* to be when he's wearing it. More noticeable. Man standing upright, flower right there, in anyone's eyeline, no need to search for it. He's given the signal. He knows you two are watching him. He sees the square and the thicket of trees, sees how he can shake you, and does it.'

'He paused, though. Explain that. At the top of Brunswick Square, he paused.'

Alastair shrugged. 'To not appear conspicuous. To make it look like he's remembering something. Or forgotten something. Reconsidering a book he saw in the window. Something from the greengrocer's or...'

'All that's true, then why draw attention to himself by entering the square and leaving straight after?'

With a single downward nod, Alastair looked up at Anna and pointed out that, according to her own account, shortly after they had entered the square it had started to rain. 'Imagine the opposite. Imagine he stays. In the square, in the rain. Everybody else scarpers. No one else around. And here's a man lingering in a downpour. No, that won't do.'

'He did it again in the park yesterday,' Anna returned to her earlier point. 'Paused before he reached the grotto. Then left his flower behind, same as at the café.'

'Different flower. Carnation at the café, marigold in the park. Makes all the difference. And was he even *wearing* it in the park?'

Anna shook her head. 'It was some distance. But we *found* it – remember? – about where he paused in the grotto. We couldn't see him, but clocked his hat.' Anna gestured the width of Mr Peters' straw boater with her hands held in line with her eyes.

'True. Okay. True. Well remembered. He paused again. To unhook the flower and leave it? Assuming he did that, still some question there, but assuming he does it, we only get to the *why* again. Why was he there when *you* were there? Chance? The odds are *fantastically* against it. And if he was wearing a flower again, why wear it and why ditch it like before? Who else was at the park? Four, five dozen people? More?'

'He wasn't out shopping yesterday. No bag. No fresh fruit. No paper or books...'

'Ah. Now. Hold that thought. You remind me. I brought you something.'

Alastair popped a catch on his rucksack, reached inside and removed a small package wrapped in parcel paper and string. He handed it to Anna.

'Do you know Gatsby?' Alastair asked before she had finished unwrapping it.

'Some,' Anna lied. It was a book on her parents' shelves; she knew the title from its spine. The copy Alastair gave her had a black and white photo on its cover of a young woman in a long dress and pearls. The woman smiled at a man leaning toward her across a table not unlike the one here at the station café.

'On the syllabus last term. A-star on the exams. My personal copy.'

Anna flipped through the pages and resisted the urge to hold the book to her nose and inhale its scent. She felt small for not having brought Alastair a going away present. She had been late returning home from their picnic and had missed the auction of her mother's print. Ordinarily, she would have been grounded and was surprised that she was not. Rising early this morning to make the station in time she hoped seeing Alastair off would be enough. 'What if I couldn't make it today?'

Alastair nodded across the concourse at the parcel and post self-service kiosk.

'But I don't have anything for you.'

Alastair mused. 'You could tell me a secret instead. Secret's as good as a present. Gift of sorts.'

Anna considered demonstrating how she liked smelling books she was reading but dismissed it as unsightly or too thin to qualify as a worthy secret. Should she confess to having not reported the gold and ruby pin she'd once found doing GoodWorks litter picking? That she found the smell of manure comforting, even savoury in a way? The family practice of Living As If? Her mother's illness? To cover her uncertainty and the red rising up her throat, she cupped both hands around her coffee cup and sipped. That she didn't sputter it everywhere gave her courage.

'Like what?'

'Such as a crush on a teacher or that you're a secret skinny-dipper...or what you did for initiation when you switched from Canterbury to Mallory.'

Anna asked how he knew she had switched houses.

'A little bird, as they say.'

'Magritte or Danny?'

'Might be aiming wide on that one.' Alastair's eyes flashed. 'Go on, spill! Or give it back.' He held out his hand for the book.

'No-oo. Never.' Anna playfully clutched the book to her chest. She debated how much Alastair already knew, and how much she should tell him. After Miss Buxted had informed her she had been reassigned to Mallory, Anna was pink with dread about what initiation she would face from her new housemates. She needn't wait long. Eight Mallory girls were grouped below the phallic pillars when she arrived at school two days later. They were a mixture of sixth-formers and girls her own year. Alice Andrews was one of them. Magritte was another.

Anna stood with her back against a pillar. Melanie Bramber, who was taller by a head than everyone but Anna, put forward that she should wait in the third floor Laurels toilets during lunch hour. Any Mallory girls who entered, Anna would offer a choice of washing their hands for them or kissing with tongues. Magritte objected to this, pointing out that if anyone was carrying glandular fever it would be transferred amongst them, deftly adding that it would slash their chances of regaining the Lady Lull Trophy if there was widespread infection throughout Mallory.

Agatha Treetinwot-Holmes suggested Anna should bow or curtsey to all Mallory girls for the rest of the week. This was given serious consideration until Magritte again objected on the grounds that, on its own, and with respect that it was already Thursday, it wasn't adequate. 'Not for Mallory standards.'

It was finally decided Anna should steal the 'Ming' vase from the mantelshelf in the administration building and, after weeing in it, return it without getting caught. With help from Magritte, who diverted the bursar with scholarship questions, Anna completed her mission late the following afternoon. She was Mallory now, and had a new friend in Magritte.

'Your turn,' Anna heard herself saying after she had finished telling Alastair about her initiation. Rather than admit she had urinated in the vase (and how it foamed and hissed beneath her, how its base was warm to the touch when she reset the vase to the mantelshelf), she conjured up instead having had to down a vile concoction of vodka, tequila and whisky from it. 'Let's have some of your Tops info.'

'I brought the book.'

'Denton reporting for duty, sir!'

'Selmeston, sir!

'Dominic. Christian.' Alastair leaned back and straightened his face. 'Address the lady.'

'Begging your pardon, sir. Ma'am.' The boys repeated their salutes for Anna. They were Alastair's year and the salutes were only for fun. Same as him, they were bound for NaTra in the New Forest. Like the other elite programmes in Little Gaddesdon, Telford and Dedham Vale, the New Forest camp was boys only. Girls who preferred single sex training (including fourteen from Lynton that summer) attended Cranbourne Chase or Waddesdon Manor. All other NaTra camps were mixed. Anna enjoyed some relief that Alastair wouldn't be anywhere near other girls. But it didn't do anything to quell the emptying feeling that she was losing him for the summer.

As the other boys started to unsling their packs, Alastair said he would see them on the train. The boys exchanged smirks.

'Save me a seat,' Alastair called after them as they headed off.

'Like fuck.'

Alastair hoisted his own rucksack on his back. His eyes were wide as he took Anna's hands in his. 'This summer is...you're here and I'm there,' he said with a rehearsed air that touched Anna all the while they were apart. 'It's only a few weeks and then I'll be back. Besides,' he nodded at the book he had given her, 'there's a line in there for us. You read it and you'll see. It goes something like, "Life starts all over again when it gets crisp in the fall."'

Sarah Fetlock finished her drink and ducked in through the balcony window. 'Catering van again. That makes four times in the past half hour.' The evening sun cast a forgotten light across the sitting room. Sarah shut the window and pulled the curtains closed. Nick switched on a lamp.

Earlier, when the van made its third pass, Nick began casually unplugging appliances. Their mobile phones were stored in the refrigerator (a 'smart' refrigerator linked by the internet to the National Grid Monitoring Service, it was itself unplugged) so their microphones couldn't pick up the family's voices, and laptops stacked one atop the other in the Towering Shitter, its door closed to the stairwell. Nick's was left playing *To Catch a Thief* from a traceable subscription service. The Fetlocks had seen the film before; in case questioned about their whereabouts and activities on that particular evening, they could each recount scenes and plot and Nick could charm any inquisitors by reciting lines in Cary Grant's moneyed drawl. He used it now,

'Same one, darling?'

'Van, plates, driver.'

'Could be just a sweep.'

'As If,' Sarah said *sotto voce*. Anna, who had been summoned from her room, stood in the doorway.

'As If,' Nick confirmed, still in character.

'Ready teddies?' Sarah clapped her hands. Anna nodded and moved to the sofa. Tucking her feet beneath her, she told herself anything could happen now.

'*Scram*, she said to the egg.'

'*Dash*, he cried to the salt.'

'*Pinch*, she told the sugar.'

And with that, they were away, Living As If, when anything could be said and done – said and done as if they were unmonitored by authorities or neighbours for infringement.

Living As If had initially been Nick's gift to Sarah, when she was ill. It was a way of helping her recover. Its origins were in something Sarah herself had years earlier told him about, the Gandhian practice of satyagraha. Satyagraha, a portmanteau of the Sanskrit words for truth (satya) and holding on to (agraha), was civil resistance. It meant insistent holding on to oneself, one's humanity. When Anna was younger, Nick and Sarah practiced satyagraha together, just the two of them a few minutes a day, whatever Sarah could bear. By and by she recovered. Later, when discovering their television had been recording them, they expanded the practice to include Anna, lest she too fall under the same iron wheel of anxiety and depression that had crushed Sarah. As freedoms constricted and surveillance metastasised, it helped them feel less frightened. It was an expression of love.

It was also defiance, pure and clean. To remind them who they were, *that* they were. Anna was instructed to never mention it to friends. It was a family tradition and secret she cherished. Living As If always began with a nonsensical prelude, a sort of limbering up, as it had tonight. Sometimes it was a cacophony of recorder, bodhrán and saucepan played with a spoon. Others it was reading aloud lines from poems and children's books backwards or talking through kazoos. They drew pictures. They sang and made music. They talked.

The outside world sealed off, all potential recording devices removed or switched off, tonight they enjoyed a sprawling conversation that took in Wes Anderson films, Yuri Gagarin (a twice annual visual arts and music night Sarah and Nick used to attend, as well as the name of the road where Susie lived when she and Nick were children: all of the streets in her estate had been named after astro- or cosmonauts), the triangular cataract of bubbles in Nick's glass of wine, Isosceles, Archimedes and his 'Eureka!', Anna's English teacher Miss Buxted, Zadie Smith essays, Dale Winton, cumulative collusion by generation, the definition of 'stoop' in the US north vs the US south (and stoop as a verb). Sarah spoke of an exhibition at the Rijksmuseum in Amsterdam – Otto Dix and Elfriede Lohse-Wächtler, the sculptors Emy

Roeder and Marg Moll. Food leftover from the Art Walk party two days earlier was brought from the kitchen. Cheese, melon chunks and crisps. Anna was issued a glass of wine (and benevolently tolerated a second). Nick did imitations of government ministers, William Shatner and what he called the 'Lynton Golfer Father'. Anna imitated Miss Rodmell, The Shrew. Malkmus marched in and out and eventually perched owl-like above them on his favourite shelf.

After two hours Nick stood and stretched. He announced he now knew the voice needed for Dr Frobisher in an upcoming radio production of *The Browning Version* and that he was going to his studio while it was fresh. Sarah seemed to say something to him with her eyes and out loud that she had better get on with tidying the mess in her own studio.

'Oh, are you two going to have sex or something?' Anna had seen the look from her mother and was on her second glass of wine. She lifted it. 'As If. When we can say anything?'

'Then...' Nick started.

'Yes.' Sarah unblushingly joined in.

The sitting room windows were opened. Anna retrieved her mobile from the refrigerator to see if there was anything from Alastair. Sarah and Nick disappeared into their studios. They took with them more food and wine leftover from the party. The outer studio door closed behind them with a click and Anna was surprised to hear the thunk of its lock.

Her late return from Saturday's picnic with Alastair was a serious infraction. She had missed the auction of her mother's print. But instead of being told off, her parents had blithely disregarded it. They were in high spirits when she had arrived home (the print, Susie exclaimed amidst the gentle clamour of the party, had raised £2,400) and inexplicably seemed to harbour a sense of relief. Instead of being confined to the house as she had been for previous offenses, her mother had all but shooed her out the door the following morning when it was time to see Alastair off. Afterward, Anna had been permitted to spend the rest of the day with Magritte and to stay the night at hers as well. And returning home the following day lunchtime, instead of being conscripted into tidying the still substantial mess from the Art Walk party, Anna's father handed her forty pounds with the solemn advice to 'immediately proceed to spend it unwisely.'

If in total it was a new variety of punishment, something to instil in her a sense of guilt for blowing out the auction, it was working. Anna felt unwanted. Alastair was gone (and no message from him since leaving for NaTra camp). Her parents appeared intent, even happy, to carry on without her. Malkmus had turned tail on their hugs. Even Susie, ordinarily enthusiastic about Anna's goings-on, seemed to cast wide of her following their momentary encounter at the party. Tonight's Living As If session was a welcome return to business as usual.

Had Anna's Rudie alertness been switched on (had it not been packed away like her mobile and laptop for that evening's round of Living As If), she would have noticed there was no amorousness in the look Sarah had given Nick. It had been furtive, and their stuttering confession to disappearing downstairs to make love was a flimsy display of improvisation. Had Anna been fully alert to it, she might have placed the look her parents exchanged as something akin to the danger and mistrust in her mother's face that afternoon weeks earlier when she had surprised her in the kitchen, and the pleading in Tommy Denton's eyes as he stood solitary sentry outside of Freddie Heathfield's beachfront party.

Anna tapped out a long message to Alastair that they were having drinks at home. Thinking better of it, she erased it before sending and instead wrote *Wine is flowing!* facetiously adding *Thirsty?* Three X's. She lay in bed reading the book Alastair had given her and fell asleep waiting for his reply, unaware of the quiet glide of the bookshelf hinges opening in her father's studio two floors below, the soft clunk as the shelves were closed again sometime later and the doors locked for the night.

They were there, the Crosses, in hiding. Frightened by the creak of the stairs all but directly above their bed, by the clicking of the water pipes. Frightened by the clatter of footsteps in the front hall and outside the studio door. They were there. Anna had no idea.

FOURTEEN

the iComm

Things changed when Morkel and I next met up. For starters, his spot had disappeared. I can't adequately explain my relief to see it gone. When we last met, Morkel was sporting a whitehead on the rim of his upper lip. All the while we talked, I kept glancing at the spot, hoping he didn't notice and wishing he would do the decent and get rid of it. We had coffee and the dusting of powdered sugar from Morkel's croissant somehow made his spot glisten all the more (and put me right off my own cream horn). I've no clear recollection of what we discussed. The Hassop Five must have entered into it though: it was the bee in his very own bonnet, his Crosses to bear, so to speak.

A week or so later, Morkel came to visit me in the shop. It was Flying Ant Day, an annual summer spectacle seeing colonies of ants erupting into nuptial flights by the thousands, livening the skies and littering the pavement in silvery swarms. Samuel cherished the event since his teens, most likely because it coincided with him meeting his first great love. We had gone to the seafront for a dip to break the noontime heat. Two or three blankets away was a red-haired swimmer named Mandy Hayling whose ice cream had been scooped whole from her hand by a gull. Samuel instantly and chivalrously replaced it with a Double 99. Until Lindsay, I doubt if Samuel, through all his conjugal meanderings, ever loved a girl so blindingly as Mandy. Their romance was short-lived. She chucked him after three weeks for a Tasmanian weightlifter with a driving license and, you ask me, fraudulent rhotacism.

Consequently, out of fraternal solidarity, I was uninclined to commemorate Flying Ant Day with anything other than a passing reflection on what might have been. It may have even gone unnoticed entirely that day if I hadn't left the shop door open to alleviate the afternoon heat. Before I knew it, flying ants had coated the window display of cat tepees and our signature collection of 'Poetry' porcelain vases, and were fashioning a run at the till. Selecting one of the beefier feather dusters I set about driving them back. I was making some progress when the duster shot from my grasp. It took out a shelf of glass tumblers and a wine cooler that leapt bodily at the ornamental pepper grinders. One of these, executing a double aerial, sent a pyramid of portable speakers crashing to the floor. They exploded with a might only just outbursting my fart of surprise (and one questions, of admiration?). A flying ant landed dead at my feet the same moment Morkel entered the shop.

'Now that you've finished having your fun,' he seemed to say with his eyes, 'maybe we can talk like grown-ups.' Morkel swiftly locked the door and pointed me toward the back. Why he was acting so gruff was unclear. We passed the till and stood facing each other beneath the racks of oversized maps. I reconsidered telling him about the Map Men. The only thing that stopped me was Morkel getting in there first.

'The Crosses. Give me what you've got.'

I asked him what he meant. Morkel made a quinny expression.

'Mark and Hannah Cross. We agreed said couple were a subject of interest.' Morkel waited. I nodded. 'We agreed you would supply information concerning said subjects.' He named the date and the special Ambrosia points he had provided 'in good faith' for his part of the bargain. This pained me. It was fabrication and I was momentarily embarrassed for Morkel, having stooped to falsehoods when he should have come to me as a friend or a brother.

'Said couple transgressed the law,' Morkel continued and waited for my reply.

'Yes.'

'Said couple have put others' wellbeing and lives at risk.'

I thought of the lunchtime power cut that same week, how I'd been forced to cancel the sale of some marmalade toast candles. The customer had yet to return. 'Yes.' I nodded solemnly. 'Yes, indeed.'

'Said couple absconded prior to sentencing.'

'Yes.'

'Said couple have known connections to our local municipality.' I couldn't answer that one but must have assented in some fashion, for Morkel went on. 'Said couple, through their present and illegitimate liberty, present a threat to the community.'

'Yes.'

'Your father, for instance.' Morkel named him and the garden flat where he lived. 'He is presently well, is he not?'

'Yes.'

'And you would of course hope that he remains so? Your father...' Again, Morkel gave my father's full name and address. A goose honked in my gut. We had never spoken about my family before. I worried Samuel was next.

'Yes, of course I – '

'You believe in helping others?'

I started to say how much it had meant to me to have helped pay for my father's care. For a long while – years – he had ruminated about my mother dying whilst holding his hand and him 'suddenly feeling the weight leave her'.

'Mark and Hannah Cross are a threat to your father. Mark and Hannah Cross are your priority.

You focus on them. Everything you listen for is about them. Everything you look for is about them. This is Grade A priority. For the country. Is that clear?' As he spoke, Morkel's voice had reassumed by degrees much of its usual ease and warmth – only now, through patterns of repetition, it also amassed a sort of patriotic heft.

I was inspired. The worry for my father's mention (and Samuel's almost mention) was quelled by having been given such an important assignment. Morkel was probably under pressure himself and, frustrated, it had leaked out before he could stop it. I straightened my shoulders and nodded.

'Out loud, please.' And it was then that I understood Morkel was recording our conversation. I told him what he wanted. But these things work two ways and I swiftly knocked the ball back over the net. Indeed, I told myself Morkel would have expected nothing less.

'About the Ambrosia points you mentioned. For the Crosses?'

'Yes?'

'You said there were special points.'

To this Morkel arched backwards as was his way and fished his mobile from the holster on his belt. The holster upset me. It was imitation leather. He deserved better; I decided to gift him a proper one before doing a flit abroad. Morkel tapped at his mobile screen. He shook his head and tapped some more. 'Consider this a down payment.'

That evening I closed the shop early and went to the beach. It was as good a place as any to look for the Crosses. The sea was green and marked in patches of brighter colour where the sun shone on the shallows – and again farther out where tankers inched across the horizon. Slow rollers foamed white as they neared the shore and rolled themselves flat into nothing. A cloud, muscular and roasted pink in the heat, nosed across and soon obliterated the sun.

FIFTEEN

Anna

There hadn't been a power cut with any punch since May. We'd had The Flicker, The Fizzle, The Hour, The On-Off (at least a dozen of these) and The Slow Fade. Nothing that hung around. You could feel it: everyone sensed we were due. When it came, it lasted forty-six hours (and longer in the countryside). But school was out and so was the sun. It was the first week of August. I met Magritte, Alice Andrews and others each day at the beach. We swam in the sea and dug trenches in the pebbles, down to the cool sand, to chill our drinks. At home, Mum improvised an air conditioner made with plastic bottles and Dad served ice cream one breakfast. Nighttime was candleland.

'Stop. Give it to me again. 18b Farnham Courtyard. You went right up the door?'

'And the window. The door, the window, then the door again.'

'And you knocked?' Alastair, full of attention.

I thought about this. 'Had to. In case someone was watching. I even waved through the window for anyone the other side.'

'And?'

'No one home. But it bought me time to see what Mr Peters might have been looking at.' Again I paused and asked myself: *at* or *for*? 'You remember me telling you how when we tailed him at Easter, Magritte saw him waiting outside the door of 18b like he'd knocked.'

'Did he?'

'Softly maybe. But there's a bell too. Magritte couldn't have heard that.'

'Go back a sec. When was this again?'

'Today lunchtime.'

'Supposing someone came to the door?'

'Easy. I had the perfect cover. I'd just tell them I'm doing GoodWorks and Farnham Courtyard is bang in the middle of things. Ordinarily neat as a pin and technically off my beat, but I wanted to...'

In my head I took it as given Alastair knew my GoodWorks assignment was litter picking and wouldn't bring it up. He did, and I would move on like I hadn't heard.

Or perhaps, I reflected, I ought to leave Good-Works out altogether. Thinking what to say instead, I scratched at a damp wad of paper that was gummed to the pavement. It came away after a few goes and I flicked it into my bin liner. It was the second bagful of rubbish that day. I had already cleared Brunswick Street, Kerrison Mews and Upper Market Street, and had worked my way round to Little Western Street, where gulls had torn open a takeaway bag that's contents were scattered everywhere by a wind. What if Alastair recoiled, saw me as a little garbage girl? No, GoodWorks litter picking wouldn't do.

All I was certain of was I needed something to tell him. He had messaged that he would try to ring tonight, and Farnham Courtyard, where Mr Peters had mysteriously cut a detour Easter weekend, was just there. I didn't *want* to make anything up; only something real would truly impress Alastair. The New Forest NaTra camp was in a tarl, where mobile signals were scarce. When we had spoken two nights before, Alastair had needed to climb a hillside fifteen minutes outside camp to reach me and sounded indifferent when I told him about going to the beach with friends. Even Danny's chatting up a trainee lifeguard and the news that the seafront road had been sealed off after a woman leapt from Bedford Towers barely drew a response. Mr Peters was my only ace.

Alastair, meanwhile, was in his element. By day, the camp studied what he had learned to call 'Astrology' (ARIES: Agent Reconnaissance & Infiltration Excogitation Strategies; LEO: Letterbox Emergency Options; SCPOS: Serious Crime Prevention Orders), advanced cryptography, steganography and countersurveillance methodology. At night there were campfires and exfiltration games. Nocturnal orienteering had them out of their tents until two in the morning. Breakfast was served only after they ran a 'quarter marathon' and the coffee was 'abominable'.

I felt dull in comparison and, wanting to demonstrate I was in on the fun too, having adventures of my own, needed a story that would make him miss me. I had also prepared a first-character null cypher message to send to him: *At night now, at last one views everything sensually and languidly. Around seaside towns, artifice is real*. It was on my mobile, ready to go. All I needed to do was press send.

Was it too much? I knew I ought to hook him on something first (unless, as I hoped, he would be the first to say it). I had zero news, nothing that made headlines. Mum's birthday was coming up and we were having a party. The next day but one there was an appointment with the Lynton Data and Compliance Officer, the DCO. I was halfway through the book Alastair had given me (I wondered, was I his Daisy or his Jordan?). There was nothing else. I began picking my way into Farnham Courtyard when I noticed the door to 18b was open.

Rudie training didn't fail me: I glanced at the open door like it was nothing and looked away, searching the courtyard floor for litter instead. Surveillance procedure 2a. There was hardly anything and what was there was too small to grasp with the teeth of the picker. But stooping to collect something with my fingers every few steps I edged towards the house and felt a surge of delight when I spotted a bottle cap near the front door, at the base of a planter. The sun was overhead and drew a sharp line across my path. Rather than bend to collect the cap with my fingers, I made a hash of things with the picker, buying me a few moments to peer through the open door.

Inside, the house was in shadow. Atop a wooden floor stained deep brown was a runner stretching into the back. The runner was thin, pale and foot worn. A landscape print hung on the wall. Something about it caught my eye. Involuntarily I stepped forward for a closer look.

'May I help you?' The voice came from behind me. I leapt out of fright, dropping the sack of rubbish and the picker clattering to the ground at my feet. In that same instant, I thought the latex gloves I wore must make me look like a thief. No fingerprints. I quickly stripped them off and held my hands up. 'I was only...'

I didn't see much of anything for several seconds. The play of sunlight and shadow across the housefronts. The mass of sheds with flowerbed roofs at the centre of the courtyard. My legs shook like they do in films.

'Oh, wait...I know you. You come to the shop.' The voice came unexpectedly low, from the nearest shed but one. It was then that I saw her face; it was the only part of her visible. A moment later she emerged, rolling her shoulders and spine upright. She held a trowel in one hand and with the other gripped the base of her back. Dressed in a t-shirt and overalls, her chest strained against the latches when she stretched. Her face was freckled and she wore her hair in an arced fringe. A streak of soil across her cheekbone I mistook at first for a bruise. Seeing I was still too startled to speak, she named the shop and, with the trowel, gestured in the direction of the high street.

Her name and all its musicality, seemingly lifted from any of the children's stories or fairy tale books at her shop, came singing back to me. Jeannie Penny-feather. I sagged with relief. Still troubled by a stitch in her back, she managed a laugh.

'I'm sorry, Miss Pennyfeather,' I started, and she told me to call her by her first name. 'I was just doing my – it's GoodWorks – and I saw...' I waved at the open door.

'Your mother's print on the wall.' She knew my parents by name and was about their age. 'You're Anna.'

For the second time in as many minutes I was speechless. Now I knew why I had been drawn to take a closer look at the print. I glanced at it again and back at Jeannie Pennyfeather. What I didn't understand was the connection between my parents and the woman who, until then, I hadn't thought of as existing anywhere other than behind the counter at her shop. When I was small and permitted to select one or two books for my parents to purchase, visiting Brunswick Books was as much a treat as Café Bertrix. Often the two events occurred in succession the same day. At Christmas and Easter there were chocolates at the till. As the years passed and armed with money given to me by my parents or Aunt Susie, I grew old enough to go to the bookshop by myself. Usually it was an assistant or another who rang me up, and only occasionally Jeannie Pennyfeather. I couldn't remember the last time I'd seen her.

'Come,' she turned and stuffed her trowel into a holster hanging on the shed door. 'We'll take a closer look. It's okay.' Jeannie brushed herself down and went into her house. I followed and stood beside her on the runner.

The print was a lithograph of the South Downs above Lewes. Green and gold whaleback swells rippling in the sunlight and marked by crooked pathways cut over time by grazing sheep. It was never anything I had paid close attention to, but rather something I once knew from Mum's studio and was now only as familiar as a half-remembered face.

'When I saw it, I had to have it. You were there, remember?'

I shook my head no.

'You must have been five or six and were wild, absolutely bananas, about a series of books, *Esmée the Purple Dragon*.' She listed several titles in the series. 'Ring any bells? Every time a new one came out, I'd put a copy behind the counter for when you next stopped in.'

For a moment I thought I would cry. I'd forgotten about the books; they seemed so long ago.

'Well, sure as eggs, one day you were there with your mother and she had with her a handful of Art Walk flyers. We always put a stack of them on the counter, for customers to take. That print was on the front of the flyer and I swooped one right up. My father had died recently and we'd had him cremated. According to his wish, his ashes were mixed with wildflower seeds and scattered on the Downs. He always loved the walk up to Mount Caburn, so we did it there. Not strictly legal, you understand. But there – do you see?' She pointed to a tiny line of orange and pink that ran along the left of the print. 'And here too. Blink and you miss them.

'Your mother had no idea, of course. We didn't know one another that well yet.' Jeannie seemed to hesitate, as though she had said something she shouldn't. She glanced at me, then away. I couldn't think how to respond. 'But there he is, in the flowers of your mother's print. She could have easily left them out, those little flowers. Or been there a different month, when they weren't in bloom or after the sheep had munched them away. But she got him. He's there. And when I told her, do you know what she did?'

I shook my head.

'She *gave* it to me.'

The letter summoning me to meet with the Lynton DCO gave nothing away. It was addressed to me, rather than my parents, stating only the time and date of the meeting, the particular building where I should present myself. Out-of-term letters and electronic notifications from school were not uncommon. When it was something important, they sent both. Belt and braces. Because there was no corresponding e-message for my parents, the letter didn't seem much of anything. Boring bit of bureaucracy, I recalled Miss Buxted saying when I'd been reassigned from Canterbury to Mallory. The summons felt like more of the same.

The day of the meeting was overcast. An early mist cleared to reveal a flat, putty grey sky. It was the first morning in weeks I hadn't seen the sun. Going to school out of uniform was a thrill. It felt forgivably illicit, a privilege of sorts. Because the day was cool, I wore a heavy jumper and jeans. Before leaving home I'd rubbed myself with a lint roller to remove the Malkmus hairs, but still bore traces of him on my sleeves. By the time I reached Lynton I wished I had listened to Mum to bring an umbrella. Trees waved in a wind and the pavement was peppered with rain.

There were no other girls in sight. Across the road, at the junior school, there were art classes and games in the gymnasium: Lynton offered summer courses that more or less operated as a childcare service for households where both parents worked. But here, on the ground floor of The Laurels, I was the only student. After signing in with Miss Matteson at reception, I checked my mobile for anything from Alastair. Through the window I glimpsed the phallic pillars, cool and sleek and free of any markings. I was relieved I hadn't been called in to explain my role in painting Alastair's initials on them. After a few minutes I heard a door close and footsteps approaching.

'I'll take this, Jennifer.' To my surprise it wasn't the DCO who came to collect me, but Miss Buxted. She looked as put-together as ever, with her hair upswept into wartime curls and a dark floral dress drawn tight at the waist by strings of the same material. She was already taller than me and her heels added another few centimetres. I stood to meet her as she came around the counter, now wishing I were dressed less shabbily and had thought to wear the Mallory badge that had once been her own.

'Did you get caught in the rain?'

I explained how I'd made it just in time but didn't have high hopes for returning home.

'We'll sort you out with a spare brolly before you go. There's practically an entire *closet* of them here. But first there's an office for us to chat in just at the back.' Miss Buxted smiled and together we walked down a corridor side by side, turning left and right every few paces before reaching the room. I sat facing a desk and, rather than taking a seat the other side of it, Miss Buxted wheeled her chair around so it was beside my own. Between us was a small table with a broken leg propped up on a book.

'First things first. Would you like a cup of tea?' I nodded yes. 'Good. I've been gasping for one. I'll make us a pot.' Miss Buxted moved to the window, where there was an electric kettle, cups and saucers atop a shelf. Rain tapped at the window. As the kettle began to whir, she explained what was happening.

'Jacqueline, Miss Stoughton to you,' she turned and smiled at me again, 'the Data and Compliance Officer, is up to her eyeballs with admin this summer, so I and a few other teachers are pitching in where we can.' Miss Buxted placed coasters on the table between our chairs, and cups and saucers for each of us. The coasters were cork and bore rings where they had been stained over time.

While waiting for the tea to brew, we talked about the weather and what I had been up to over

the holidays. I thought she'd like it that I was reading and told her about the book Alastair had given
me.

'Oh, how *wonderful*. If ever there was a story that
sums up the season, it's that. You're reading it precisely
the right time of year. There's a line near the beginning... "And so with the sunshine and the great bursts
of leaves growing on the trees, just as things grow fast
in movies, I had that familiar conviction that life was
beginning all over again with the summer." I think of
that every May. Narrowly speaking, May isn't quite
summer. But it does *feel* like it's already here. They
ought to re-order the seasons, whomever *they* are.
May, June, July and August are summer months, all
four of them. Make it last that much longer, an extra
month. Sugar?'

I shook my head and replied no thanks.

'Good. Now, as Mallory girls, we'll do things
properly.' Miss Buxted poured the tea, milk first,
then reaching into her bag on the desk in front of us,
she removed a box of biscuits. Shortbread fingers:
she offered me one. 'There are standards to uphold.
Not like those Canterbury Cretins, as we used to call
them,' she said with a wink.

'Your GoodWorks assignment is what precisely?'

'Litter picking.' I made a face to show her what
I thought of it. For a moment I thought she would
blanch and inform me that it was beneath Mallory

standards, and I would need to return the badge she had given me.

Miss Buxted nodded and blew softly on her tea. 'And for how long now?'

'Four years.' Although I knew it by heart, I counted it out on my fingers. 'Since I was eleven.'

'What would you say about testing something different? It would *be* a test. In the beginning you would still need to continue your present duties. But eventually, perhaps as early as sometime this autumn, it will be entirely your own.'

I saw my chance and took it. 'That's in the book, too. *The Great Gatsby*. I haven't reached the line yet. But I know it: "Life starts all over again when it gets crisp in the fall."' I don't think I'd ever seen so astonishing a smile before, certainly not from any of my teachers. It rivalled, somehow even outpaced, Mum's.

'You are truly wonderful, Anna. And you deserve this. It's not an *easy* assignment, you understand. It will certainly take some doing.' Miss Buxted nodded. 'Unfortunately, there are many people who, through no fault of their own, find themselves alone. Many of them are older. They've lost their partners, their children, if they have any, are busy with lives of their own and live elsewhere. They're lonely and could do with some company, someone to talk to or drink a cup of tea with once or twice a week. Is that something you think you could do?'

I felt myself burning red beneath my jumper and couldn't speak. But I think my own smile must have said it all. It said yes in a wet gush and I had to wipe my mouth.

'Now, the question is who? Usually things work best if you're already familiar with someone. Takes the load off getting acquainted with them first. I don't suppose you know anyone who...?'

I did. Terry Peppers. Terry, my neighbour up the street. Terry and his dogs, Molly, Golly and Ollie.

By the time I'd finished my tea and thanking Miss Buxted, the sun had burnt through the clouds and the day was bright. I sailed home in the sea breeze and sunlight.

SIXTEEN

Anna was on the landing between the ground and first floors when the wasp stung her. She took the stairs two at a time. The first floor bathroom was closest – closer than the Towering Shitter one floor above – and where the first aid kit was kept. It was Saturday; she would see Alastair the next day but one. His family had extended their stay in Charmouth by two extra nights. It wasn't the trains this time, the wrong kind of sunlight. She'd checked. There was no reason given. Only the message, *Returning late Sunday eve instead. Sent a card. Monday is ours. X.* She was counting the hours until they met. After six weeks apart, the last thing she wanted was a freakishly swollen hand for Alastair's return. The wasp had got her on the fat of the thumb. How she cherished that *X*.

She held her hand under the tap. The water gurgled past the stopper left in the drain. It was the third time that week she had found it there. Ordinarily the stopper sat in a soap dish, topside down to dry. The first time she had found it in the sink she thought it was nothing. Probably her parents' cleaning had knocked it. But there it was again two days later, and again now. Anna puzzled why. She lathered the sting with soap and rinsed it with cold water, telling herself she was lucky: the wasp had started in her hair.

Whether it was the recurrent oddity of the stopper or a sort of sixth sense trickling through her, Anna looked around her now for anything else out of place. *Question the curious,* the line from Rudie training came to her, *to uncover the spurious.* Something wasn't right. Something had changed. There, as always, the toothbrushes in a tin cup, the toothpaste rolled forward from the end. There, as ever, her mother's array of make-up and creams jumbled atop the chest of drawers wedged between the sink and the bathtub. The enormous faux-gilded mirror multiplying the size of the room by half, the grooves of its scrollwork dulled by dust. Anna rattled through the chest of drawers until she found the burn gel and rubbed it into the sting. A worm turned in her gut.

The night before last she had woken in the small hours when hearing a noise somewhere in the house below. Attuned to the sounds her parents made in the night, to the ta-*tump* of Malkmus having leapt from a bookshelf or windowsill, she listened and heard nothing more, as though the noise itself, upon realising its existence, was now holding its breath. When neither of her parents stirred, Anna slipped out of bed and into her robe.

She checked first the loo next door and there was nothing. Looking there was little other than self-encouragement. The noise had come from below and something inside told her she needed to ready herself before braving a look downstairs. The runner padded her footsteps as she descended to the first floor and went from kitchen to sitting room, to the box room at the back. Windows in each were open a crack to draw a breeze. Anna tested them against the metal governors in the frames to ensure they didn't lift any higher. The noise played over and over in her head. Only the quiet from her parents' bedroom told her it wasn't sounding again for real. A single noise might be slept through, but not a series.

She crept further downstairs and stopped. Peeping over the banister she peered through the dark to make certain the front door was closed below. Streetlight shone in the transom window above the door. The front hall was empty. In her head she began constructing a narrative to tell Alastair. How she had heard a bump in the night and, alone in the dark, investigated. As the narrative took form, the thrill of it amplified her tension and bolstered her confidence. Her movements were predicated by the tale she was constructing, adding colour to what was otherwise her Rudie voice.

The front door was double locked. Goosebumps raced up my spine when I tested it. I had this awful feeling I'd made a mistake. Mum and Dad's studios were behind me now; why hadn't I checked them first? What if someone was already there and I had my back to them? I spun round in a flash. The corner by the stairs was in shadow. It used to be bigger, even more shadowy, until Dad and Aunt Susie blocked up a chunk of it redoing his studio last year. Now it's only half the size but still doesn't get any real light.

I played it like it was nothing. Heading as though back upstairs, I reached out and tested the outer studio door was locked. All good. But something stopped me. Something was wrong. There was the noise – I'd heard it – and now there was a different feel or scent. Something cool, like old dust blown up from somewhere and also strangely sweet, like honeysuckle or toffee.

Before I had time to think it through, I pushed my fingers beneath the stairwell runner for the studio keys. I was careful to pull them out slowly so they didn't jingle. There was just enough light for me to see what I was doing; the real trick was turning the locks so they wouldn't wake Mum and Dad. A five or six second job took ten times as long. But I was in and closed the door behind me.

Mum's studio was dark. Nothing moved. I'd heard it though, whatever it was, and forced myself to keep going. There was light through the curtains in the front window and after a few moments my eyes adjusted. I could make out Mum's easel in the window and the bulk of her worktable, the old armchair in the middle of the floor. I counted to twenty and moved forward,

*careful not to knock anything. Every other step I paused
and listened for the noise. Or a new one. Something
nearer. Someone in the room.*

Anna shook her head. Her breathing was shal-
low, like after a hard cry.

*Instead of going straight for Dad's studio at the back,
I found myself standing in the streetlight through the
curtains. It was for safety's sake, I guess. Now I needed to
cross the room again and my eyes readjust a second time.*

*But above Dad's studio door is one of those ON AIR
lights that beams red when he's recording and can't be
disturbed. When he's not recording, it still has a faint
glow, and I marked my path by that. The sound of his
studio door locks didn't matter so much, but I still took
care to turn them softly. If the window at the back of
his studio was open, I would know straight off someone
was here. Closed and we were okay. I pushed the keys
between my fingers and made a fist. Not Rudie training: Personal Safety, Miss Hollingbury's class, when
someone's cornered you.*

*Why I didn't turn the lights on before, when enter-
ing Mum's studio, I can't explain. Neighbours across
the street were probably used to seeing lights in there at
odd hours, if they were awake and watching. But I did
it now in Dad's. There was no choice; the darkness was
complete. The switch is just inside the door. I took care
to reach across with my left to flick it, keeping the keys
between the fingers of my right.*

A shot of air left Anna's mouth. There in front of her was what had made the noise; she stood for a moment taking it in. A box file of typescripts had fallen from the shelves and splashed across the floor. On the fourth shelf up, the slender void where the file had been, like a gap in a row of teeth. Anna turned to leave and stopped. Half a minute later, she had gathered together the papers and slid the file back where it belonged. The lights turned off and all of the doors locked, she pushed the studio keys beneath the runner and returned to bed. Only later did she ask herself what could have caused the file to fall. But by then she was already asleep.

The following day when Anna returned from swimming with Magritte her father was in the kitchen. It was early evening and Nick was preparing a pea and prawn pasta (a Fetlock Family Favourite, as these things were known and recorded). The aroma of garlic and butter had caught Anna on the stairs. The saucepan sizzled. Anna raced across the room to inhale its steam.

'You're just in time.' Nick lifted a strand of spaghetti from the pot, bit into it and nodded. When she was younger and her mother was ill, Nick had made Anna laugh by teaching her you could tell if pasta was cooked by throwing it against a wall. If it stuck, it was done. There was a section of wall beside the refrigerator still marked with traces of noodles Anna had thrown. 'Ready in a sec.'

While lunches were a free for all taken at any time, the Fetlocks invariably ate dinner together, and breakfast on weekends. Anna hurried to her room to change out of the swimsuit beneath her clothes. She admired the tan lines on her shoulders where the straps had been. No one could report her for being burnt (a prospective cost to the NHS that drew a fine).

When she returned to the kitchen, her mother was leafing through a sketchbook. It was one of Anna's great memories of her mother, the trips they took, just the two of them, to spend an afternoon at this or that exhibition, drawing what they saw. Her mother's own drawings and her mother teaching her, Anna, how to draw, how to see and render shapes and light and shadow.

A Friday night, there was wine with dinner. For a while they talked about planned redecorations in their upstairs quarters. Even with Susie's trade discount, savings had to be made before work could begin the following spring. Then they moved on to maintenance and building works downstairs.

'If you could keep clear of the studios for the time being, darling.' Anna's father chomped a piece of garlic toast, swished it with wine and swallowed. 'Don't go down there without us.'

Anna was about to reply *Do I ever?* when she remembered the previous night. It had been a non-incident in the end and failed to live up to its promise of something to tell Alastair. She felt her mother looking at her.

'It's just that there's a crack in the ceiling. Right above your head,' Nick went on.

'It's been there for years.'

'Yes, darling. But it's growing. It's every time someone closes the door.'

'Well, it's not me. It's you two. I haven't been in –'

'Not even last night?'

Rudie training on cover stories ran through Anna's head. She twirled up some pasta with her fork and adjusted her voice. 'I only went to the kitchen for a glass of water when I thought I heard something.'

'Like what?' Her mother this time.

Anna shrugged. 'Malkmus. He must have caught a spider or something.' And for several moments the silence was bare.

'Almost forgot. Letter arrived for you,' Sarah raised her eyebrows and nodded at the envelope on the countertop. The postmark was Dorset. It was dated the previous day and sent special delivery. Anna hurried with it to her room. A postcard was inside. On the front was a photograph of fossilised bones arranged in the shape of a long-tailed dino-saur, and on the back three ballpoint lines about the creature in capital letters that Anna guessed at once to be a rail fence cypher, signed at the bottom AX. As she set about decrypting the message, she thought her parents knew she had lied about investigating their studios last night.

Later, when the studio keys were missing from beneath the stairwell runner, she was certain of it.

Returning the burn gel to the chest of drawers, Anna spotted what was out of place in the loo. What had changed. The bathmat, a multi-coloured rug crocheted by her mother, was folded twice over the side of the tub. All her life it was folded only the once, a simple drape. Anna pressed her hand to it, ran her fingers over it, as though reading its bumps and weave for clues why things were different, when they had changed. In the tub, three hairs lay curled like thin snails. They were too dark, too short and too curly for anyone at home.

Two nights before, the noise. Then her parents, their studios and the missing keys. Now this. Suspicion had entered the blood.

Anna removed the takeaway coffee loop from between the slats of the park bench. The bench overlooked the playground of St Anne's Well Gardens, alive with playgroups and parents. An ice cream van jingled nearby. Pop Goes the Weasel. There was a good seventy or more metres between where Anna was seated and the copse that carved a wedge into the corner of the park. She knew someone could watch her from the trees but, at such a distance, not closely enough to make any difference. She was just someone perched in the midday sun. What remained of the tree stump where she had found Malkmus was nearby. In times past Anna had visited the stump and whispered words of apology to the mother cat, should she somehow be tuned in and still wondering the fate of her kittens. Anna had told her Malkmus's name and about his mannerisms. She had told her about their hugs, but not that they had stopped. The coffee loop was cardboard and folded in two. Breaking it open where it was glued together, Anna glanced inside. The encrypted message Alastair sent by post had guided her to the bench where he had secreted the second half of their rendezvous instructions. She knew where to go now, where Alastair would be waiting.

She was to meet him at the Duke of York's cinema in Preston Circus. The cinema was old and squatted above the street like an enormous wedding cake. Its Baroque façade and archways gave it an air of permanence and grandeur. People had visited it to watch films and live performances for more than a century. Through the generations, romances had blossomed on its screen and in its stalls.

Now it was Anna's turn. Her heart bounced. She checked her hand where the wasp had stung her. No swelling, no discolouration. All was good. She didn't know why the secrecy, why the coded messages from Alastair. It must be something big. Should she tell him her own stuff? Should she tell him something odd was going on at home, or wait until she knew exactly what? She had started keeping an eye on her parents. Other than instinct telling her something was happening, there was nothing definite. Tearing the coffee loop in pieces, Anna pushed the bits into separate recycling bins at the edge of the park. Letterbox Procedure 4c: memorise and destroy.

The cinema was teeming with parents and children. A matinee of *Frozen*. Several children were dressed in character. The air conditioning drew a shiver from Anna as she waited beside the ticket booth. She had seen the film enough times when she was younger to know its songs by heart. Lines and melodies came to her now. When the appointed time for Alastair to show came and went, she looked for him upstairs. She checked first the bar, then the outdoor balcony overlooking the street in front. Alastair was in the far corner standing with his back to her. The balcony was crowded and Anna had to squeeze past tables to make it to him. Alastair turned just as she neared. Quadrilles of his hair shifted in a breeze. Anna touched his hand and he kissed her quickly.

'Show starts in a few minutes. Wait until everyone goes in.' There was a peculiar light in his eyes. Something there but masked. It was a dark light. Anna didn't know what to make of it. She had drawn him larger in their weeks apart – and so he was. Alastair's lips, by her measurement, were a centimetre, perhaps two, above where she remembered them. His skin was deep gold from the sun. Alastair's greeting had been perfunctory, far less than what she had hoped for after six weeks apart. She told herself it was everyone else, the balcony's busyness that held him back. When people began filing inside, Anna's fingers found Alastair's, ready to be led to their seats. When he stayed put, she asked if they weren't seeing the film too.

'Sold out.' And Anna could see straight away Alastair wasn't telling the truth. 'Or actually, we could see it, but we'd have to sit apart. Do you want...?'

Anna shook her head no and did her best to smile. She wore a blue and white striped top that she knew showed off her figure and arms, a favourite skirt that displayed the length of her legs. Would it be enough if Alastair wanted to meet her here, somewhere public, where she was less likely to make a scene, to tell her things were over? It was what felt like was happening. He looked like he wanted to be somewhere else. To Anna's eye, he almost looked ill.

Alastair glanced around and raised his chin at the other end of the balcony. 'Table free now.'

They pushed the used cups and saucers to one side and sat next to each other at the corner. Alastair fished his mobile from his trouser pocket and quickly, almost absently checking its screen, rested it facedown between them. The last few people nearby swallowed their drinks and disappeared indoors. Anna told Alastair she had finished reading the book he had given her. She quoted its ending, as though doing so would somehow ward off their own. First, whatever it was at home, whatever it was her parents were up to. Now this. The end was coming, it was happening, she was certain of it. '"So we beat on, boats against the current, borne back ceaselessly into the past."'

"What? Oh, yes. That.'

'I meant to bring it with. Give back your book.' Anna lied for something to say. 'Next time,' she added hopefully.

'No. It's yours.'

'And we have the autumn, like it says. The fall.'

'Listen.' Alastair hesitated and Anna held her breath. 'Do you promise not to run away if I show you something?'

Anna nodded.

'And do you promise not to say a word to anyone?'

The fear Anna harboured that Alastair was going to break up with her had ebbed with the first request and all but vanished with the second. He was entrusting her with something. That was commitment. It was a future. She thrilled in relief. Her chest and throat burned red. But this time she didn't mind.

'I need to hear you say it. I promise...'

'I promise.'

'To not run away...'

'To not run away.'

'Or tell a soul.'

'Or tell a soul. For ever and ever. Amen.' Anna felt giddy now that the fear had passed. Only the grave look on Alastair's face drew her back to earth. He took up his mobile from the table and tapped at its screen.

'Anyone comes to clear this mess up,' Alastair gestured at the empty cups, 'you start talking about the book again. This is...You're the only person I know who...'

'It's Mr Peters, isn't it? You've found something on him. Something big.'

'Who? No. No, not him.' Alastair glanced at the doorway leading inside to the bar. Anna followed his line of sight. The doorway was empty. Alastair leaned forward. 'If only it was, I wouldn't feel so... No, it's my mum.'

Anna swallowed and pushed her hair behind her ears. She was relieved it wasn't her mother, her own parents. She wouldn't say anything about them. Not yet. Not now.

'The facts are these.' Alastair flicked his lip with a thumb. 'We had a power cut down in Charmouth. The winds were high and the flags were up for no swimming. We'd been putting it off the whole time, but finally got down to doing a big clear up. The place needs redoing. New paint and the floors sanded and that.'

'Same at ours. There's a crack in the ceiling and the whole ground floor is falling to...' Anna stopped when she saw Alastair's eyes were fixed on something through the balcony door. She looked over her shoulder, but again there was no one there.

'Anyway, it had to be done,' Alastair went on. 'A big clean and throwing stuff away and boxing up the rest before the decorators can get started. Donatello recommended some people. We'll be here, in Brighton, but he can let them in and supervise things, as need be. He already has keys, to water the plants and so on.' Alastair exhaled deeply and didn't speak for several moments. Anna reached for his hand. Alastair stared trancelike at the face of the building. They didn't need to see the film; it felt like they were in one. It felt like something Anna had seen in a film, the two of them sat there in love and weight and silence.

'I finished doing my room and thought I'd tackle the closet off the kitchen before lunch. The closet is where we keep our wellies and the badminton set and all sorts of junk. Piles of it, actually, and all of it not half thick with cobwebs and dust. I'd hauled most of it out when I noticed a loose floorboard. It sort of slid into the wall when I was standing on it and must have spun round on my toes.'

Anna felt Alastair glance sideways at her, and for a moment everything he had described began to crumble. He rushed the term 'loose floorboard', as though recognising it for the hackneyed trope it was, the bridge of the tale that, however many times it had been rehearsed, still clanged off key. Anna fought away the disbelief.

'Just the one floorboard?'

'No surprise, really. It's an old cottage and its foundations are eighteenth century. The area was absolutely *famed* for smuggling way back when. People bringing in tobacco and rum, gold bullion and whatnot. Makes perfect sense there's an old hideaway. Three boards in all.' Alastair held his hands about half a metre apart and formed a square.

Anna waited. She glanced at Alastair to see if he was winding her up. But the way he chewed his lip persuaded her otherwise. Her mind scurried for what he had found – found and that in some way implicated his mother. Letters from a secret lover? A murder weapon? A stash of false passports and pills?

'The picture isn't great – I had to rush before anyone found me – so you can't see everything. Didn't want to touch it either. Fingerprints and that. But I managed to blow away most of the dust. Here. Look.'

Alastair showed Anna his mobile screen. On it was a photo of a stack of papers; after a moment Anna recognised the top sheet as an Ambrosia points printout. To the left and right were scratched wooden floorboards. A shadow obscured the top corner of the sheet where the name and address were printed. The Ambrosia logo and account number were visible however, and down one side a rolling total with more than forty thousand points showing. Anna marvelled at the sum. To think that one person could have amassed so many points. Between the three of them, the Fetlocks were lucky to own half as much.

'Now look at this.' Alastair scrolled to the next photo. 'A screenshot of my mother's Ambrosia account. Notice the difference?'

'Only twelve thousand points this time.'

'And?'

'And that's a lot less than before.'

'And what else? Look.'

'Give it here.'

'No. Just look.' Alastair scrolled back to the previous photo, then forward and back again between the two pictures. Anna leaned closer to the screen. She reached over and enlarged the image of the papers found beneath the floorboards. Through the shadow and dust, she could just about make out the name Clara Broyle.

'Move it forward again. Now back to the... Ah!' Anna beamed up at Alastair. 'The dates are different. The one you found in the floor is from four years ago. She's spent a bunch of points since then.'

Alastair shook his head in exasperation. 'No. You're missing it. Look again. The account numbers are completely different. This one is UKBS55 and so on, and the other starts UKBN34. Different addresses too – I know you can't see it so you'll have to take my word for it. One account is for our place here, in Brighton, the other for down in Charmouth. Same person, two accounts. It's...'

It was big trouble, Anna thought. A great swarming mass of it. From time to time there were stories on IcePie of people caught operating multiple Ambrosia accounts, and warnings about the illegality and dangers of doing so. It was an extra identity, of sorts. Like a bank account or property registered under a false name. Anyone caught with a surreptitious account was subjected to investigation and faced penalties ranging from confiscation of points, to fines and imprisonment, depending on the scale of deception. Anyone who knew of somebody running an extra Ambrosia identity and who turned them in was rewarded. If proved someone had knowledge of a fake account, or even suspected one and didn't report it, they faced punishment for complicity. Fines and prison sentences again. Inspections. Neighbours informed on neighbours, shopkeepers on customers, friends on each other.

'I've got to get her out of this. You won't say a word. You promised.'

And with that, any doubt about Alastair's commitment to her evaporated like a cloud in the sun. She could see it all now. The hidden compartment beneath the floorboards in the centuries-old closet filled with junk. The necessity of an encrypted message sending her to the park bench to collect further instructions. Alastair's mechanical greeting on the balcony in the eyes of heaven-knows-who was watching, and his pensive, watchful demeanour. The soaring clear blue of the skies.

SEVENTEEN

the iComm

I examined myself. In the days following Morkel instructing me to find him the Crosses, I took stock of me. I looked at how others might see me, the things I did. Once, when I was a boy, I pushed my bike up from the seafront, past the racecourse, to the top of Manor Hill. The day was clear and as I looked out over The Channel I thought I saw land. For the next week or more I told anyone who would listen I had seen France. Schoolfriends, neighbours, ice cream men, the lot.

Later, when trying to figure out which bit – Normandy? Picardy? Dieppe? – I discovered it was impossible to see that far, even in the best conditions. It had been either a flotilla of cargo ships or a dark, low-lying cloud beached on the horizon. Whatever it was I'd seen, I haven't seen it since and, for that matter, stopped looking long ago.

That, in a nut, sums up my approach to searching for Mark and Hannah Cross. I would seek a vantage point from which I could observe logically, with clear eyes, and not be taken in by the fantastical. I would see what was actually there. Lesson learnt. And if anyone thought they saw me looking, I wanted them to ascribe it to something else, something likely and reasonable, and let it go.

After several attempts browsing faces at random, the manner in which people hurried or ambled along the seafront or drank in pubs, I returned to the system that afforded the most promise. I would focus on the shop's customers and competition. Top of the list was Gavin Hercules who ran Glass Brades, the homeware shop in Gardener Street. Gavin, I had reason to suspect, borrowed readily from my stocklist and copied my window displays. He was twice my size, drank at the Gloucester Arms more or less across the street from my shop and was hairy as a coconut. I kept my eye on him two nights running. By the way he mixed with others, I could see Gavin was scarred by his failure to master the trombone, traded favours for a reduction in rent, had been jilted by a children's television show presenter and was sexually aroused by packing peanuts. But a harbourer of fugitives, no.

Araminta Wilde and I had been at primary school together. We hadn't been friends; and now that her plant shop had branched into selling outdoor cushions and garden lighting (and scooped exclusive local rights to the new line of Wordsworth picnicware), there was no reason to strike an accord. Araminta, I could see, sneaked her shop rubbish into public bins, sold items at cost to IcePie influencers and had tried to top herself with pills. Her hair was luxurious. I made a record of what I saw and moved on.

Of the customers, several stirred my suspicions. The couple who would have divorced if not for their Airbnb income. The former Radio 1 DJ now property developer. The psychology lecturer and her wife, a stage actress, with a summer house at the end of their garden. The hairdresser who worked off the books in his kitchen. The middle-aged widower and estate agent. A long ago ex with whom I feigned cordiality.

Keeping an eye out was no bother. I could see or read people easily enough, and any of the leads could be the one. But was I alone in my assignment? Wouldn't Morkel have others doing the same? It got up my nose someone might beat me to the Crosses. I wanted them for myself; I wanted it to be me. The Ambrosia reward would come in handy for the overseas flights, especially now that I was considering bringing my father along too. With my mother dead all these years, Samuel long gone and settled overseas and now me doing a flit to boot, he would be stuck on his own. I convinced myself that his coming with me wasn't too big a wave and may even be written off as something of a win. It was mostly economics. Older people weren't earning anymore and cost the NHS something dear. Let some other country take the expense! Let New Zealand pony-up for his care! Meanwhile his flat could be repossessed and sold, the money going to the state, the good of everyone.

Convincing my father to leave would be the difficult part. He wasn't one for change (when Cussons Imperial Leather, his lifelong favourite soap, updated its logo he couldn't function for weeks). And we would need to take my mother's ashes with us. But there, at least, I had a solution. We carried a range of Kilner jars at the shop and any of the two litre ones would do the trick. Bundle her up and send her special delivery. I set aside a roll of bubble wrap and a Russian doll of boxes for the job.

That sorted, I was making the most of my final summer at home. The seafront gelato. Hikes across the Downs. Al fresco drinks in the North Laine. Once when I was feeling particularly wistful and out for an early morning wander I caught sight of my father jogging. Flush-faced and lips flecked with slobber, his limbs pumping and head hammering back and forth (and him not so much gliding, but thrusting forward), I had a sudden vision of my conception and had to look away. Our beginnings aren't always pretty.

For instance, I wouldn't have known Morkel at all if not for the Household Accordance Act. Linked to personal credit rating, a revamped Ambrosia system, housing options (leases, mortgages, council flats), improved interest rates, insurance, broadband speed, shopping discounts, school and university selection, and ultimately status, an estimated eighty-five per-

cent of the population were outwardly compliant
with it. The Act was administered by public-private
partnerships. Preferred providers were contracted by
the Home Office and operated regionally. Agencies
subcontracted by regional providers collected data on
individuals on the local level. All information was fed
upward and stored centrally at the Ministry of Public Safety. Morkel worked for Segovia, a local security enterprise whose operations spanned the coastal
stretch between Littlehampton in the west and Bexhill
in the east and the lives of three-quarters of a million
people. Relatively small when held in balance against
agencies monitoring the capital and other metropoli-
tan areas, Segovia could still boast an Intercommunity
Communicator for every two hundred people. Every
sizable business, every school (and every couple of
streets) had at least one. No iComm broadcast their
role. It would have been counterproductive to information retrieval. We kept our identities to ourselves.

Likewise my father had never told me he had
taken up exercise. But if he was open to things oner-
ous and new (if he had invested in flash new trainers and, Jesus wept, a Lycra unitard that left nothing
to the imagination), it meant selling him the idea of
going abroad wouldn't be as tricky as I first imagined.

'That's it?' Morkel glared at me like a man about to
comment on the darts. 'That's all you've got?'

'But there's tonnes there,' I protested. Having given him a rundown of everyone on my list, I expected some thanks. 'Consider. Any one of those leads could land you the Crosses. Some real gold there. Take a closer look. These two,' I pointed at a pair of names on the list. 'Their summer house, perfectly habitable for a couple on the run, with running water and electricity. It's got a bed, they've got blankets and just bought a new whisk. I've got sales records to prove it. On paper.' In my head I could hear Morkel repeating my father's name and address again. I went on. 'Or what about the estate agent with access to all those empty properties – check *him* out and I bet you find he's had *this one place* on his books for months now. Or several. One property sells and it's off to the next with them. They move from flat to flat every time somewhere new opens up. Perfectly logical. Perfectly...'

'Bunk and dribble.' Morkel turned away from me. We were at the shop. His eyes roamed the shelves of merchandise. For a dreadful moment I worried he needed to look elsewhere when informing me an inspection team would shortly be visiting my father. He was facing the direction of his flat.

'The place next door selling sausages.'

'And cheese.' Ordinarily my mouth watered at the thought of their raclette, their goat and Sussex Charmer. But not now. I stuck to the facts. 'Moo and Oink, yes.'

'Floorspace of – ' Morkel named a figure. He had a surprisingly good eye for it.

'Exactly the same as here.'

Morkel stamped a foot. 'Except they have a cellar. You don't.'

We looked at each other. Morkel nodded slowly. I asked if he thought the Crosses were hiding in the Moo and Oink cellar. It made sense. They could have slipped in as customers and been ushered downstairs when no one else was around. There was a kitchen, a toilet, an endless supply of meats and cheese. Biscuits. Fresh bread and eggs. Condiments, too, now that I thought about it. Olives.

In response, Morkel shoved aside a box of soaps on a shelf. The soaps were handcrafted; they sold like nobody's business. Morkel rapped his knuckles on the wall. He made an appraising purr. 'Solid. Probably load-bearing. But with the right support you could open this up.' He gestured with both hands, indicating wall's width. 'Double your floorspace, double the goods for sale, your income skyrockets – *whoosh*.' Morkel gestured again. I followed it through the ceiling with my eyes. 'Yes, you could have a real nice set up here. You would like that, would you not?'

I went for a walk. With Morkel's suggestion he could get me the shop next door, New Zealand suddenly seemed a long way to move. I asked myself, if I could uncover the Crosses' hiding spot, score the shop next door as a reward, make a pile of money, couldn't I just go and *visit* Samuel? Test the waters, as it were, rather than chucking everything and vanishing overseas. What if I got there and Lindsay didn't like me? What if she was jealous of Samuel's and my bond? I'd be living off them for the foreseeable; what would happen if they got fed up? Was I even permitted to work? And weren't the seasons there the wrong way round, with snowbound summers and torched armpits for Christmas?

Rather calling things into question about expanding next door was Morkel's history of building works. His house had all but toppled in on itself (and him inside it, his neighbours in theirs). When it came to it, I made a pact with myself, I would find my own builder. Expanding next door was seriously tempting. Samuel was offering me a home; Morkel was offering me a chance to build my trade and income. Profits grew and I could get an assistant, cut down my hours. As I walked, I read more into Morkel's offer. Moo and Oink was as much a reward as it was an apology. A reward for when I found him the Crosses, an apology for his implied threat to my father and the fear he must have read in my face. We were on the same side again.

In St Anne's Well Gardens a bumblebee stopped me in my tracks. It was crawling across the pavement and in danger of being squashed. As a boy, Samuel had been bonkers about honey. Honey on his breakfast cereal, honey on cheese, honey drizzled on yoghurt or on his tongue, straight from the squirty jar. You name it. It was no wonder he'd fallen in love with a flower grower. He must be swimming in the stuff now. Before Samuel left and in his letters he sometimes talked about bees. Two things he told me came to mind.

The first was how people believe bumble bees shouldn't be able to fly, given their non-aerodynamic shape and frankly oafish bulk compared to wing size. But because bumblebees don't think about it, so the theory goes, they don't recognise their inability, achieve what physics says they can't, and fly. Was this bumblebee too smart for its own good? Was it the philosopher of its hive, weighed down with thoughts of its own existence? Why wouldn't it just get on with things like all the rest? Why couldn't it just be?

Out of brotherly love, I shovelled it onto a business card from my wallet and dropped it on a flower. All it had to do now was snuffle up some nectar to go biffing off back to the hive.

Which reminded me of the other thing Samuel had told me. Where it concerns bees finding food it's not down to luck. Flowers emit an electric charge that bees can sense or see. The electric charge tells bees there's pollen here, like a menu in a restaurant window. No one else can see it. But bees can. They have special sight. They see things others don't.

EIGHTEEN

Anna

August was over. Mum's birthday was that coming Sunday. School began a day later. The nights were hot and nobody slept. Autumn was around the corner. The fall.

For Mum's present, I was making her a pair of bangles. The idea came from an art magazine she had shown me years earlier. In it was a photo of a twenty-million-year-old grasshopper preserved in amber. The amber was pristine, only eight or nine centimetres in height and half as wide. Within it, standing as though reaching for something on a high shelf, was the grasshopper looking just as it had when alive, its antennae stretching upward from between oversized eyes, its armoured body, its hind legs crooked backward above sleek, latticed wings. Mum sketched and painted it – and later destroyed the painting, when she was ill. It was in her studio, then the stairwell landing, then it was gone. But the idea stuck with me, of preserving something so others might look back at what once was. A life. An event. A season.

Making Mum a present was also a diversion from fixating on whatever was happening at home. I'd caught myself watching for signs of things afoot. Mum and Dad knew I was looking for something, but didn't know what. The studio keys were still missing from under the runner. Twice Mum asked what I was up to when I was pretending to read in the sitting room. When I spotted her on errands in town one afternoon, and followed her back to work at the Courtauld, I knew I needed to stop. She'd seemed perfectly ordinary, just someone going about her business. That raised my suspicions even more. She's good, I told myself. Whatever she's doing, she's good.

The bracelets helped put a stop to that. They kept me busy, gave me something else to consider. Before casting them I sketched the bracelets again and again. Each on its own, the pair of them together, or modelled on my own arm. I suppose they were a way of saying sorry, too. My snooping didn't entirely stop. I would make Mum her present and still keep my eyes open *just a little*.

In any case, they were now impossible to close.

From the art supply shop across from Brighton Dome I bought tubes of epoxy resin and hardener, and a silicone bracelet mould. Unlike the dark gold of the amber, the resin, once hardened, would be clear; I wanted to fill it with as much natural colour as I could find. For a week I collected cornflower and poppy blossoms, Spanish daisies and red campion that I kept alive in a glass of water in my bedroom window. Unwilling to sacrifice a living creature, I kept an eye out for any that had already died and felt like I had won the Ambrosia lottery when I found a pair of lacewings on the back patio, and a day or two later a mayfly on my windowsill. There was a dead wasp on the kitchen floor but I didn't use it. Lacewings and mayflies have delicacy and beauty. Wasps are only ever a menace.

The resin and mould I paid for using Ambrosia points. Paying purely by Ambrosia transfer was more costly. But it was Mum's birthday and I was earning more now that I was visiting Terry Peppers every few days in my new GoodWorks assignment, an extra sixty a week for maybe three hours of my time.

Terry's flat was ten doors up, on the first floor. There was a separate flat above him and another below, occupying the ground floor and, like most houses higher up the street, an accessible basement. The top and bottom flats were seaside getaways for Londoners who came on weekends. Terry was the only fulltime resident. From the beginning, we had a routine. I would help him with whatever housework needed doing – dusting picture frames and books, washing windows, spraying the vine tomatoes on the patio for greenfly (too small and fragile to use in Mum's bracelet) – followed by a cup of tea and a chat. I could scarcely believe my luck. Terry, while always appreciative of the company, seemed entirely capable of managing on his own.

Every visit required a report logging anything of note. What we did and things we discussed. Likewise Terry would counter log the hours we spent together, the dates and times of my visits. Of all my friends I was the only one whose GoodWorks assignment meant Viennese fingers and a cuppa in a stuffed chair. Terry was seventy-eight and his flat smelt of the lemon curd shampoo he used to bath his dogs. 'Otherwise,' he explained, 'they stink to high heaven.' I couldn't help noticing Terry smelled somewhat lemony himself.

Only two things from any of my visits stood out as noteworthy. Because both occurred on an unofficial visit, when I went round to arrange things with Terry the morning after seeing Miss Buxted, neither made my reports. Terry's flat was not unlike our own first floor quarters, with the sitting room and a narrow balcony at the front, his bedroom up a short set of stairs beside it, and a box room through which one had to pass to reach the patio at the back. But where in ours the kitchen was a separate area altogether, Terry's was joined with the sitting room through a wide archway. Sunlight and fresh sea air breathed throughout.

Beside the front windows was a glossy black piano with framed photos and a maquette of Degas' *Little Dancer* arranged on top. Nearby, nestled amongst a bank of potted ferns, was a large white-wire birdcage.

Inside it was an imperious red- and blue-feathered parrot Terry introduced me to as Miss Jean Ross. When she wasn't in her cage, used mainly for resting, she hopped and marched across the back of the sofa or perched on Terry's shoulder, like something out of a children's book or cartoon. Miss Jean Ross had been a wedding present Terry and his late husband had bought themselves along with the cage, a replica of Brighton Pavilion's onion dome.

'Molly, Golly and Ollie I got as pups from a breeder,' he said, offering the bird a grape; the curtsey she performed accepting it tickled me no end. 'But Missy here was a rescue mission. She was three when we brought her home; her plumage was a mess, not the radiant coat you have today, was it, dear? No. No it wasn't.'

I asked wasn't he afraid she would fly out the window. Terry tucked his thumbs under his arms and drummed his fingers on his chest, saying that her wings had been clipped long before they brought her home. And as though guessing my next question, he explained there was every chance she would outlive him.

'She's thirty-one-years-old. With the right care, they can live up to forty, fifty even.'

What'll I do? What'll I do?

'That's Franklin.'

What'll I do when you are far away?

I looked at Terry. Franklin had been his husband's name.

'Well, not Franklin. Franklin's voice. Or not his voice,' Terry shook his head. 'Just one of the old songs he liked to sing. She's remembered it all these years.'

The piano had been his husband's, Terry went on to say. He and Franklin had been married for twenty-eight years, before he died. 'Me, I'm hopeless with that sort of thing. Tone Deaf Terry, Franklin used to call me. And he was right. Can't sing or play a note. But it meant whenever he would sit down at the piano of an evening, my role was to pour the drinks, put my feet up and enjoy. He had a wonderful voice, like September, full of sunshine and shadows. I only keep the piano because it reminds me of Franklin and because it was such a bitch to get up here. See for yourself.'

Terry guided me to the front windows. Like ours at home, his windows were a many-paned bowed set of three running floor to ceiling. 'Despite every assurance the movers could do it, the piano wouldn't fit past the turn in the stairwell. We had to take the windows out here,' Terry traced a finger along the window casing on the right. 'To the middle one there. Balcony railings needed pulling out, the street blocked off. Then they hoisted it up by crane and eased it inside. I kept waiting for it to drop and the sound when it hit. A *big* bang and the cacophony of every key sounding at once. But it was all right in the end. Franklin played *Let's Face the Music and Dance*, while I mixed a pitcher of Pimm's, his favourite. Then everything had to be put back. The windows, the railing. You know who did that, don't you?'

I shook my head no.

'Susan Reid.' Terry was enjoying himself. There was magic in his eyes.

I was about to ask him if he meant my Aunt Susie when I saw a figure shuffling along the street. 'Here comes Peer Glimpse.'

Terry looked where I was pointing.

'*That* fucker.' He rested his fingertips on my arm, telling me to lower my hand.

As we watched Peer Glimpse go from door to door and check the Household Accordance plates, Miss Jean Ross warbled in the background:

What'll I do? What'll I do? Velveteen collars... Velveteen collars all the rage.

I was to hear the same words here and again, from one visit to the next. But it went no further than a passing mention in the report on my first official visit two days later. Terry's parrot talks, I wrote, and left it at that. Anything more, Terry might not seem so lonely and my GoodWorks visits with him would never get off the ground, my wings snipped like Miss Jean Ross's. I didn't mention what Terry's parrot said or that one of the things it did was half-familiar to me. It wasn't until weeks later come the autumn, come the fall, that I remembered Mum repeating the same phrase to the boy at the café she had dragged me to in the early stages of her illness. Only then did I realise the significance.

Terry's exclamation at seeing Peer Glimpse I also omitted from any report. I had heard the same and much else besides at home.

Mum's birthday party was scheduled for Saturday night. Aunt Susie and a few family friends were coming round. There would be music and drink into the small hours. Dad, Susie and one or two others would disappear to Dad's studio to smoke a spliff, as though the room was airtight and I couldn't smell it. Sunday there would be a birthday breakfast and presents. Mum was particular about that. Even those presents brought to the party by friends she would wait until midnight before opening. Family presents were only ever on her birthday itself. Because I could afford only a single bracelet mould, I needed to make the bangles one at a time. Each would take twenty-four hours to dry. I'd make the first that Wednesday night and the second the following evening. If one didn't take, there would still be time to do a replacement. After that, I'd be out of resin and flowers.

Casting the bangle was easier than expected. I layered the mould with blossoms and insects I'd collected, mixed the resin and hardener in a plastic measuring cup gleaned from Mum's studio, and poured it into the mould. The measuring cup was the only difficulty. Not realising until the last minute that I needed something in which to mix things, I had to turn to my father. His and Mum's studios were still off limits and locked. Dad brought the cup to my room. When I showed him what I was doing, his eyes smiled and he kissed my forehead.

After Dad left me to it, I wondered how Alastair would react if I told him about the present – and what he himself would make or buy for his own mother when it was her birthday. I had dreamt of him the night before. The dream vanished but for the memory that, in it, he had smelled like my father. After seeing Alastair at the cinema and him telling me about the documents he'd found (and swearing me to secrecy), we went to the park where we'd weeks earlier seen Mr Peters. I tried asking him questions about NaTra camp and Donatello, but Alastair was preoccupied with his thoughts, only giving quiet, monosyllabic replies. When he bit his lip, I kissed his mouth. When he chewed his knuckle, I kissed his hand. We sat side by side on a bench near the duckpond. I stroked his hair.

'I ought to lie down for a bit,' Alastair nodded to himself. A breeze pushed across the water. 'And I want to check on one or two things while my parents are out. Listen,' he stood quickly and, taking my hand, pulled me to my feet. I moved my face closer to his and waited. 'I know I just got back, okay? And I know I should be...' Alastair gestured with his free hand, making the muscles of his arm bob and dance. 'But I really need a few days to process everything. I need a plan. I may be...*incommunicado* while I figure a way out of this. It's not you. Don't think that, okay? The opposite.

'You realise...,' Alastair shifted his weight and stood contrapposto. 'You realise I'm only telling *you* this. No one else. It's just you and me. It's our secret. Mum, Dad, me, we could be in *real* trouble. I could lose everything.'

I started to say that Alastair wouldn't lose me, but he stopped me short. 'I know you already promised not to breathe a word of it. But I need to hear you say it again.'

I did, three times over. Once for him, I told myself. Once for me. And once for the two of us and everything we would have together. Alastair had shared his secret with me. The solemn enormity of it – and his trust in me to keep it to myself – was exhilarating. I never felt closer to him than that afternoon.

Having made the first bracelet I left it to harden atop my chest of drawers. I covered it with a tented sheet of paper to protect it from Malkmus and dust. I would tell Alastair about it only after he had sorted things with his own mother. Until then, the subject of mothers was off limits. I didn't want to cause him any more anxiety (and I was still feeling guilty about following Mum). Alastair and I were due to see each other Friday evening. If he asked to see me again the next night, when Mum's birthday party was on, I had a story at the ready, one not mentioning mothers. And it was just as I was checking if Alastair had posted anything on IcePie, that I heard the crash below. The house shook with it. A door banged open. Then another. A rush of feet and voices on the stairs. I ran to the landing and shouted for my parents. When no one replied, I hurried down a level. Then the next again, toward the sound of grunts and slapping.

They were all there. Mum, Dad and the two others. The man I didn't know. But the woman I had seen before, alone in our kitchen at the Art Walk party. Mum was helping her brush the man down. Her swollen belly shone creamy brown where her tank-top had rolled up to her chest. She wore pyjama bottoms I recognised as Mum's. Dad hurried to the front door and watched through the eyehole. 'Clear,' he said in a coppery whisper.

All at once the four of them turned to look up at me on the landing. Dad switched off the light.

NINETEEN

'Miss Fetlock?'

   'Yes, Miss?'

   'Have we lost you already?'

   'No, Miss. Just...'

   'Do you require the nurse?'

   'No, Miss.'

'Then perhaps you would be so kind to do as requested and repeat for us the Four P's you will have learned last year in this very classroom.' It was the first day of Tradecraft 2.1, five days after the Crosses crashed out of hiding. They had stayed that night upstairs, in Nick and Sarah's room. Hannah Cross had escaped the wasps beneath a blanket; Mark Cross was stung on his neck and arms. When he turned clammy and collapsed, Sarah raced for the first aid kit and jammed an adrenaline injector into his thigh. The anaphylaxis passed and the hole in the Tokyo's Suite's rear wall was patched. The following day lunchtime, the Crosses returned to their hiding place. On Friday, Alastair messaged Anna he was ill and couldn't make their date. Sarah Fetlock's Saturday night birthday party was cancelled. Sunday she turned forty without fanfare. Anna flung the bangle she had made for her mother out the window. Now it was school. Anna felt like an actress – she felt like an actress alone on stage with an audience ready to hiss her into the wings.

'Prevent...'

'Standing, please.'

Anna rose from her seat. Her knees trembled and she had to steady herself against the table. Miss Rodmell asked a second time if Anna required the school nurse. Anna shook her head no and breathed deeply.

'Prevent – Protect – Prepare – Pursue.'

'And now, if you would, kindly furnish us with the primary elements of Prevention, beginning with the need.'

Anna felt the eyes of the class on her. For a moment she thought she might pass out, when a thought came to her – a thought that spoke to preventing anyone seeing through her (seeing through to the secret drumming inside her), that would protect her and would stop cold any pursuit before it began.

'If I might, Miss, I've been considering a fifth P.'

Miss Rodmell cocked her head. 'Go on.'

'Profiling, Miss.'

'Explain.'

'It's looking for patterns. Patterns in people and using that information to generate profiles predicting who's going to do what, who's likely to engage in community-adverse behaviour and activities.'

'For example?'

'For example people in certain professions or who have particular hobbies, things to do with credit and where people live. To build up a picture of how someone might appear or behave prior to committing an act.'

'Prior to?'

'Yes, Miss.'

'And afterward?'

'Miss?'

'You suggest employment of profiling prior to the pursuit of persons and imply positive results from said pursuit. What becomes of the profile afterward? Dismissed? Given a pat on the head and a biscuit?'

'No, Miss. Afterward profiles can be added to others of the same or similar suit, to fine tune things. For the next time.'

'And these profiles, this repository of data, would it be kept private, for use by professionals, or in your learned view made public?'

Anna sensed a trap. She thought for a moment. 'Public, Miss. Public access to profiles might serve as a guide for those – ' she stopped herself from saying *those of us* – 'in need of support, people who might believe they are doing something acceptable but are in fact in breach of societal norms. Thereby preventative. It protects a person from making a mistake and at the same time protects us – ' how relieved she was to get in that *us* – 'from people taking adverse actions. It also allows the authorities to better prepare and focus, now having a clearer picture of whom they're pursuing, thereby avoiding time spent chasing dead ends and reducing spend on the public purse.'

Anna stood glowing. An actress she was.

'And what, might I inquire, compels you to believe profiling is not already integral to the process?'

Anna had gone to see the secret room for herself. The Tokyo Suite was compact and considerable, cluttered and sparse. Windowless, it managed to somehow convey the outdoors. There was an earthy smell to it, like potatoes. The bed was immediately the other side of the hidden door, a mattress on a low platform. Covering the wall behind the bed was a mural, a trompe l'oeil of the South Downs' whaleback green hills and chalk trails, a distant church steeple. Anna examined the mural. She considered the detail, the hours and weeks it would have taken her mother to complete. The leaves and nettles. The buttercups amongst the wheat grass tilted westward in a breeze (judging by the sunlight, the shadow). The whites of the clouds and the varying blue of the sky. In the top right corner obscured by a hawthorn in bloom was the hole where the wall had crumbled and the wasps had arrived. The Crosses came through one hidden entrance, the wasps through another.

Biting into the adjoining wall was the underside of the stairs up to the Fetlocks' own quarters. The stairs up were mirrored by a slender set of steps down to a lower level; viewed together, they looked like a set of teeth opened in shout. In the room belowground was a table and two chairs, a mini fridge and electric kettle. On the table were two plates, two bowls, two cups and cutlery. Pallets of bottled water and boxes of dried fruit and nuts were stacked nearby. The area beneath the cellar steps was sealed off by plaster-board and a narrow door. Through the door was a toilet and sink. The Tokyo Suite was only intended to be a temporary stop, a secret staging post for a few nights, a week at the very most, before its travellers moved on. Not the Crosses' forty-six days before the wasps drove them from hiding. Ideally built for one person, it made do for two.

At night and when during daylight hours it was deemed safe, Hannah and Mark Cross had the added luxury of Nick's studio, a doubling of their seques-tered world. There they could stretch and enjoy what natural light filtered through the milky glass of the studio's rear window. On days Anna was out, they were brought upstairs to bathe. Care was taken they weren't seen. A handwashed shirt or jumper was left to dry on a hanger in the landing window, blocking any outside view of the stairs. Anna was the real worry. Eyes were kept on her while she was out with friends, with Alastair or doing GoodWorks. Amongst the watchers was Gordon Peters of 17 Vernon Place, whose traffic light system of buttonhole flowers and scarves had helped the Crosses (and others before them) disappear. An orange flower meant caution and to read the scarf. A green scarf meant stay alert and proceed; red meant danger – stop. Terry Peppers was another. Not so much a watcher, but a minder, someone who occupied Anna's time and kept her out of the house. Any movement by Anna toward home was instantly conveyed to her parents. For her own good, for safeguarding her future, she had to be protected from any knowledge of the Crosses.

As planned, they had arrived at the Fetlocks' separately. The Art Walk party was the cover. With people coming and going, wandering out and returning, the Crosses would appear ordinary partygoers, there for the food, the drinks, the art. Hannah Cross arrived first, along with two friends of the local bookshop owner, Jeannie Pennyfeather. Three women on a Saturday out. Some half-hour later, Mark Cross strolled up with a young woman on his arm, a friend of Anna's Aunt Susie. The woman wore high cut shorts and a low-cut top to draw any attention from him to her. Mark Cross had shaved his head and beard. He looked years younger. Hannah Cross had shaved her hair too. Gone was the green dye-job she had in online news stories about the Hassop Five. She wore Jackie O's and an enormous floppy sun hat. Mark had lost weight in the months of hiding. Hannah's belly had grown, her breasts swelled as her due date neared. They were moved from safe house to safe house when at the most recent their host was hospitalised with a stroke. With no one to bring them food or news, they were evacuated. The Tokyo Suite was the Crosses' final harbour before escaping to asylum abroad. First the Continent, then beyond. What few belongings they possessed were brought by others in backpacks and shoulder bags.

Off script and requiring improvisation on the Crosses' arrival day was Anna. Her leaving home to meet Alastair in Queen's Park had been delayed. That in itself might have been easily remedied. The Crosses could have been ushered from one studio to the next and into the Tokyo Suite as planned, so long as Anna wasn't in the room. Everyone else at the Fetlocks' that day lunchtime was part of the plan. Between eleven and two, the party was a private view, only for people known to Anna's parents and Aunt Susie. Like-minded friends and associates in on the operation who could be trusted. Before anyone realised it, Anna, in the dark about things, had admitted some half dozen or more visitors who could have been anybody. Scouts. Informants. Chancers. The Crosses kept apart all the while they waited for Sarah Fetlock's studio to clear of the unknown visitors. They couldn't be seen together, lest any of the uninvited guests peg them for the fugitives they were.

Hannah waited upstairs for the all-clear. She acted like any other guest. Considered the art. Enjoyed the food and drink. Mark Cross did the same in Sarah's studio. By the time Anna finally left to meet Alastair, Mark had been whisked from Sarah's to Nick's studio and through the bookshelf door. Twenty minutes later, after encountering Anna in the kitchen, Hannah joined him.

Anna finished throwing up in the school toilets. She held her wrists under the tap and rinsed her face. Leaving The Laurels through the rear door, she made her way through the teachers' car park to the street. Her mobile pinged. It was Magritte asking her to the Dome café: be there for four o'clock. Danny had a new crush; he wanted someone to observe the boy's body language to see if he was for real. Anna paled at the thought of it and was sick again behind a tree. Magritte, Anna, Danny, a target to observe, just the same as the June day after school three months earlier when she first met Alastair. She knew he wouldn't be at the Dome this afternoon. After school swim practice. Anna didn't think he wanted to see her anyway.

Alastair hadn't been ill like he claimed when breaking their Friday date. That, or he had made the swiftest of recoveries. There were shots of him on IcePie the next day. He was clever enough to not post anything himself, but he was there in the background of friends' videos taken at a gathering in Queen's Park late Saturday afternoon. Alastair flicking a football off his heel. Alastair spinning a frisbee on one finger. Alastair with a group of girls and boys heading toward a path through the trees in the early evening light. Anna convinced herself he was still messed up about his mother and was doing what he needed to burn off steam, while as far as he knew she herself had family plans she couldn't think how to tell him had been cancelled. Saturday night Anna messaged him three X's and received no reply.

She told herself his silence was nothing. Alastair was keeping distance to protect her. He had, after all, confided in her and her alone. If things blew up, she would be questioned, like Tommy Denton. Alastair wouldn't want that: he wanted better for her. He saw he shouldn't have said anything and now he was shielding her. His going to the park with friends was a cover, Alastair acting normal in the face of uncertainty and fear. It was not unlike what Anna's mother had said to her when the Crosses were safely back in their hiding place:

'Hold on for just a little longer. Act as though nothing's happened. It's the same as seeing friends after Living As If. You already know how it's done.'

Anna knew it was far more than that. It was a command performance of indefinite length that couldn't (and could, at any moment) go wrong. She was frightened of what would happen next. One morning before assembly she would be escorted from school to a car waiting at the kerb, the last she would see of Lynton, her friends and Alastair. They would lose their home, Malkmus taken away and put down. There were accusations. There were tears. Anna jerked away when her mother tried to kiss the top of her head.

Her father tried a different tack. He came to her room with a thick slice of birthday cake. Which was when Anna flung the one bracelet she had made for her mother out the window.

Aunt Susie was summoned. She sat at the top of the stairs, between Anna's room and the Towering Shitter and spoke to her through the closed door. Susie told her the story of making Sarah's wedding dress.

'She was pregnant with you and kept changing her mind. I would get halfway through one pattern and your mother would go right off it. Material was wrong. Neckline too high, too angular, needed rounding. A-line, strapless, Empire line... Drove me up the proverbial. Ask her yourself and she'll tell you she changed her mind four times. But I'm here to tell you it was nine. I was ready to push her in a puddle, in whatever goddamn thing she wore. But I didn't. Point being that your parents' wedding, and you inside, were more important than anything I was feeling. You just have to face up to things. Be strong in the face of it. I know you can do it.'

When Magritte messaged again about meeting at Brighton Dome, Anna switched off her mobile. She had barely spoken all day. Rather, she had sought an equilibrium from the everyday school sights and scents. And kept alert, watching for any sign that her classmates were treating her differently. They wouldn't know about the Crosses (not yet), but if Alastair wasn't shielding her and was dropping her instead... During lunch in The Laurels' front lawn, a helicopter seed pod fell into the tangles of Anna's hair. Maize Addams pulled it free and held it up for everyone to inspect. It was a rare triple pod. Maize proclaimed it good luck and returned it to Anna, declaring, 'Now all your problems are solved.' Anna's heart popped and it was all she could do to not burst into tears. Twice between classes she thought she noticed girls exchange glances and whisper as she passed them in the corridor. She felt their looks on her like ruined sunlight, felt them inside like spent air.

The feeling of being watched didn't vanish after school. Anna headed in the direction opposite the route Magritte would take to the Dome, also keeping clear of Waterloo Street and home. She didn't want to be anywhere near the Crosses. She wanted them out – out of her house and out of her head. In Somerhill Road, on the edge of St Anne's Well Gardens, she noticed a couple turn away from her as she neared the park gate. The couple carried tennis rackets and were dressed for a match. Both mid-30s. Him, more than a foot taller than her. She, with a braided ponytail hanging stiffly over the band of her visor. He, with a red rash on his left forearm. Her, with a slight but noticeable pigeon-toed step. The man was leaner, darker against his tennis whites than Mark Cross, who had paled over the months of sunless concealment, bald but for a dusting of sandy stubble running from ear to ear. The woman was lighter than Hannah Cross, who was born of a Kittian mother and red-haired Ayrshire father (and had a saddle of freckles across her nose as though to prove it). Seeing them together the weekend before, Anna had guessed who the Crosses were on sight. Photos of the Hassop Five had been everywhere online, the trolling of them unrelenting and vicious.

There were death threats, vows of rape. A noose was hung outside the Crosses home, in their back garden. The manhunt for them headline news. Then they were in her front hall, straight from her parents' studios and frantic.

In the park, now, she hastened past the couple, doubling back alongside the tennis courts and scorched bowling greens. As she exited the park, she glanced over her shoulder and saw the couple again. Again they paused and turned to each other as though suddenly sparked into conversation. Their resemblance to the Crosses was incidental, but Anna couldn't dismiss their twice being there, twice turning away when she faced them. Who were they? Were they there for her? Her phone was off; she couldn't be electronically traced; so how did they know where she was? She couldn't take any risks. Anna hurried back through the park, taking a squirreling route through the trees. Only once she was certain the couple were out of sight did she circle past the play area and onto the street.

The same night the Crosses emerged, Anna began keeping lookout. She pulled a chair to her bedroom window and sat watch until four when finally, her head rested against the glass, she slept sitting upright until dawn. Once, when she was small, her father had spent a week in the same chair beside her bed in case she was woken in the night by the roseola fever that burned a rash across her chest. Nick was a legendary sleeper, known to slumber through films, car alarms, even Malkmus's nose-to-nose demands for breakfast. To make certain Nick would wake when Anna did, a length of thread (it never occurred to her to enquire what colour, but she always imagined it red) was tied to her wrist, and its other end around her father's index finger. If Anna cried out and moved at the same time, it would be enough, along with Nick's paternal devotion, to wake him and soothe her back to sleep, a dampened flannel to her forehead and reciting lowly whatever scripts he had recently recorded or was learning. According to Fetlock family lore, the lines Anna found most soothing were for a nose trimmer ad: *Hair you go. Smooth, tug-free precision grooming from Phillips.*

The words came to her again the morning after her first night watch. She supplanted them by noting people and cars on the street. Parents pushing buggies. A plumber's van that twice crawled past. The gas man and postie. Every morning and evening Terry Peppers preceded by Molly, Golly and Ollie on rainbow leads. Late Saturday afternoon (while Alastair was with friends in Queen's Park), her heart flew into her throat. Across the street a man in a checked shirt and work boots consulted his mobile phone and vanished down Little Market Mews. Anna counted thirty seconds before turning her attention to a white van paused up the street. Moments later the check-shirted man re-appeared, glancing at the Fetlocks' house and studiously away. He spoke into his phone. His work boots, Anna noted, were new and unmarked. The white van slid forward. Again the man looked in the direction of the Fetlocks' front door. He stood at the kerb. The van pulled up. Anna scrambled under her bed and clamped her hands over her ears, saying *No, No, No* and kissing the floorboards goodbye.

Now, having shaken the tennis couple, as Anna ventured up to Seven Dials, she grew aware of a man following her same path. The man was across the street and twenty yards back. He wore a grey-blue jacket and a moustache three shades darker than his hair. Through Rudie training she knew about working in teams, handing off the trailing of a quarry from one set of tails to another. She told herself that if the tennis couple knew or suspected themselves blown, the man behind her had taken their place.

Anna strode quickly ahead. At the next street she came to a halt, unslung her rucksack, knelt and dug inside the main compartment. Then unzipping the front pocket, she removed her mobile phone and switched it on. Messages pinged. Anna stood and turned so the man was in sight. Holding the phone high and dropping her head to one side she pouted at the camera. One picture, then considering it, another, in a different pose. Then pretend to send. It was a natural enough thing to do.

The man appeared to take no notice and was soon ahead of her. Anna crossed the street and picked up his tail. She had turned the tables and wished Miss Rodmell had been there to see it. In Leopold Road, the man pushed open a garden gate and jogged up the steps of a house. Anna slowed. The man fished a set of keys from his pocket and unlocked the front door.

Just then, Anna saw a figure passing along the street ahead. Mr Peters pulled his seersucker jacket closed against the breeze and, buttoning it, carried on past the junction and out of sight.

TWENTY

the iComm

Chance – asked me before I would have scoffed. I would have told you that chance playing a pivotal role in anything was fanciful, the stuff of fairy tales and films. That was denial talking, unthinkingness and grief. I give you my mother's death as case in point. What but chance could explain it? What but chance could have shaped the set of occurrences spanning my parents' friends inviting them to lunch for that particular afternoon, at that particular seafront restaurant, for them to finish their meal at a particular hour, to forgo a second coffee (or any of the banoffee pie, a pyramid of profiteroles with four spoons and whipped cream), to pay the bill when they did and then elect to bus it home rather than walk, just as the wind sucked a sheet of glass from a window frame on the seafront tower, sending it not just anywhere (not into the sea, the car park, the A259) (and not catching the two of them both), but narrowing in on my mother's slender neck alone? What else could explain the window belonging to the newly established branch office of my parents' very own life insurance company?

Thinking about it made my head spin. To consider the capriciousness of chance was to allow all potentialities, an unfathomable parade of possible events rivalling the galaxy of milliseconds since we began measuring time. It was bewildering, incomprehensible. I left it well alone.

But the absurdity of chance, I gradually accepted, was eclipsed by the absurdity of dismissing chance as inconsequential. I give you my meeting Morkel, his entering the shop on the heels of the customer who so reminded me of my brother. I give you Samuel meeting Lindsay ten thousand miles from home (and him not botching it like he had countless times before, Lindsay's immeasurable capacity for patience and forgiveness and to love). I give you my father finding love again twenty-odd years after my mother's death. I give you closing time at the shop one late summer's day.

When my father told me he was seeing someone I produced a startled gurgle. Then the hiccups. I crouched in two with my head between my knees and held my breath. A bit of wind squeaked out. After I came up, my father explained. They had met at a party in early spring. She had got him doing yoga and taking exercise. All the physical activity – he raised his eyebrows then shooed away my blushes – had helped him get over losing my mother. They were moving in together, this woman and my father – she into his. He was anxious the news might upset me.

I wasn't. Then I was. What if she was a secret poisoner, a temptress preying on lonesome older men and quietly offing them with mandrake or bleach? What if she was some operative or another of Morkel's, someone assigned to gather information on him? What if she was a homeopath? It was only when going through the shop records that I stopped worrying. She had a distinctive name that rang a few bells; I found her amongst my orders eighteen months earlier. She had bought a pair of eiderdown cushions with aquamarine slips. I took it as a sign she wasn't a lunatic.

What struck me most about her was how unlike she was to my mother. Typically, as with Samuel, born of our father's flesh, people have a type or seek a set of features reminding them of an ideal concocted in first love's blossom. Brown hair or red. Broad shoulders or slender. A lopsided smile. Where my mother had been pale and elfin, someone so delicate you wanted to pop her into your pocket for safekeeping, the woman my father was now doing the downward dog with, and with whom he was readying to set up a common home, was tonk and buxom. She had the bravado, accent and vernacular of a middle-aged Welsh barmaid.

As it happens, she did run a pub. Before we officially met – a grilled pepper and halloumi luncheon on my father's patio (she was vegetarian, the only fault I could peg her with alongside a penchant for wearing enough rings to fill a call centre) – I scoped her out at work. The Mermaid's Tail was some distance from home, but it was tidy and placid, a quaint and chatter-filled neighbourhood establishment with clean windows, potted ferns and immaculate urinals; and when *Nothing's Gonna Stop Us Now* came on the pub speakers, followed by *This is It*, two songs on a compilation album Samuel had entrusted to my care when he left for abroad, I took it as another sign she was above board. My heart swelled for my father. She would keep him here, keep care of him. She would keep him from being lonely. They would live together. Together they could visit Samuel and me overseas. I drew up a list of housewarming presents I would gift the two of them before I left.

Good things, Samuel once told me, come in threes. Afterward, I began to see the pattern for myself. Bean salad. Destiny's Child. Sheets to the wind. The third and final sign that my father was safe in his new love was my bumping into Lucky Emmitt, a fabled character from boyhood whom I hadn't seen in years and long ago presumed dead. It was Samuel's theory that spotting Lucky Emmitt was on its own a favourable omen; if he so much as said hello, you were bound for good fortune, no mistake. Much of it had to do with his carrying a shepherd's crook taller than he stood, combined with a Tolkienesque appearance. He had a wispy beard and sparkly eyes, white hair that waved like semaphore and a job lot of teeth pointing right round the compass. One of the many characters or eccentrics about town, there was something especially magic about Lucky Emmitt. Samuel would always have a serene look in his eyes whenever he had spied him hunching along in his cloak and sandals, or in a park dreaming gnostically amongst a whirlwind of crows. Every time a new girl came into his life, Samuel sought him out, a talisman that this one, this girl, would be the one.

I was returning home from the Mermaid's Tail when I bowled into Lucky Emmitt rounding a corner. I suppose I had tanked up a good deal at the pub (the assurance about my father, the two-forone craft lagers, the foot-tapping tunes) and, consequently, didn't notice the laurel bush that presented itself in my path. I might have freed myself from it with some grace if not for the bird nesting inside who took exception to my intrusion and delivered a series of pecks where it hurt. Dancing away pretty sharpish I collided with something that hadn't been there before – a man, I soon discerned. The force of our impact knocked him flat. Like a flipped beetle, he moved his limbs in a helpless attempt to right himself. I flew into action. After a nearly successful go I was forced to abort on account of the bird land-

ing a mighty one on the side of my head, I managed
to right the fellow. We stood face to face.

'A sparrow got me,' I explained.

'Tit.'

'No, a sparrow, I'm certain.'

The man looked me in the eye, his lips quiver-
ing with what in other circumstances might have
been mistaken for incomprehension. Only then did
the truth break on me that I was in the presence of
Lucky Emmitt.

For a moment I was dumbfounded and merely
watched as he stooped and, with a crack that pained
my own back to hear, scrabbled for his shepherd's
crook from where it had clattered to the pavement.
Lucky Emmitt's cloak was coated in bits of feather
and twigs. With him bent in two, its hood flopped
over his head and covered his eyes. I tried peeling it
away to help him see better and somehow managed
to yank him backward (again, that lumbartic crack).
But Narnian genius that he was, Lucky Emmitt
braced himself with a downward stab of his crook
(at the time I hardly noticed it on my toes) and all
but yodelled the word again, 'Tit!'

And with that, was on his merry way. But knowing who he was, the poignancy of our encounter was
colossal. It arriving just as I had been rejoicing about
being reunited with Samuel, my father and his new
love. Chance again. The good fortune of chance.

Lucky Emmitt had spoken. His words, the pair of them, pointed and pronounced, ballooned with an enormity almost impossible to get to grips with, and sent me reeling.

Unfortunately, this reeling was in the direction of the laurel bush once again. And as I lay there on my own back mustering the strength to climb to my feet, I was elated, knowing with certainty that everything was now falling my way. I couldn't wait to tell Samuel the news.

It was practically closing time when I noticed I wasn't alone in the shop. I had a cut in my ear – never mind from what – and was busy examining it with a pair of dental mirrors when the man must have slipped in. I knew from experience that last minute customers typically flew two ways. Either they were merely killing time before meeting someone for a drink or would take an age deciding on a gift. Wanting to get home and take the weight off the foot Lucky Emmitt had caught with his crook two days earlier, I began limping over to the man to offer my help.

Here's a tough one, I thought. His hair, smooth and dark blond, was recently cut and anointed with what I detected at distance to be sandalwood cream. He wore a seersucker jacket I would have thought slightly too late for the season, with an orange spray in the buttonhole and a red cravat. There was an air about him that spoke of bookishness or at least learnedness in a particular field, like song-writing or statistical analysis. He was pushing hard at fifty if he was a day, and single. Beyond those few points, however, I could see nothing more about him. He was a jumble of misdirection and smart little walls thrown up somewhere inside, lest some secreted truth leak out.

But that in itself is telling. What was he hiding? Rather than offer my services helping him select a gift or something for himself (I couldn't discern which he was after), I hung back and watched. The man didn't once look in my direction and instead was making some small show of examining a pair of salad tongs, then our pearlised sippy cups, whilst skinking glances through the front window. A voice told me he wasn't here to buy anything and had come to rob me – whether of items or cash, I wasn't sure. Was he keeping an eye out for a clean getaway or to signal an accomplice lurking on the street outside?

With no desire to go down easy (all that paperwork, all the counter-suspicion and questioning), I turned to grab arms. An angle-poise lamp suggested itself, but was not only plugged in out of reach but also too unwieldy to swing when it came to it. A half metre pepper grinder instead. The paisley one. But as soon as I had it in my hands and was spinning round just as the man was no doubt readying to set upon me, he was gone through the door.

Minutes later, I had closed the lights, set the alarm and locked up. Knowing there was nothing at home for dinner, I debated a Chinese or Indian or something from a shop along the way. My heart sank at the queue outside Moo and Oink and I started across the street when I saw the man again. He peeled away from everyone waiting outside the sausage shop and joined the queue trailing from the patisserie two doors along. Again my suspicions were raised. Who wastes time lingering in one queue, advances up the line only to abandon it and join another? Who goes from one shop to the next and on to a third and each time comes away empty-handed? Despite the sunlight having disappeared behind the buildings higher up the street, the man had removed his jacket and cravat. And now, having waited momentarily outside the patisserie, he was on the move again.

My thoughts turned to Morkel and to the Crosses. This was something, I was certain of it. I took up his tail.

As we neared Queens Road the man seemed to drop off his pace before picking up speed to cross the street. There were plenty of people flowing down from the train station and it wasn't difficult to keep out of sight amongst them. The man's seersucker jacket, I noted, was turned inside out and had a golden lining almost the same shade as his hair.

He carried it under his arm with a hand tucked into his pocket. I gave him a lead of perhaps forty paces. When he paused to let the traffic pass on Dyke Road I kept out of sight behind a wheelie bin in case he chanced a look back.

Where we were heading I couldn't guess. But because the man maintained an even stride, only occasionally hurrying or slowing down, it wasn't difficult to stick with him. All of the streets were now residential, and with every house I grew hopeful he would turn inside one of them, providing me with an address to give Morkel. I told myself to not get over excited, that the man might not have anything to do with the Crosses and the whole thing could add up to nought. Yet I could sense there was something coming, and that something was big.

A short while later we were in Victoria Road. The numbers of people returning home from work had thinned. I noticed we weren't alone on our chosen path. Ahead of the man was a young woman, by about the same distance he was ahead of me. I had glimpsed her before on the far side of the road while keeping out of sight behind the wheelie bin, then again far ahead on Clifton Terrace. Even at a distance I could see she was tall, almost my own height, with dark blonde hair. She was dressed in a green skirt and grey blazer and had a rucksack hanging from her shoulder. It was only when she lingered for a moment outside the gates of the girls' school at the next corner, as though she had reason to enter the grounds, that I twigged her outfit was a school uniform.

There was nowhere to hide this time, no wheelie bin to duck behind. I carried on, in plain sight of the man and the girl both. The girl rested her hand on one of a pair of pillars, gazing up at its domed peak. As she did, the man seemed to hesitate, and I understood that his being here, keeping a constant distance behind the girl, was no coincidence.

It explained why he had popped in the shop and kept stealing glances through the window while pretending to browse. It explained why he had slid from one queue to the next outside the food shops up the street, abruptly abandoning each. Every move, from shop to queue, from queue to queue, was to blend in, like a bishop stalking a queen amongst the pawns. It explained why he had removed his jacket, his cravat, both instant giveaways for anyone wanting to go unseen. When after a few moments and a false turn inside the gates, the girl recontinued her path, the man surprised me. Rather than following her along Temple Gardens, he turned instead and went uphill, toward Seven Dials.

I now had a choice, the man or the girl. He was cater-cornered to me and she just ahead. What interested him so much in her? The man was up to something; of that I had no doubt. My eyes danced between them. The man turned his jacket outside right and slipped his arms through the sleeves. The girl crossed the street. The man removed his mobile phone from his pocket, dialled and held it to his ear. The girl looked back at the school. I made up my mind. Never before had I seen someone so obviously harbouring a secret and at the same time thinking it best if it were somehow brought to light.

I followed the girl. I followed her all the way home.

TWENTY-ONE

Anna

According to the astronomical calendar, summer begins with the solstice in late June and runs through to the fourth week of September. In that way, it is a season of descent, each day shorter than the one preceding it, the darkness creeping ever longer. Contrary to this the meteorological calendar and popular convention maintains a different measure, seeing summer build from the first of June and, hitting its peak, carry forward until the end of August, when at midnight autumn begins to unfold.

However it's taken, the party was drawing to a close or already over, the atmosphere and light we told ourselves to recognise and enjoy, lessening or, as we understood in the corners of our hearts, already gone.

On the third day of school, Miss Stoughton, the Lynton Data and Compliance Officer summoned me to her office from ten o'clock English with Miss Buxted. It wasn't uncommon for girls to be called in to settle some bureaucratic point or another. Indeed, a few enterprising upper sixth-formers ran a book on the number of times we would collectively be pulled from class. They offered huge Ambrosia pay-outs to anyone who landed the trifecta of summons by class year, month and term. Miss Buxted, perhaps in an act of Mallory sisterhood as much as ordinary kindness that suggested she was unaware of the reason for my visit to the DCO, said I might leave my rucksack at my seat, an offer implying I would shortly return. In other circumstances, I wouldn't have given it a thought. Today I told myself it was a sign that whatever was coming would be of little substance and I would survive. I rose from my seat and headed out, masking the fear unfurling inside me with a bemused smile. Closing the classroom door, I took a last look around. Miss Buxted asked a question and a number of girls raised their hands. Outside, through the open windows, the thrum of a single engine plane somewhere over The Channel.

'Ah, there you are.' Miss Stoughton was seated behind her desk, her eyes moving busily across the computer screen facing her. She glanced at the wall clock before returning her attention to the screen. 'I began fearing it would be a search party.'

'No, Miss.'

'Do sit.'

I did as told. Miss Stoughton was in her mid-fifties, five foot three in heels and every inch of her devoted to the minutiae of her profession. Her skin had a dry melancholic look, like old cheese, and she wore her eyebrows plucked in thin arches.

'May I begin by apologising for pulling you from class?'

'Yes, Miss. Thank you, Miss.'

'The formalities first, shall we? Good.' She named the time and date, having first checked the wall clock against the computer. It was 10:16, the ninth of September. 'Fetlock, Anna Marion. Mallory House. Predicative grades mix of B's and A's. Bursary Level 2. School Meals Programme 2. GoodWorks sufficient. Ambrosia count moderate...Dramatics this term I see?'

'Yes, Miss. As a supplement to Tradecraft. To sharpen character portrayal in the field.'

'Many girls do the same. One point to note is projection. Please speak volubly.' With an upturned palm she indicated a small obelisk on her desk. It was a microphone; the blue light at its base indicated it was on. 'Temperamental thing. I've requested a new one, but we shall make do with what we have today. So. Where were we?' Miss Stoughton raised an eyebrow and resumed reading from the screen. 'Chemistry, good. Sociology. Tradecraft, as previously noted. English Lit, Miss Buxted's from where you have been regrettably dragged this morning. French. *Connaissez-vous la raison pour laquelle vous êtes ici?*'

'*Non, Madame. J'espère que je ne te dérange pas.*

'*Non. J'espère que je ne vous pose aucun problème.*'

J'espère que je ne vous pose aucun problème. Not of *any* trouble to you.'

'Good. That's good. Let's hope that is indeed the case. You appear to be progressing well at Lynton. My commendations.'

'Thank you, Miss.'

'Happy here?'

'Yes, Miss.'

'Plenty of friends?' Her eyes glanced again at the screen.

'Yes, Miss.'

'I expect friends at other schools as well?'

'Yes, Miss.'

'See much of your friends over summer holidays?'

'Yes, Miss. Several friends. Most days.'

'Good. That's good. Summer holidays...' Her mouth closed, Miss Stoughton ran her tongue across her top teeth and opened her lips with a pop. 'Friends might sometimes – shall we say, compromise you.'

'Miss?'

'Invite or pressure you to perhaps do or participate in something you mightn't have done without their inducement.'

I went pale; where was this leading? I pictured the hidden room at home, my parents being taken into custody, my removal from school before a Goldilocks of classmates.

'Miss?' I said no louder than a whisper. Miss Stoughton asked if she needed to fetch the school nurse. I shook my head no and Miss Stoughton again indicated the microphone on the desk between us. My fists clenched in my lap. With some effort I managed to swallow.

'No, Miss.'

'"No, Miss" you don't require medical attention or "No, Miss" you haven't been compromised by a classmate or a peer outside of friends here at Lynton?' A telephone rang in another room and abruptly stopped. The wall clock ticked on. It was the only sound.

Your friends, I told myself. She's not talking about your family, she's only asking about you and your friends. My thoughts raced. What could I give up? What could I give her to deflect scrutiny of what was happening at home? What did she already know?

The spliff smoked with Danny and Magritte on the beach?

The illicit drinks from the Bedford Tavern on Pride Weekend – Danny and Magritte again, Prisha Kumari, Alice Andrews and others?

Twice following Mr Peters outside of assignment, the aborted attempt in the park with Alastair and then again after the first day of school? Did they think Magritte was in on it too?

Try as I might to bury it deep beneath all the rest for fear it would somehow show, I thought of Alastair taking me into his confidence and the last message I had sent him. It was still on my phone. After waiting for him to message me first and hearing nothing, I sent it the night before school began. *Will never. Always true.*

On its own, it was ambiguous enough to elude punishment, a message easily ascribed to my love for him, while secretly delivering the assurance Alastair needed that I would keep quiet about his mum. The only bit I didn't think he would understand were the four X's at the end, one for every month since we'd met. Rather than wipe the message from my mobile, I had saved it with all the other messages, photos and videos to and from Alastair, a cover in case things were ever checked. Nothing saved would look suspicious.

Don't falter, I said inside. Play it smart and don't falter. I told Miss Stoughton who Mr Peters was, how he had come to my attention as a Rudie and about following him two days earlier, outside of assignment. It was recent and therefore I reasoned most likely what she wanted to hear. I told her no one else was involved. I said Magritte wasn't part of it. I had acted alone. With a downward glance I hoped looked repentant, I said it was to impress a boy. Something to talk about.

'I see. And this boy, he was not present?'

'No, Miss.'

'Name?' She glanced at her computer screen.

'He was at swim practice.'

'Noted.' No look at the screen this time. 'His name?'

'He didn't do anything. He wasn't part of it.' Going back over what I had just told her, I repeated how I had followed Mr Peters only briefly, before losing him amongst the shops in Gloucester Road.

'The more you avoid supplying the boy's name, as has twice been kindly requested, the less likely he appears to be uninvolved.'

I asked how someone could be part of tailing someone else if they were at swim practice. Miss Stoughton tubed her lips. I took a chance and said, 'You must already have his whereabouts on record.'

'Yes. Correct. That is indeed the case. Perhaps unfortunately, not only for the day you have high-lighted. I shall need to be frank with you. The day you have named, Monday 7th September, was of no concern. Any unauthorised tailing of a tradecraft quarry is, of course, an infraction and will be dealt with accordingly should, please understand me, Miss Fetlock, *should* that be deemed necessary.'

Again the wall clock, its incessant beat.

'On Monday 31st August at approximately 14:00 hours you attended the Duke of York's cinema. Do you recall what was showing?'

I nodded. Miss Stoughton raised her eyebrows and pointed her eyes at the microphone. I named the film.

'You attended said picture?'

'No, Miss.'

'You are in the habit of visiting cinemas and *not* attending the screening?'

'No, Miss.'

'What then? You were passing by – ' Miss Stoughton consulted the screen. 'The day is on record as hot, twenty-eight degrees, and you decided to pop in on a whim?'

I remembered suddenly that I had not only not bought a ticket for the film, but there could also be no record of me purchasing any food or drinks either. I wasn't sure where this left me. For a moment I considered denying ever visiting the cinema that day until realising with a sickening dread that I already had confessed as much.

'Begging your pardon, Miss, I went to the cinema not knowing it was sold out and shortly after arrival learnt it was.'

'And this information you gained precisely how, the ticket office?'

I shook my head no. Miss Stoughton didn't motion to the microphone this time.

'Perhaps you discovered there were no tickets by consulting your mobile phone? If so, we could corroborate that by examining its data.'

'I believe someone said it, Miss.'

'Someone?'

'Yes, Miss.'

'This someone being...?'

'Someone at the cinema, Miss. The lobby was busy to bursting and I must have heard it there.'

'Must have?'

'I believe so, Miss. I can't think how else I should have found out.'

'I see. And once you heard from this unknown someone in the lobby or elsewhere about the cinema that the film had sold out, you did what precisely? Exit and go about your day? Stay for a cooling drink, an iced coffee or fizzy lemonade? Twenty-eight and sunny, summer holidays...'

I glanced at my hands still balled into fists on my lap. Sweat leaked from them, making dark patches on my skirt.

'You arrived at the cinema on your own, correct?'

'Yes,' I nodded, forgetting myself for a moment and picturing Alastair waiting on the balcony above the street. A story was forming in my head, almost within grasp. 'Yes, Miss.'

'Remain on your own?'

'I went upstairs, Miss. To the outdoor balcony.'

'Reason?'

'To do as you suggested, Miss. A cooling drink.'

'Which was what precisely?'

'It never got that far, Miss.'

'Hot day. You arrive alone. Air conditioned cinema. Discover show has sold out of tickets. You climb the stairs to the outside balcony in full sunlight with the intention of enjoying a cold drink and abandon the idea moments later?'

'There was nowhere to sit, Miss. All the tables were taken.'

'And then?'

'I saw someone. A friend.'

'By chance?'

'I believe so, Miss.' I thought of the postcard Alastair had sent me with the coded instructions telling me to go to St Anne's Well Gardens, and the second message secreted in the slats of the park bench. The latter I had destroyed minutes after retrieving it and the former I would burn as soon as I returned home. 'I mean, yes it was chance. We hadn't seen each other in several weeks.'

'A friend from Lynton or another girl you know socially?'

'Neither, Miss.' I could tell she already had his name and didn't see the point of pretending otherwise. 'Alastair Broyle, Miss.'

'Ah. Now we have arrived. You saw your friend Alastair Broyle, latterly of swim practice and uninvolved with the following of tradecraft quarry Peters, and you...?'

'Nothing. We chatted for a bit. Just chatted. The balcony was crowded, there wasn't anywhere to sit. We said hello, talked a few minutes. That's everything.'

'Any memory about what you spoke of?'

'NaTra camp, Miss. National Training. He was there all summer.'

'All summer?'

'Or however long it lasts.'

'You are good friends?'

'We'd seen each other a few times before, Miss. Four times, I believe. At parties and picnics. Then he went away.'

'To National Training.'

'Yes.'

'After which he returned home?'

'I believe he also went somewhere in Dorset after NaTra camp. Or possibly before,' I embellished. 'Bournemouth or somewhere. His family has a place there. I've never been.'

'I see. You encounter this boy here and again. Summer holidays arrive and he attends National Training, followed or preceded by additional time away with his family, after which he returns home and, as chance would have it, you bump into each other at the cinema, he on his own as well as yourself, neither of you booking ahead and each of you discovering separately tickets have sold out. Making the most of it, you engage in chat. For how long did you converse, ten minutes, fifteen?'

'About that, yes, Miss. Ten minutes or so.'

'And nothing of note about anything he told you?'

'Not that I recall, Miss.'

'You are certain?'

Unclenching my fists I held my palms up and made a face.

Until then I thought I had kept just ahead of whatever was happening. But swivelling her computer screen so that we could both see it, Miss Stoughton tapped at her keypad and an image popped up. It was a picture of Alastair and me seated at the balcony table. I was in profile and Alastair head on. The photo, I could tell, was taken from inside the doorway to the first floor bar.

'That's right,' I said as steadily as I could. The wall clock hammered on, second by second, as though giving measure to the fear rising inside me. 'When the film was about to start everyone went inside and we sat down for a couple minutes. All that,' I indicated the cups and glasses bunched together on the table, 'was left behind by the people there before us. None of it's ours.'

'That much we already know. Let the record indicate that Fetlock, Anna confirms her presence in Image AF/3108/A.' Miss Stoughton tapped a key and a second image appeared on screen. I recognised it straight away as the photo Alastair had shown me of his mother's Ambrosia statement found hidden beneath the floorboards. 'Is this familiar to you?' I felt her eyes on me. 'Think carefully before answering.'

Larger now than it was on Alastair's mobile outside the cinema, I could make out his mother's name, address and account number with greater clarity than before. Pretending to squint to see through the dust and shadow that obscured some of the lettering I groped for what I could say to get out of this. I leaned closer, swallowed and dug deep for my Rudie voice.

'An Ambrosia statement. Logo at the top is clear enough. Forty thousand points total. Name is a bit tricky to make out.' I squinted. '"Broyle" I can see. But not Alastair. Someone named Clara, I believe.'

'Is that name familiar to you?'

I shook my head. 'If it's some relative of Alastair's, or even a misprint, I don't know.'

'The image itself, have you seen it anywhere prior to today?'

I could only think to lie and deny. If I was going to save Alastair, keep my promise to him, it was my only chance. If I was going to get out of this without further scrutiny, without investigators checking up on me at home and everything happening there, it was lie and deny. Every other hope fell away.

'I can't think of where, Miss. I mean no, Miss.'

'Let the record indicate Fetlock, Anna states Image AF/3108/B is unfamiliar. And this?' Miss Stoughton clicked up the image I knew was coming, showing the clear printout of Alastair's mother's Ambrosia account with only twelve thousand points. Again I feigned ignorance. 'Name appears to be the same. Fewer points total this time.' Pieces of Alastair's and my conversation that day floated back to me. I shrugged. 'Looks like whomever it is has spent a bunch. Or saved a tonne, depending which comes first. This one is...recent. June of this year, and the other...can we go back to the previous picture?'

A tap at the keyboard and the dusty image re-appeared. I told myself I was winning again.

'Four years between the statements.' I made a show of counting it off on my fingers. 'Probably a big holiday or something. Or medical reasons,' I added, thinking of my mother.

Miss Stoughton waited. I kept my eyes on the screen as though puzzling something more out of it.

'You are aware that, at Lynton, data compliance is paramount to the health and safety of your classmates and to the school itself?'

'Yes, Miss.'

'Thus, any breach of data compliance puts Lynton and every girl enrolled here at acute risk.'

'Yes, Miss.'

Miss Stoughton tapped at her keypad. A black box appeared on screen. Inside it was an audio wave image not unlike those I had seen on Dad's recording equipment in his studio. The wall clock clicked ahead. Miss Stoughton pressed another key and the wave danced to life, yellow and green.

The first thing I see when I arrive home that lunchtime is the open studio door. On the stairwell landing a knit jumper is drying on a hanger in the window. In my jacket pocket is a form my parents will have no choice but to sign. The form outlines the charges against me: failure to report fraud and conspiring to conceal fraud. Penalties include fines of Ambrosia points and money, my record marked. There when reapplying for my Lynton bursary. There when trying for university, for jobs. There when needing a doctor's appointment or booking travel. There for life. In my favour is the absence of any evidence I stood to benefit from Alastair's mother's scheme. I was 'relieved of attendance' at Lynton for the remainder of the day. Miss Stoughton warned I faced a lengthier exclusion, contingent on the adjudication of the school disciplinary committee when they convened in two days' time. An electronic copy of the form would be sent to my parents, along with a recording of my interview with Miss Stoughton. She herself, as an officer of the Ministry of Public Safety within the Department for Education, would oversee the case. If deemed necessary, it would be referred to court. In different circumstances the charges could be challenged, opening a lengthier investigation and improving my chances of exoneration or a reduction of penalties. But not now: the Crosses. Any investigation would be intense, and their discovery was too great a risk. I had taken my mobile phone with me when summoned to Miss Stoughton's office. My rucksack I had left in Miss Buxted's classroom. All I could think now was to get to my room and hide.

Climbing the stairs I pass the jumper in the window. Water droplets stretch and fall from it, making a damp patch on the floorboards. Then the sound of someone approaching from the first floor above. I tell myself it is Malkmus when I know it can't possibly be. The tread is unfamiliar and too heavy. Whether the steps are coming from the kitchen or the front room I can't tell.

'Ow. Ow-ow,' a woman's voice sounds from inside our quarters. Then three rapid breaths and Hannah Cross is at the top of the stairs ahead of me, one hand holding hard to her stomach, the other pressed to the wall. She sees me and stops short, holding her hands up. 'We can't – ow, *fuck*.' She grabs for the banister to steady herself.

Involuntarily I hate this woman, her very presence; and involuntarily I am compelled to offer her help. Before I realise it I am up the stairs and beside her, guiding her arm over my shoulders and holding her up from behind. She is wearing my mother's robe and smells of her shower gel. Standing upright, I would be taller than her. Stooped to allow her weight across my shoulders, she stands above me. Her stomach swells bulbously, ridiculously forward in the manner that people once claimed meant carrying a boy. Evidently she feels some need to assure me. 'Don't worry,' she manages between winces. 'Only kicking, only kicking. Not yet.'

A window closes inside our quarters, my parents' bedroom by the sound of it. I dread telling them what's happened. A water droplet from the jumper dangles insufferably long and eventually falls.

'We have the same name, but for the H's either end of mine.' Hannah Cross smiles brilliantly, her eyes alight and wondrous and the freckles across her cheeks radiant as a constellation. She smooths my hair. 'A pair of palindromes, us.'

All manners and compassion desert me. 'Nobody wants you here.' And I hurry to my room.

Dad pushed a pink pinwheel in a flowerpot on the front balcony. Within minutes his mobile pinged and he went out. There was a conference in the kitchen when he returned two hours later, everything switched off and unplugged, Living As If rules. Mum, Dad and the two Crosses. From what I overheard, I learnt two things.

One, following a convoluted trek across town via foot and bus, entering and exiting shops to shake any tails, Dad had made his way to what later proved to be Jeannie Pennyfeather's bookshop round the corner from home, where he met someone whom he referred to as 'the GP.' Dad pressed the GP for an emergency extraction, having first 'explained the situation with A', as I had tearfully told it to him and Mum that afternoon. The GP said it was impossible, arranging any operation would take seventy-two hours minimum. Dad argued for a swifter intervention. The GP held firm and reminded Dad that he knew the risks. Seventy-two hours at the very best. Dad would receive a call telling him a book he'd ordered was now in stock, whereupon he was to return to the shop for instructions. There could be no contact between now and then. They left separately, the GP first. Dad took a different labyrinthine circuit home.

Two, the GP wasn't a doctor, as I or anyone would have presumed. 'The signal is reversed here on out,' Dad explained. 'Green flower and orange bowtie means go,' he said and straight away I understood who he meant.

That evening Alastair's name was everywhere on IcePie. The first I saw it was a post from Danny. Then an explosion of messages coming every few seconds as word spread. Finally, Alastair himself, like a festival headliner taking the stage after the warm up acts have the crowd in a state. He thanked everyone for their well wishes. He thanked his parents for their 'unintemporal love and support'. He thanked his teachers, his NaTra camp counsellors and drill instructors for their work getting him this far. He singled out friends who had stood by him, who were like brothers to him and that he 'wouldn't ever forget'. Alastair had been accepted that very day to the Adler Institute, an elite tradecraft training programme that, to date, no other Hanover Park boy had achieved. State-sponsored and operating out of a former Hampshire boarding school, he would transfer from Hanover at the end of autumn term. Look as I did, my name wasn't anywhere amongst everyone he thanked.

At first I couldn't believe it. My heart went to pieces. When in the morning I would need to return the form signed by my parents and by me, admitting my role in covering up Alastair's mother's Ambrosia scam, thereby nailing him, all this, everything he had worked for, all the praise, his admission to the Adler Institute, would be ripped away. I was the wrecking ball.

That's when it came to me. It came in the form of a question. Why was I in such hot water and Alastair, who stood to lose even more than me, suddenly soaring? Surely if I had been pulled from class for questioning and sent home from school, he would have faced the same or worse. It was his mother, after all, not mine.

Until then, my head was spinning so that I hadn't asked myself who had made the recording of the two of us on the cinema balcony. I hadn't asked myself how the recording had made it to Miss Stoughton. She had everything, from when Alastair and I sat down at the table and I quoted the final line of the book he had gifted me, to my promise to keep his secret safe. And the photos, not only of the two of us in conversation on the balcony, but also those of the conflicting Ambrosia statements Alastair had shown me on his mobile phone – who had provided *those* to Miss Stoughton alongside everything else?

I saw, then, that everything was Alastair's doing, a plan he had cooked up to at once demonstrate his allegiance to society and to the system, and his tradecraft cunning, garnering him the big reward of the Adler Institute. Only someone blinded by love could have missed it. The plan was simple and, in sickening afterlight, risible, the second (and faked) Ambrosia statement hidden beneath the floorboards in an ancient house. How could I have fallen for it? We had learned, even been warned about it in Rudie training. When you set someone up, someone on the known opposition or some dupe, you *dangle* them. That the dangle, in this instance, was baseless, that the second Ambrosia statement had been faked, a concoction of Alastair's with all the finesse and originality of a fifth-hand rumour, made no difference. I had been informed of the infraction, knew its illegality, believed in the fraud, was recorded promising to not report it and, in keeping my promise, had been exposed as a conspirator.

And with all of that, somehow worse than all of that, Alastair was gone from me. It sounds incredible, but I didn't cry. The deception was too stunning. Sweat flowed out of me all that night. The bed was damp with it and I had to change clothes. My sleep was broken what seemed every few minutes. My dreams were frightening, fleeting and raw. Once, when I woke, I went to the window to stand in the breeze. On the roofs across the street dozens of gulls were roosting for the night. I bent forward out the window, my arms stretched either side of me like I could fly. With a noise that sounded almost mechanical, a hundred wings beating the air, the gulls erupted into the sky. Only one remained, emitting a red screech. The seventy-two or more hours until the Crosses could be moved would be too late. By then, Miss Stoughton would have made her ruling, the damning black mark applied to my record. Mr Peters, Gordon Peters – the GP to Mum, Dad and the Crosses – was at the centre of it, the malign and dark agent. But for him, there would be no Crosses. But for him, the charges against me could be fought. If he had an inch of compassion, an ounce of morality, at the very least the Crosses would be moved without delay and I would be saved. He had something on my parents, I told myself. Some line on some slip up years past, and he twisted them for his own gains, extorting them to harbour fugitives.

If only I had done better! Three times I had followed him, three times I had lost him. I stood on the tips of my toes and leaned further out the window. A bit more...a bit more...If I fell, I wouldn't need face any of this. The lone gull across the way stretched its wings, as though mirroring my arms, craned its neck up and cried into the night. I knew who Mr Peters was, I said to myself. I knew who he was, knew where he lived and, crucially, now understood the buttonhole flower signal. I knew he went unlistening to my parents' pleas. They were compromised; he was exploiting them because of it. Whatever it was he had on them, it was big. Big enough to push them into harbouring fugitives. Big enough to blackmail them to construct the secret room. All that expense. All those hours. He *forced* them to hide the Crosses. And after he finally consented to moving them on, when would the next lot arrive? The next after that?

That's how it works. He had his hooks in my parents and, because of it, into me, when I should have succeeded at any of the three chances I'd had at stopping him. If only I had done better! If only I hadn't failed! I needed to do something now. Something with counterweight and force. There was still time. And when I did, when I punched back, Alastair would know it, see just how well I knew how to play and score. It would win him back. *I'd* win him back. The pair of us: the golden couple.

In the morning I left for Lynton before anyone else was awake. Teachers, I knew, arrived at school early. As I passed through the phallic pillars and headed for The Laurels, words from yesterday's meeting with Miss Stoughton came back to me. Don't falter, I told myself. Don't falter, and said my name out loud. Straightening the Mallory badge on my blazer I opened the door.

At 6:28am the following day, after a four hour labour in the hidden room, the Crosses' baby was born. Nathaniel. Forty-seven hours later they came and took everyone away. The Crosses' capture was headline news. So were Mum and Dad. They were tried quickly and found guilty. There was no hope of appeal. They were jailed. Eighteen years each, released after fifteen. We sent each other Christmas and birthday cards in the beginning. Then they stopped. There was nothing to say. They looked older the time I saw them at the halfway house –

older and washed-out by incarceration, exhausted by a decade and a half of disbelief. They were moved on or moved themselves, I don't know which. The Crosses lost their baby. He was taken away and never returned.

TWENTY-TWO

William

Anna and I met twice and arranged to meet a third time. My notebook filled with her recollections, her girlhood summertime story – and with the strange and often scarcely credible meanderings of the shop-keeper, the one-time iComm informant who, like so many others in want of attention or personal gain, had reported on whomever they reasoned paydirt.

When I arrive at Café Voltaire, née Bertrix, the morning after drinks with the shopkeeper, my head is heavy from the previous evening's pints, so much so that I elect to not wait for Anna if she is again running late. I swiftly decide a Full English (or the Candide, as the menu has it) is the only hope of cure, my tolerance for alcohol not what it once was.

To my surprise, when the waitress comes to take my order she hands me an envelope. Pushed through the top corner, almost like a stamp, is a small badge with an ormolu oak leaf at its centre. The badge is worn of shine, held in place by a clasp at the back. Inside, folded in three, is a single sheet of paper with a handwritten message that, even without a morning-after lager haze, I would have struggled to decipher. The note, signed by Anna using her full name, says she won't be coming to see me today. She has decided to go further along the coast, to Beachy Head. A walk. The chalk path, the grass and skies. The note has an air of finality, of goodbye.

Puzzlingly, the final line reads:

Songbook: four down – three across.

I am annoyed. Annoyed at Anna's not showing. Annoyed at her mysterious note and my inability to grasp its meaning. Annoyed, too, I must admit, for spending all the money and time I have over the past three days that will necessitate extra frugality and dedication in the coming weeks if I am going to get back on track financially and with my music hall research. And finally, annoyed at the waitress for her own annoyed look at my taking up a table to myself and hesitating with my order when discovering I am to breakfast alone.

If not for craving quick sustenance I would have left there and then, heading home for the oblivion of the duvet and pillows of my rented summer bed. The enigmatic line of Anna's note reads like a crossword. As luck would have it, through the café window are copies of that morning's papers fanned across a table near the till. Each has crosswords, cryptic or easy, none of which shine any light on solving the clue, as I hear myself calling it, that has been left for me.

If not for another glance through the window as I wait in climbing desperation for my breakfast (is the waitress punishing me for my delay in ordering or is it simply a glut of orders all at once?) do I see where Anna is guiding me. A set of bookshelves against the wall. Is it a holdover from Café Bertrix as Anna described it? I hurry inside. On the fourth shelf down from the top and three volumes across is an oversized book with a cracked spine. My head tingles at its title, The Novello Music Hall Songbook, writ in gold font. All of this – Anna, the shopkeeper, the expense and hours – has not been for nought.

The songbook I already know, albeit in its modern, spiralbound form. That it is here, that Anna has led me to it, races through me. Is it a first printing? Is it by any chance annotated – my heart skips ahead at the question – in Max Miller's or one of his contemporaries' own hand?

Flipping through its front pages to the publication date (1968: five years after Miller's death), a thick envelope sequestered at the back falls free and bounces off my feet.

It bears the initials NC. It is for me.

Inside are diary entries and dozens, more than a hundred undated pages of notes I see at a glance were written as and when, in different pens, on sheets of paper varying in size and colour and in the same but changeable hand. The notes, random and orderless as they may be, are packed with voices, packed with detail, about Anna, her family, her schooldays and friends. They also provide me with missing points of a history I have been searching for longer than I know.

I am nothing if not the son of my mother and father – my mother and father who raised me and also my biological parents whose combined Afro-Kittian, Scottish, Saxon and Danish DNA comprises my genealogical chemistry. At first and often second glance I am seen for the Scots, the Scando-Germanic in me. Others see the layered whole of me, that non-white part of me, and draw a definition of who I am, my tastes and behaviour based upon that. My Yorkshire vowels give nothing away of my homebirth, as I have now come to know it, in a room beneath the stairs of a house here in the city grown over the centuries from its beginnings as a small fishing village by the sea.

I am nothing if not the son of my parents. For almost two full days, I was Nathaniel, named for my maternal great-grandfather, who, in writing this book, I discovered arrived in the United Kingdom by boat when he was five-years-old. As an adult, he worked on the railways, knew his off spin and off cutter, and parented my grandmother, his only child. After six decades, he was deported by plane for want of documentation he and his own parents had been told upon arrival at the docks in Tilbury, Essex they wouldn't ever need.

The street outside the café is busy. People coming and going, sitting down to eat. The waitress leaves a plate at my table, collecting others from those behind. Somewhere amongst them a pause in the chatter as a child begins to cry. Anna never asked; it's that what cuts me so. She never asked and she really should have. She really should have asked what it felt like now, touching that original wound.